C000184622

Children of
Darkness and Light

Children of Darkness and Light

Nicholas Mosley

Secker & Warburg LONDON

First published in England 1996
by Martin Secker & Warburg Limited
Michelin House, 81 Fulham Road, London SW3 6RB

Copyright © 1996 by Nicholas Mosley
The author has asserted his moral rights

A CIP catalogue record for this title
is available from the British Library

ISBN 0 436 20216 6

Typeset by Deltatype Ltd, Ellesmere Port, Cheshire
Printed and bound in Great Britain by Clays Ltd, St Ives, plc

'The children of this world are in their generation wiser than the children of light.'

Luke 16:10

'Without an object on which light can fall we see only darkness. Light itself is always invisible.'

Arthur Zajonc, *Catching the Light*

Children of
Darkness and Light

One

You know the story of the children in Yugoslavia who said they had seen the Virgin Mary: she appeared to them on the side of a hill and went on talking to them in the village church in the evenings; the hillside and the church became a shrine. I did a piece on this for the newspaper I was working for at the time — about the susceptibilities and projections of adolescent children, the local political situation from which the authorities might welcome a diversion, church rivalries in which the Franciscans might be using the children in their battle with the state-backed clergy. My editor said 'But people don't want this analytical stuff; they want a piece about children who say they've seen the Virgin Mary.'

I said 'But people don't believe that, do they?'

'Part of them will want to believe. Part of them will think it's rubbish.'

'So they won't have to think at all.'

'You'll learn.'

So I went and wrote a piece about the wonderment of the children on the side of the hill; the ruthlessness of church and state authorities in their treatment of the children. I managed to make the harassment of the children seem vaguely sexual.

My editor said 'You're learning.'

I said 'But the interesting thing is what the Virgin Mary seemed to be saying. She said that humans, with their greed and violence, are in danger of destroying themselves: this is the last time she's going to appear to give warning.'

The editor said 'You don't believe that, do you?'

'She goes on and on about the need for prayer and fasting. But people have been trying that for centuries, and it doesn't seem to work.' I added 'I mean, I think this language is some sort of metaphor.'

The editor gave me a look as if I might not last much longer with his newspaper.

I wrote yet another piece on what I myself felt about the story – in terms of it being a metaphor. I said that the Virgin Mary must know that her instructions weren't working because they had been tried so often and had been ineffective; what she must really want was for us, her children, to recognise this and grow up and start working things out on our own. I added that a metaphor was a way of talking about practical things that could be looked at in no better way.

I had become friendly with a local clergyman who was on the editorial board of an avant-garde religious magazine. I rang him up and said 'Why is it that what the Virgin Mary says in these appearances is always so boring?'

He said 'Perhaps she wants us to see that it's boring, so we'll begin to work things out for ourselves. But she can't say that, or we wouldn't be working things out for ourselves.'

I said 'But that's just what I'm saying!'

He said 'Then it seems to be working, doesn't it.'

He got my piece published in his religious magazine. It seemed that no one paid much attention to it.

I had a girlfriend at the time who was called Melissa. Melissa was a student at an art school: I had just started in this my first job with a newspaper. Melissa and I were living together in two rooms in north London. Melissa became pregnant. I said 'Now what do we do – a bit of fasting and self-laceration, or do we think for ourselves.'

Melissa said 'It's me we're talking about, not the Virgin Mary.'

I thought – What's the difference?

So in this way our son Billy came to be born – with the help, it is true, of what might be called a bit of anxiety and trusting.

I had first seen Melissa at her art school when she had been standing in front of a pedestal on which there was a lump of clay. She was squeezing the clay with her hands; she was wearing a T-shirt and jeans. I wanted to take her in my hands and squeeze and mould her. I remembered the idea that when you are doing a piece of sculpture, you are not so much forming an object as discovering what is there.

When our son Billy was born he emerged as if he were a sun rising above hills. Then he was left on the edge of the bed while the nurse and doctor attended to Melissa. I thought – Poor old sun, you don't get much help from us, do you.

I said to Melissa 'I suppose now we'd better marry.'

She said 'I wondered whether you were going to say that.'

'I didn't want you to think I felt trapped.'

'Don't you feel trapped?'

So Melissa and I marrried: and we lived with our son Billy for what indeed seemed sometimes for ever after.

I don't want to write much about the early years of Melissa's and my marriage. A wedding used to be taken as the end of a story: more difficult to see, but more interesting, would be what happens after. During the early years of a marriage often nothing much seems to be happening: roots are being put down; growth or decay goes on underground unseen. With a child or children it is apt to be anyway a bit of a long winter. The compensations are those of being able to be wrapped up close in bed; of holding out hands on either side of a fire. But there is also inescapably the anxiety that it may never be spring again. Marriage, all right, should be a nurturing of roots and seeds; but what of the flowers that one once so boldly or tremblingly displayed – have not they been cut as it were and put in a vase, with not much prospect of new life between this and the bonfire?

Sometimes during these years – I am talking of the seven or eight years after Melissa and I married – I had the image of myself as an old monkey sitting on the stump of a felled tree, but its roots going deep into the earth as if they were an extension of the backbone of the monkey; and there still reaching to primitive needs and desires and wanting to feed from these – poor old monkey! He scratches his head: he had such hopes that he would no longer feel anything of this – that some higher state of consciousness would emerge to flower above his head like one of those *chakras* that are supposed to arise from meditation –

– But now here he is still plagued like St Anthony in the desert and wanting to scratch much more than his head; in which case whatever seeds might have flowered would be blown away on the wind –

– but seeds have to be scattered of course –

– and does not old ground have to be broken up before new flowers can grow?

Melissa and I sometimes fought. We fought because we each wanted our own ground, we each wanted the other to be out of our own ground, we each wanted the other to be contained and held safely within our ground. Sometimes our needs complemented one another; sometimes they did not.

All this, I mean, seems to be natural to marriage: what else is the point of two people each wanting to invade the other; to complete themselves by possessing the other? Thus indeed there is the impression of earth being broken up: but so that something new may grow?

Often the requirements of our son Billy were the area over which we fought. At other times Billy seemed the obvious justification for our marriage. When it was my turn to watch over Billy or to comfort him at night I would think – I am some Frankenstein's monster with a defective brain which sometimes wants to cast what it might love into a river like the petals of a flower: but since I know this, then might not this be some new growth in a not totally defective brain – do you hear me, Billy!

I sometimes tried to talk to Melissa about this. But Melissa would feel that my efforts at reason, at detachment, were moves by some ape-man to drag her into my cave. I would say – But if you do not like detachment, then you are some ape-woman wanting to prevent us from getting out of our cave.

She would say – And you think that by being clever you can

keep us half in and half out of the cave. And now you'll say – Yes I do.

I would say –Yes I do. Then – That's half of it.

– And what's the other half?

– We'll see.

I lost my job on the first newspaper I worked for: I had begun to drink too much; I had such contempt for people who wrote what they thought people wanted to hear rather than search, like a sculptor, for what might be true. And anyway, what was it that people might want to hear? If they wanted dirt, then might it not be about this strange desire that they might like to hear?

I said to Melissa 'Now I'm unemployed I can do more of my share in the home.'

Melissa said 'God forbid.'

I said 'That's what St Paul said when he worked out that in order to have grace, you had to sin.'

She said 'You're drinking too much.'

I said 'That's true.'

Thus, some time before that at which I will begin my proper story, life had begun to run down. There was some breaking-up of old ground, indeed, but where were the signs of when new life might begin? I wondered – Something is required other than just trying to be clever; one must watch for which way the wind blows?

I was offered a job – more reputable than my last – by the Features Editor of a national newspaper whom I had known briefly at school. I thought – This is luck? I said to Melissa 'I think he was a bit in love with me at school.'

She said 'I thought you said he had read and admired your work.'

I said 'That's true.'

I achieved some success in my new job. I was away from home much of the time doing stories in foreign places. I established some corner in the business of writing articles about the connections between what was going on in the world and current ideas in the mind. I enjoyed success. But I was pursued by the question – What was I doing making out that I was reporting objectively on events and ideas when one of the ideas I was writing about was that the observer in some way formed the images that he saw? And had I

5

not had the idea that humans should learn to be responsible – and not only for themselves?

At the time when I begin my proper story Melissa and I were living in a tall thin house in a terrace above the canal in North London. Billy was twelve and went to the local school; Melissa went out to work most days to do designs for ceramics: Billy was quite often looked after by helpers and friends. I had been making efforts to stop drinking but in fact was in danger of falling down on my job –

(Have I succeeded in giving the impression of things both not happening and happening during these years? the sense both of aimlessness and of commitment; of sometimes waste and sometimes the trust that things might after all be growing underground secretly: hope even that perhaps one day there might be a flowering like that Tantric *chakra* above the head – some state of higher consciousness in which potentialities and hopes might be held in suspense like the condition of Schrödinger's both-alive-and-dead cat; waiting for some act of recognition, some chance event, to resolve the condition this way or that; and then –

– This is alive? that is dead?

Or – Are you joking?)

I was summoned one day by my old schoolfriend, Jack, who had recently been promoted to being Editor of the newspaper, who said –

'Didn't you once do a story on those children in Yugoslavia?'

I said 'Oh God, I hoped no one would remember that.'

'Why?'

'Because it was an impossible thing to write about. The children went on saying they talked every evening with the Virgin Mary. They believed this. So what can you say: that you don't?'

Jack said 'Did you believe it?'

I said 'I didn't and I did. I believed that they believed. What more can you write about that?'

Jack was looking at some press-cuttings on his desk. I sat on a chair facing him. He said 'There's a group of schoolchildren in the north, in Cumbria. They're said to have had some message from the Virgin Mary. Except that these children now seem to be saying that this isn't true –'

I said 'That might be interesting.'

'Why?'

'Because that's what the Virgin Mary might have told them to say. I mean that's what they might have said the Virgin Mary told them to say. I mean all these things are stories.' I thought I might add – Then they might get on with doing what they wanted on their own.

Jack pushed the press-cuttings across the desk to me. They were from a local newspaper in Cumbria. They told the story of a group of children, aged between seven and thirteen, who had set up in some sort of commune on their own in the hills. They were not being prevented from doing this by their families or the local Social Services. There had been the story that the Virgin Mary had instructed them to do this in a vision; then the leader of the children, a girl called Gaby, had said that she had made this story up. When the reporter had asked her why, she had said – Why do you think? The reporter had been unable to decide what she was or was not making up –

I said 'You see – !'

Jack said 'What do I see?'

'Nothing.' Then – 'They might be able to go their own way.'

There was a photgraph of a young girl with a round face and short fair hair. I thought – Such a girl is nowadays an archetype in people's minds: a sort of younger sister of the Virgin Mary.

I said 'What was interesting about the children in Yugoslavia was that their visions and messages about destruction and self-destruction happened just in the area where for the last few years people have in fact been tearing themselves to pieces –'

Jack said 'And what do you think might be interesting about these children now?'

'If they've gone off on their own, perhaps they want to survive.'

At the end of a second piece in the local newspaper there were scarcely veiled hints that there might be connections between this story and an earlier story of satanic cults involving children and parents and indeed Social Services people in the area. I thought I might say to the local reporter – You're learning!

Jack said 'You see the sexual connections? Why aren't the families and the welfare people butting in?'

I said 'You mean, the children might have some hold over them?'

Jack said 'That's not what I meant –'

I said 'Everyone's got this abuse stuff on the brain.'

I had begun to wonder why Jack might be wanting to involve me with this story: it seemed too small a story for me to go on. But Jack knew I had been drinking; I had not done much serious work for some time. Also of course it was true that this might be my sort of story –

I said 'You want me to go up there?'

He said 'Rather up your street?'

I was thinking – On the other hand, Jack knows that I have recently been having a difficult time with Melissa, and it has sometimes struck me that Jack might be after Melissa –

Jack said 'You can take a photographer.'

I said 'What photographer?'

'Janice?'

I didn't think that Jack knew about Janice. Janice was a girl, woman, girl (what's the difference) that I had been in vague pursuit of for some time. (I will be saying more about this habit of the pursuit of girls.) The fact that Jack had mentioned Janice was evidence, surely, that he might be after Melissa –

I said 'Jack, you're entering the destruction or self-destruction business!'

He said 'I thought you were suggesting that messages might be about how to survive.'

'You mean, a weekend for two at that four-star hotel in the Lake District, what's its name, the one with the good food?'

'I'm sure Janice would do it.'

There is a pub called The Sailing Junk where people from my newspaper and from others whose offices have moved to the area like to congregate in the evenings – a gathering of the tribes like that of apes round their tree-stumps: a chattering, nudging, scratching, screeching; an exercise-yard for the phantoms that are imprisoned in people's minds. These phantoms are to do with power, prestige, vainglory, money; but above all, for men like myself at least, to do with girls (women, girls – you think words can make a difference?), an archetype of such phantoms being Janice.

Janice wore short tight skirts above long legs; Janice was like a bud waiting to burst; Janice had long fair hair like the sticky fronds of plants that attract insects. Janice was setting herself up as a free-lance photographer: she was herself like one of those sleek photographs of models that lodge in people's minds. It was to The Sailing Junk that I would come in the evenings in my pursuit of Janice – like some odd bee with his proboscis or whatever between would-be prehensile legs.

What is there to be said about this enlurement, wonder, curse, that gets itself dolled up in romantic or appalled images? Men are monkeys on their tree-stumps; they have lines going to and from the earth and their guts, minds, balls – all right, if they had not, how would they have taken the trouble for thousands of years to ensure that the race survived? And how can the institution of marriage be expected to make much difference to this? Marriage is a phenomenon of the heart and head and does have much effect on the genetic life of the balls. Janice was a genotype as it were and reached up to the mind by a direct line from the guts. I sometimes tried to talk to Melissa of this: I would say –

– It is not as if anyone wants this sort of curse! Men should be pitied, not blamed, for lustfulness. These phantoms that haunt us are disasters, catastrophes, that go back to Adam and Eve and that tree –

Melissa would say – You see, you blame women!

– I don't, I thank God for them –

– Well please thank God a little more for me.

It sometimes seemed to me that my drinking was in order to get rid of these images – or perhaps to become at home with them. But then what sort of world might it be in which one might be at home both with them, and with Billy and Melissa?

At the back of The Sailing Junk there was a long covered terrace with plate-glass windows that looked out over the river. Here one could watch an occasional barge going past, like a leaf that presaged autumn. At the bar there was the pumping of elbows and chatter like machinery – the racket that had taken over from the age-old traffic of the river. I knew quite a number of the people who came to the pub; but since I had been trying to stop drinking I found it almost impossible to have much contact with them – and they, I

suppose for the same reason, seemed to keep clear of me. I thought
— One drinks in a desperate effort to be at home with other
humans; sober, there is the fearful realisation that there might be
just oneself, and the whole.

I sat on a stool on the covered terrace and looked again at the
cuttings that Jack had given me. The story about the children
stopped, as usual, just when it might have become interesting. It
had apparently been the father of Gaby, the leader of the children,
who had spread the story about the vision of the Virgin Mary; the
hints were that this had been done to cover up dubious
relationships between the families and the authorities and the
children. I thought I might say to the local reporter — But you do
see, don't you, that all such phantasms themselves might be a
cover-up —

— A cover-up of what —

— Of learning about any journey, search, that might be being
undertaken by the children — or oneself?

I saw that Janice and a man called Malcolm had come into the
bar in the main part of the pub. Janice was wearing one of her skirts
that was like no more than a bandage round her behind. Malcolm
was the Science Correspondent of a rival newspaper; he sometimes
wrote stories that were in competition with mine. I might be
jealous of Malcolm: however — he might rescue me from Janice?

Each time I saw Janice the old monkey within me began
jumping up and down on his stump; scratching at his root that went
down into the earth; wanting to pull it up, pull it in, pull it off: or as
if it were the bandage that was wound round Janice's behind —

— A wound, a scab, a healing — give it air.

I wandered through to the main part of the pub. I said 'Hullo,
Janice.'

'Oh hullo —'

'Malcolm, there's a message for you from Scotland, you're
wanted there rather urgently, they're having a bit of trouble with
the king.'

'Oh hullo, Harry, I see you've been reading some good books
lately.'

I said 'Janice, I've got a job, if you'd like to come. In Cumbria.'

'Yes I know, I've spoken to Jack.'

'You've spoken to Jack?'

'He rang me.'

I thought – You mean, in that case, Jack really is keen on Melissa? There is indeed a whole tribe of us gibbering on tree-stumps?

Janice said 'Malcolm, be a love, and get us a drink.'

I said 'I'll do it.'

'No, let Malcolm.'

I was wondering – So what is Janice's relationship with Malcolm? I had not seen them together before. She seemed to be treating him with some disdain: but this might be just familiarity?

Malcolm went off to the bar. I said 'I didn't quite know whether to say that in front of Malcolm.'

She said 'You think something might go wrong?'

'You'll come on this job?'

'Of course.'

Because all this suddenly seemed to be so easy, I began to have doubts. Of course I should worry about Melissa! Had I not said to Jack that this sort of thing was a carry-on towards destruction? How on earth had I worked out that never to risk this sort of thing was also some form of self-destruction –

I said 'There are some children who say they've seen a vision of the Virgin Mary. Or this might be a manoeuvre. They've set themselves up as a sort of commune in the hills. I thought it might be of interest, but I didn't know if it would be to you –'

'Of course –'

'Yes?'

'Anyway, who cares about the children!'

With Janice's small soft face a few inches from my own it did not seem indeed that anything much mattered except that I should get Janice to a four-star hotel in Cumbria as quickly as possible; and there, in a bedroom overlooking a moon–lit lake, who indeed would care about destruction or self-destruction –

Janice said 'But you mean, what about Malcolm?'

I said 'You do have to worry about Malcolm?'

'I mean, won't he tell Melissa?'

Then for a moment – as Janice's face resolved itself into something more distinct, more wary – I had the impression that I was to have increasingly in the days that followed: that there might be something going on just outside my range of knowledge, but it was just this, perhaps, that might be the point of our journey.

Malcolm was coming back with the drinks.

Janice said quickly 'I'll try to fix it with Melissa.'

I thought – For God's sake, you fix it with Melissa?

Malcolm was setting down the drinks.

He said 'You'd better watch out in Cumbria.'

Janice said 'Why?'

Malcolm said 'Nasty things coming out of the woodwork.'

I was still trying to work out – Malcolm might tell Melissa? Malcolm knew Melissa? –

– Something was coming out of the woodwork?

Janice was saying to me 'Did you read Malcolm?'

I said 'What?'

Malcolm said 'The invasion of the body-snatchers. The end of this planet as we know it.'

I managed to work out that what Malcolm and Janice were talking about was an article that Malcolm had written recently about the dangers of radioactive contamination coming from the nuclear reprocessing plant and power station in Cumbria. There was some evidence that leakages were occurring, that there was a threat to the health of children in the area, that the genetic systems of adults were affected; though of course all this was denied by the authorities –

I said 'You think that all that might have something to do with these children?'

Malcolm said 'What?'

'Nothing.'

Malcolm said 'Aren't you going to drink up? I didn't know whether or not you were on the wagon.'

'Yes I am.'

'On the jolly old tumbril to Cumbria.'

Janice said 'Oh bugger off, Malcolm.'

Malcolm had put a glass of what looked like whisky and soda in front of me. I stared at the glass. The bubbles rose to the surface, burst: they seemed to represent infinite possibilities: one or two might be captured; might contain this or that universe –

Malcolm said 'When are you going?'

Janice said 'Tomorrow.'

Malcolm raised his glass. He said 'Here's looking at you, children.'

I stood up. I raised my glass. I said 'Thanks for the drink, Malcolm.'

Janice said 'Don't go.'

I said 'I'll see you tomorrow.'

I went back to my stool on the terrace with its windows over the river. I took my glass. I had not drunk from it. I thought – You have to admit that drink is stronger than yourself: then if you do perhaps you are freed from it –

– This is what happens with any form of trusting?

There was an old-fashioned sailing-ship going past on the river, its brown sails furled. On it, standing looking out over the rail, were people in what appeared to be fancy dress – men in frilled shirts and knee-breeches, women in dresses with lace collar and long skirts. It was as if they were on some voyage to discover the New World; or more likely re-enacting this for television – the hopes of peace and harmony; the reality of hardship and fighting. I thought – But people choose what they like – what they see on television?

I looked down at the bubbles in my glass. I thought – Come on, I am like a denizen of dry and stony ground; do I not need some breaking up?

The people at the bar were clattering and raising their arms like machinery. I thought – This is the invasion of the body-snatchers: I need some protection. I drank a sip of whisky.

I had gone out to Yugoslavia some years after I had written about the children who said they talked with the Virgin Mary: I was to do a follow-up on the story. In the local village I had found all the razzmatazz of a Catholic shrine – the trinket stalls, the soft-drink stands, the groups from America and Germany with their cheer-leader priests and set smiles. And I thought – These people will surely not divert whatever fire and brimstone is due to fall on stony ground! But then I had walked across the fields to a rocky path up the hill to where the children had seen their first vision; and there everything was still and silent, people were kneeling or sitting or treading with bare feet, there was a space where the rocks had been made smooth and gleaming by people's knees and feet. Stuck into cracks and pockets of earth were innumerable small crosses that were, yes, like a crop from seeds – ones that had fallen on stony ground but whose roots had thus dug all the deeper into the earth to produce – what – flowers that might emerge from the top of the head like the sun?

In the pub I had drunk only a sip or two of my whisky. It had seemed – I need to be in partnership with something stronger than myself.

In Yugoslavia I had been one of a small group who had been permitted to interview two of the children who were still in the village and who were still having visions or visitations. These children, a boy and a girl, now fifteen and sixteen, were courteous and attentive; they listened to questioners as if striving to have sympathy: it was as if they were saying – You can think we are suffering from delusions or you can believe us, as you like; what does this matter? everyone will have, has to have, his or her own experience. And this was what I had felt when I had been on the hillside: this was a place to which people came properly to enquire not about the children, but about themselves.

I was sitting on the terrace of the pub. It was growing dark outside. I had drunk no more of my whisky. I pushed it away. I thought – What firmness! or confession of delusion. But I still found, as I so often found at this time, that I was reluctant to go home. There was that cartoon image of one's wife like a gorgon above roof-tops –

– But is not a gorgon in a mirror in which one looks at oneself?

I had got into the habit of travelling to and from work by bus or Underground because I had once been caught for drunken driving and I now drove as little as I could in the town. In the Underground I joined the great army of those who appeared to be defeated – whose hopes had fallen and faded on stony ground. I thought – But my hope has always been to be an agent in occupied territory: this is a metaphor that might be true?

I wondered whether Billy would be asleep when I got home. Sometimes I looked forward to seeing Billy: sometimes Billy got in the way of the ludicrous fights that Melissa and I appeared to have a need for in the evenings. In these Billy was sometimes a peacemaker and sometimes a victim. I thought – And sometimes it is as if Melissa and I should be on our knees on the side of that hill.

I walked to our terrace of neatly refurbished houses. Melissa might be lining up her sights on me from an upstairs window: Melissa might come running into my arms in flight from whatever were her own ghostly pursuers. Such images are in our minds: they get blown there by the wind.

There was no light from our downstairs window: Melissa might have gone to bed; she might be upstairs with Billy. I could explain – I have been working late; don't you know that people in newspaper offices have to work late? Or – Oh all right, it's true that I am reluctant to come home: do you blame me if you are like a gorgon lurking above the rooftops? Do I blame you? Oh no! Or do I?

There seemed to be no lights on at all in our house. Melissa might be waiting behind the front door with a rolling-pin: if she hit me the seeds of my brain might spill like those of a melon onto the floor – and there grow again from dragons' teeth like angels. And then I could take my oh-so-lonely wife into my arms and hold her tight – so tight that she could not get a knee up into my groin – and we could prance like monkeys round our tree-stumps.

I put my head round the front door. The hallway was dark. I turned on the light. There were what seemed to be two extra uprights by the banisters at the top of the stairs. I realised that these were legs; in a film this would be shot to induce terror – the expectation of someone garrotted and propped at the top of the stairs. I quite often saw things in terms of film-shots at this time: this was a way of recognising some of the rubbish that went on in the mind? I realised that the legs were those of Melissa: how well I knew Melissa's legs! they were shapely and sturdy, indeed not a monkey's legs: thought what would be wrong about a couple of loving old monkeys? The view of her body was cut off by the line of the landing at the top of the stairs; she might be wearing one of her short nightdresses, or nothing. Perhaps I could make out that I had been hit by a bus on the way home: then I could crawl up the last few steps and throw myself at her feet; claw my way up her to reach her waist, breasts, face. Or she could put a foot on me, trample on me, which people are supposed to enjoy in this sort of predicament –

I went on up the stairs. There was Melissa indeed in her short dressing-gown that made her look like a mediaeval archer. I said 'Co-ee!' She said nothing.

I reached up and put my arms around her. She was wearing nothing underneath her dressing-gown: there were the miraculous formations and substances that I had long since discovered as it were in her clay. I was still a step underneath her, so she could not get a knee at my groin. I began to think – I might get away with this! But of course, I must have known that this is when one is most exposed. After a time I looked up and saw the Melissa was doing something with the inside of her mouth: she was about to cry? she was fighting to keep back laughter? I wanted to say – Oh Melissa, you are after all the only person I have loved, or will love, you must know! Then she spat in my face.

I got hold of her hands and held them behind her. I said 'If you do that again I shall hit you.'

She said 'That's what you want to do, isn't it?'

I said 'No, that's what you want me to do.'

She seemed to be preparing another gob in her mouth, so I freed one hand and put it over her mouth and said 'Shh, you'll wake Billy.' She bit my hand.

I thought – Well now surely my way is clear to go with Janice to Cumbria.

It seemed that I might get a hand between Melissa's legs and lift her off the ground and carry her through to the bedroom; I had seen men in the Middle East do this sort of thing to donkeys. Then I could fall and lie on top of her on the bed. But Melissa and I had in fact never been much good at the rough stuff as a prelude to making love; either it was all too serious, or else we got giggles.

I took my hand away from her mouth and she said 'You creepy bastard.'

I said 'I'm trying, but I don't seem to be succeeding.'

'Billy's not here.'

'Where is he then?'

'He's with friends.'

'Why?'

'Why do you think?'

'Because his father's such a creepy bastard?'

I thought this quite witty. But Melissa was making writhing movements inside her mouth again.

I said 'You're drunk.'

She said 'I'm drunk!'

I said 'Yes you're drunk.' Such conversations, in this sort of situation, were apt to go on for some time. But it was true that Melissa also had recently been drinking too much, as if not to be outdone by me.

Perhaps because I was holding her so that she could not get at me with her hands, Melissa landed another gob of spittle on my face. This time I hit her. I had intended it to be a slap on the face, but it came out harder than I intended. You imagine you are in control, and then you are not.

I let go of her. She ran towards the bedroom. I thought I should retire downstairs and think about what to do: I could ring up Janice? But it was as if the enraged monkey within me prodded me with a stick and I went after Melissa; she tried to slam the bedroom door and I got a foot in; we remained like this for some time with Melissa heaving and kicking at my leg and me acting as if it were made of wood. I was trying to remember – All right we are not in control; but can we not do something with this knowledge?

I shouted 'Stop it!' and pushed the door violently so that Melissa was flung back on the bed. She lay there with her legs apart. I thought – That's better: but I should not just jump on her? I paced up and down like a wrestler on television.

I said 'What is all this? I'm sorry I hit you.'

She said 'You know what it is.'

'I don't.'

'That fucking bitch rang you.'

'What fucking bitch?'

'Janice.'

'Janice rang me?'

I thought – But Janice couldn't have rung me!

Or – She said she'd try to fix things with Melissa?

Melissa said 'She said you wanted her to go on some trip with you tomorrow.'

I said 'It's work. It's a job. It's somewhere in Cumbria. I didn't fix it, Jack fixed it. I expect she was ringing to try to make it all right with you.'

'What do you mean? What was she trying to make all right with me?'

I thought – Now keep my head, and remain calm, and perhaps I can get both Janice and Melissa.

I said 'I'm not interested in Janice. It's a sort of illness, being interested in Janice. I think I'm not doing too badly. If I was up to no good, why should she ring you?'

Melissa said 'Yes, why should she?' Then – 'Does Jack know about you and Janice?'

She said this in a far-away voice, as if she were thinking of something else. I thought – Oh yes, yes, haven't I been thinking, there may be something between you and Jack?

I said 'What do you mean, what might Jack know about me and Janice?'

Melissa said 'I just wondered.'

She was lying on her elbows on the bed. There did not seem to be any mark where I had hit her. I sat down on the bed beside her. She looked hot and dishevelled. I thought – Indeed, one might take advantage of whatever turns up –

I put out a hand to touch her. I said 'Your poor face.'

She said 'It's not your fault.'

I thought – What do you mean, it's not my fault?

She said 'I just think it's so pathetic that you have to ask my permission to go off with Janice, that's all.'

I made a grab at her, but she seemed to have been expecting this, because she twisted away and made a dash for the bathroom; I was left holding her dressing-gown. There was a glimpse of her for a moment in those miraculous shapes like liquids held in air: then she was in the bathroom with the door being banged and locked behind her. This time I did not go after her. It seemed suddenly – There is a part of her that wants me to go off with Janice.

I thought I should pack a suitcase and set off quickly without further ado. When Melissa and I reached this stage in a battle it was apt to go on all night: and now there was no Billy to pour cold water on us as if we were dogs. My car was parked outside. I could drive all night. I like driving long distances; I could be in Cumbria by morning. And then I could decide what to do about Janice – and indeed like this it would not seem that I had gone off hand-in-hand with Janice –

I got a suitcase down from the top of the bedroom cupboard. I put in pyjamas and socks and a shirt or two: I could buy things I needed from the bathroom later. I thought – So I am, yes, a bit of a creepy bastard –

– But did I really want to go away from Melissa?

– Though it was true that Melissa, if she wished, could have stopped me?

There was no sound from Melissa. Once when she locked herself in the bathroom she had said she was about to take, was already taking, an overdose of pills: it had never become clear how far that had been true. But there would be no point in Melissa taking an overdose if I were not there to be threatened; so for everyone's sake it did seem best if I just got away quietly.

I placed my suitcase beyond the open door on to the landing.

But did I not really love only Melissa?

The games people play! to find out, as if by chipping away at a piece of stone, what on earth of their true feelings might be hidden inside –

– And as if it were not quite them that were doing this.

I went back and put my ear to the door of the bathroom. I thought – Poor old monkeys! with these riddles like tumours rather than flowers bursting out of the top of their heads –

There was still no sound from Melissa. I said 'All right I won't go! I'll stay and be sacked from my job and go back on the bloody bottle.'

I thought – Is it really so impossible to stop being creepy?

I said 'I'm sorry I stayed on late at the office. But I had to talk to Jack. And all right, with Janice. But how else am I supposed to work? And it's true that I often dread coming home, we're getting on so badly.'

I moved away from the bathroom and went towards my suitcase on the landing. It still seemed it was not quite up to me to choose what would happen. Melissa suddenly appeared at the door of the bathroom. She had a towel wrapped around her; she looked very young and vulnerable. I thought – So all right, this is what is happening –

I said 'You don't really want me to stay.'

She said 'You don't really want to stay.'

I said 'Have you got someone else?'

She said after a time 'Not really.'

I picked up my suitcase and went towards the stairs. There did not seem any point in saying – What do you mean, not really?

This time it was she who came after me and made a grab at me as I clattered down the stairs. Then she stayed where she was and shouted 'All right go and don't come back!'

I thought – But of course I can come back!

Then – That doesn't necessarily mean that she's got someone: does it?

In the street there were all the cars lined up as if for a funeral. I hurried along the row of them. I thought – Melissa and I may want us buried: but only for a day or two; and then some sort of resurrection?

Two

I drove through the night. I did not pay much attention to my driving. The lights of the cars coming against me were like bullets, like meteors; like those particles that knock bits and pieces out of a genetic code.

I had once done a story on the helmets, mechanisms, that you fit over your head and you see coloured shapes and lights coming at you like bullets; this was called virtual reality. I was told that one day you would be able to choose your own reality; you would not have to wait for random bits and pieces to be knocked out of your genetic code.

If I crashed my car into the central partition of the motorway of course I could get the whole redistribution process over quicker.

I had once tried to explain to Billy why Melissa and I had fights. Billy and I had been walking on a grey and wind-swept beach. I had said – There's something built into people that makes them behave like this; once humans had to fight to stay alive; now their need for battles may destroy them. Billy had said – Can't you just stop? I had said – One day something might happen and one might just stop.

Once when Billy was little and Melissa and I were quarrelling, he had run out of the house and onto the road. Melissa and I had gone after him. I had said – We must stop! Melissa had said – All right you stop!

I pulled up at a service station on the motorway and tried to sleep in the car. You try to make your mind a blank but this is impossible; your mind has a helmet round it through which images come like bullets – Janice in knee-length breeches like those of a matador; Melissa with her arms round Billy on the pavement. Sleep comes when you have accepted that it will not come; but if you think of this it does not come. I had some coffee and drove on.

I tried to consider the story to which I was going. The children came from a village by the sea: they had left their school and their families and had set up on their own. But this was at almost the beginning of the summer holidays, so why should they not go camping? But then what had been the point of the story of the vision of the Virgin Mary: the local reporter was surely right in suggesting that this was a cover for something further. After a time my mind got taken over as it were by programmed images coming in – those to do with the current obsessions that people seemed to have about children: the tales of black magic and terrible manipulations; the stories told by the children themselves of things done to them for instance with the trunks of elephants and the tails of giant fishes. All this was representative surely of an imagination clamped like an iron skull around the head –

I had nearly driven off the road. I had been asleep. I stopped on the hard shoulder and jumped up and down and banged my fist against my head.

While it was still dark I turned off the motorway and drove into the southern edge of hills. I tried to remember what I knew of the reprocessing-plant that Malcolm had talked about. To this was sent nuclear waste from all over the world; from the waste was made plutonium for the construction of thermonuclear bombs; this process used up the original waste but left a further residue that might one day be a threat more virulent and permanent even than that of bombs. In this way, yes, humans might be creating their virtual extinction. There were the stories also of leukaemia in children and infertility in men – the results of leaks and contamination. But the evidence for these stories depended on the assessment of statistics; and notoriously it was possible to juggle statistics as one wanted, so that in this sense too humans seemed to be choosing their reality. Significantly, it was people who were strangers to the district who argued passionately that the plant should be closed; local inhabitants were more concerned that they should not lose the jobs which provided them with exceptional money.

My mind went on its way. What were the details of the story of the destruction of Sodom and Gomorrah? God had sent down angels to see if there were any good people left in the cities, in which case the cities would not be destroyed –

– but the local people had tried to bugger the angels, which had been the last straw in God's statistical analysis and which had resulted in the cities being destroyed?

I was driving out of the hills towards the sea. I turned north on to a road just inland from the coast. The road wound past inlets and mudflats. On the left there were notices giving warning of a military firing-range: on the right the sun began to appear with a red glow behind the hills. I thought – The sun is the bringer of both life and death: how you take advantage of it is what matters?

I drove through the village from which some of the children were said to have come, but where they were now no longer. At certain times of history I remembered – in Russia after the revolution, in some countries of Eastern Europe even now – children had banded together after grown-ups had landed them in this or that fearful calamity: these bands had gone off to try to learn to survive – in the forest, in the hills, in the alleyways of cities. They had scavenged in dustbins; they had run and hidden like deer. Grown-ups had mostly chosen to pretend they did not exist. It was as if they were shadows from the grown-ups' unconscious – that might tell them both of self-destruction and of the style of how to survive.

There were small clouds with gold and pink edges like bits of paper on fire. I thought – Fire and brimstone are ready to come down: but first, have those angels landed? There was one cloud larger and lower than the rest which bulged above a hill like a genie stuck half in and half out of its bottle. I thought – But I know what that is! I drove to the brow of the hill and stopped; there below me, yes, on the narrow plain between the hills and the sea, were the four huge cooling-towers of the power-station by the reprocessing-plant; it was above them that steam hung like a sluggish and overweight spectre. I sat and watched the pink and gold above the mountains turn to silver and grey. I wondered – One might come across the Virgin Mary in this setting?

I drove on. I was coming to the small town which, I remembered, had once been an up-and-coming seaside resort, but then holidaymakers had been driven away by the rumours of radioactivity. It was here, however, that the local people did not complain because the nuclear industry offered such secure jobs and prospects, and protesters had been driven away with threats and stones.

I wondered – What if the children have simply been contaminated and are being kept out of sight by the authorities? But this is the sort of conspiracy theory that is more virtual than to do with reality.

At the far end of the town there was a car-park; to one side of it was the beach, with a hotel just above it, and beyond this the railway line along which radioactive waste trundled to and fro by the sea. It was too early in the morning for me to check into the hotel – I had quite lost any idea of spending the weekend in a grand hotel in the hills – so I thought I would go for a walk along the beach.

I could not remember what I had read about this beach: was it or was it not contaminated? certainly there might be some danger in the cold grey sea. No one was on the beach; and although it was early, there might have been expected to be one or two scavengers or people walking their dogs. I thought – If I walk along it I will be showing some trust? that there might be virtue in danger? that this piece rather than that might be knocked out of my genetic code –

– And if these are fairy-stories, such stories are often about the need for trust?

There was a path down through the sand-dunes. The tide was on its way out; there were runnels of water hurrying over pebbles and sand. I remembered an early science-fiction story in which a man in a time-machine landed on a strange and desolate beach; the time was either far into the future or far into the past; human life was extinct or had not yet begun. What would have been the difference? Was not human consciousness always an excrescence likely to be snuffed out: or was it rather, as some scientists now seemed to claim, that without which in some sense the universe could not have begun –

I had walked for some time along the beach and nothing seemed to be getting any nearer or further away. The cooling-towers had disappeared behind the line of dunes, though the genie still swelled lethargically out of his bottle. I thought – The towers are like those of an ogre's castle: it is in the nature of ogres' castles to appear and disappear; we make up such stories to explain our experience. Is it really by the light of such explanations that the universe is formed –

I had read stories about ogres and castles to Billy. He would say – But are they true? I would say – They are shots at talking about things than can be said in no better way. Billy had said – But is that true?

I came to a place on the beach where the tops of two of the cooling-towers had become visible again; they appeared now to be quite close. There was a high security fence along the line of the sand-dunes which separated the beach from the precincts of the reprocessing-plant and the power-station. The fence dipped down at a place parallel to where I stood; at this point there projected through the fence a large pipe, or culvert, across the open end of which was an iron grille. From this pipe there ran water which flowed in a shallow stream across the beach. I had stopped just short of this stream because I did not know whether or not I should step through it. The stream had presumably started in the hills and ran through the grounds in which were the power-station and the plant: if anything was contaminated, it would be this stream. It was indeed as if I had stepped into a landscape of magic water and ogres' castles. I thought I might say to Billy – Yes, you can say that such stories are true. Then – There is something about this place, this stretch of sand, that is like the smooth and gleaming rocks where people were exposed to visions on the side of that hill –

There was a small boy standing by the grille at the end of the pipe or culvert; I had not noticed him before; he might have come through a gap in the fence, though this seemed unlikely. He wore a white T-shirt and jeans. He was younger than Billy, though he might be the same age as Billy had been when he and I had walked along that other beach. I thought – All right, we are in a strange country: we can at least make connections.

The boy was peering down into the water: he began to move towards me along the far side of the stream. He was carrying in his hand something that looked like a container into which one might put small fish. It did not seem that he had noticed me; it was as if he were too intent on the stream. I thought – Or perhaps it is as if we are the sole survivors of some nuclear disaster; we have wandered the earth alone till now; what sort of recognition will it be when we meet –

The boy came up opposite me and stopped. What he held in his hand appeared to be a plastic carton such as might contain yoghurt; this appeared to be empty; it had a transparent covering fastened by an elastic band around the top. This reminded me of something I had once seen, or read about, though I could not just now remember what. The boy looked up at me; we faced each other across the stream. He had brushed–up fair hair and a freckled face. I thought – He is indeed somewhat like Billy; more foreign perhaps – or like an angel? He had been holding one hand in his pocket; now he put the hand with the plastic container in it behind his back and held this other hand out to me with the fist clenched: it was as if he might be playing some game, or testing me with a riddle: I was to guess what was in his fist, or choose between that hand and the one that he held behind his back. I pointed to the fist he held out to me. He opened it and on the palm there was what appeared to be a shell. The shell was unusual – I could not quite see – I was still separated from the boy by the four or five yards of the shallow stream. I thought I might say – You are wanting me to look at the shell? You are giving it to me? You want me to buy it?

– You want me to step through the waters of this stream?

The shell, so far as I could see, consisted of two spiral cones, or whorls, the one growing out of the other. I thought – All right, some sort of deformity, mutation, arising from radioactivity?

Then – This is ridiculous

The boy had not said anything. But this did not seem strange.

There was the sound of a siren, or alarm, starting up suddenly: this came from the direction of the power–station and the plant: I had put the toe of one foot into the water as if to test it. I stood still, balancing, as if I were on a wire; as if the wire had become alive and I was responsible. I thought – Though this is, indeed, unlikely. The boy continued to hold his hand out to me across the water. The siren wailed and rose to a crescendo; water was coming through my shoes. I thought – Well anyway, it is too late now; let whoever or whatever it is come and get me. I stepped through the water, placing my feet carefully one in front of the other. I took the shell from the hand of the small boy. There were two whorls like horns, yes, with a small bump like an embryonic eye in the middle. I thought – Something like this I have surely seen before: but in the mind? in reality? I did not know if I was expected to keep the shell: should I offer the boy some money? The siren had reached the high pitch of its screech and was staying there; it was as if my feet might be in some sort of trap, I might fall backwards into the water. The boy suddenly turned and ran off towards the fence. I was waving my arms to stop myself overbalancing; or as if I were wildly signalling – but to whom – for help? as a warning? There was a small swirl of dust or sand on the beach in the distance ahead of me: this was such as one sometimes sees in deserts, as a whirlwind or mirage. I went twisting and leaping back across the stream: I still held the shell. The noise of the siren began to abate. I thought – It is possible that the alarm might have something to do with the boy; it was he who was close to the fence. The whirl in the distance was coming closer with a faint buzzing like that of a trapped bee: the siren had stopped. I was now standing at the side of the stream where I had been before. I looked round for the boy but he seemed to have disappeared. He might have got through the fence where it encircled the pipe or culvert; but again, this seemed unlikely. However what else? This did not seem a place where such questions would be answered. The commotion in the distance was turning out to be a vehicle approaching across the sand; it shook and shimmered like something emerging out of a cloud; I thought – A mirage is, is it not, a reflection, refraction, from what is going on elsewhere?

I put the shell in my pocket. It seemed I should protect it as if it were some talisman, some secret.

The vehicle on the beach was turning out to be an open Land-

Rover with two men in front and two at the back facing inwards. The man in the front passenger-seat wore a dark-blue uniform and a beret; he was young; he appeared to be an officer. The driver was an older man in blue overalls and a woollen cap. The men in the back were soldiers in camouflage uniforms and they held automatic weapons between their knees. The Land-Rover had official insignia on the bonnet. It pulled up, confronting me at the far side of the stream.

The man like an officer stood up and began to raise a loud-hailer to his mouth. Then he lowered it and smiled. I thought – It is as if he knows me; as if he expects me to know this. I thought – This is a mark of this strange country?

He said 'This beach is out of bounds.'

I said 'There's nothing to say it is.'

'I'm saying it is.'

'It's dangerous? Contaminated? I mean, do you say it is?'

He continued to smile. The driver was looking in the direction in which the small boy had gone. He murmured something to the two soldiers, who climbed out of the back of the Land-Rover and set off in the direction of the fence. The officer paid no attention to them. He gazed at me.

I said 'You're security? That was an alarm?'

He said 'You'd better come along.'

'What set it off? There's a scare?'

The two soldiers reached the fence by the opening to the pipe or culvert: it seemed that they were inspecting the wire that fitted round the grille. They did not seem seriously to be looking for the boy.

The officer was not looking up the beach towards the town. I said 'You don't answer questions.'

He said 'This is routine patrolling.'

'And the alarm?'

'Testing.'

'There's been a leak?'

'No.'

'Someone trying to get in?' Then – 'But you wouldn't say, would you.'

The two soldiers had set off along the fence towards the town.

The officer was watching them. He said 'You're staying in the hotel? You've checked in?'

I said 'It's too early.'

'You've just arrived?' Then – 'You're on your own?'

I thought I might say – You're mistaking me for someone else.

He said 'Get in, I'll give you a lift.'

The Land-Rover started up and splashed its way through the stream. It stopped beside me. There did not seem to be any reason why I should not climb in. I sat in the back. The officer was in profile in front of me, his arm over the back of the seat; he was good-looking; with dark eyes and dark eyebrows and carefully cut hair.

I thought – You don't mean, you really did not see the boy?

I said 'Who are you on the look-out for, terrorists?'

He said 'You can get all the information you want from the desk at the site.'

'I don't really want that sort of information.'

'Oh, what sort of information do you want?'

'Do you know anything about a group of children who have set themselves up in the hills?'

The Land-Rover had moved off and was heading towards the town across the beach. The officer did not answer for a while; then he turned to me still with the look as if we might share some complicity. He said 'Oh I think I can say truthfully that I don't know much about that!'

I said 'That boy was one of them?'

I expected him to say – What boy? He turned away and looked ahead.

The Land-Rover was bumping over pebbles towards the car-park that was down a slope just beyond the hotel. I hung on to the metalwork. I thought – I am being shaken like dice: when I am cast out, I will present by chance this or that face to this strange world.

The young officer said with his back half to me – 'Will you give a message to someone in the hotel?'

I said 'What?'

'Though perhaps it doesn't matter so much now if you're on your own –'

'Will I give a message to someone in the hotel?'

'And there may not be anyone up yet, anyway.'

The Land-Rover was edging between bollards into the car-park. My car was where I had parked it not more than half an hour ago. But it was true I seemed to have stepped into a different world. I thought — This might be one of the effects of radioactivity? or with such a threat hanging over one, little bits and pieces are anyway knocked out of expected codes —

I said 'Look, if there's a scare, of course you can't talk about it. But why won't you talk about the boy; or the children in the hills —'

He said 'Will you give a message to the young lady behind the desk?'

'Yes.'

'That perhaps it's all right after all. That everything is for the best in the best of all possible worlds.'

'You want me to tell her that?'

'Yes.'

'And that's all?'

'Yes.' Then — 'Who said that, do you know?'

The two soldiers who had been walking along the beach were entering the car-park; they were approaching the Land-Rover holding their automatic weapons. The Land-Rover had stopped. I thought — Perhaps the young officer is mad and the soldiers are his keepers, but appearances have to be kept up —

I said 'Leibniz, I think: and Voltaire made fun of it.'

'Why did he make fun of it?'

'Because it seemed unlikely, I suppose.'

'Oh yes I see.' Then — 'But it's a metaphysical problem.' Then — 'And mind you get the sand off your shoes.'

I was climbing out of the back of the Land-Rover. The two soldiers climbed in. The young officer waved at me. The Land-Rover set off across the car-park.

At the edge of the town across the road there was a line of shops like that which might belong to a model village — a grocer's, a café, a newsagent, the frosted windows of an office that might be that of solicitors. A few people had appeared — a newspaper boy, an old man on a bicycle, two women talking on a corner. I thought — If this were in a film, the very ordinariness would be there to signify something sinister. Then – Perhaps the young officer thinks he has recognised me from another planet.

I got in my car and drove the short distance to the hotel. The hotel was a squat stone building like the clubhouse of a yacht or golf club. There was a Union Jack on a flagpole in the centre of a circle in which cars could turn; I parked my car by some bushes and got my suitcase out and went to the front door which was ajar. I thought – And once you start to see things like this, everything can appear to have some portentous meaning –

Inside the hotel there was a hallway with a lounge with armchairs on one side and a bar with tables and chairs on the other. At the far end on the left was a reception desk: to the right of this a staircase went to the upper floor. Between these a passage went through to the back.

I thought – And out of this so ordinary woodwork will suddenly burst monstrous genies with the trunks of elephants and the tails of fishes –

I went to the reception desk. Behind it was a man crouched over the screen and keyboard of a computer. He was wearing a dressing-gown. He was a large middle-aged man, bald, with spectacles. I said 'Good morning, I'm afraid I'm a bit early, I'd like a room.'

He said 'We're not open.'

'A man on the beach said you were.'

'You've been on the beach?'

He gave his attention to me for a moment; he peered over the desk at my shoes. Then something dragged him back to his computer: I could not see what was on the screen. He tapped on the keyboard. It was as if he were in one of those routines in which he would go on tapping until what he wanted came up on the screen.

I said 'I've got all the sand off.'

He said 'I mean we're not open just now for guests.'

I looked round the hallway and the lounge. Some of the chairs were stacked; nothing was untidy or out of place at the bar. I said 'Look I've been driving all night, haven't you got a room, I'm tired.'

He said 'How did you get in?'

'Through the door.'

'Who opened it?'

'I don't know.'

He left his computer and leaned over the counter again looking towards the door. I could see that on the screen there were rows of figures. I thought – He is a computer freak? He has got up early because there has been a scare? He is monitoring something?

I said 'Look, I'm nothing to do with the power-station or the plant. I've come to do a story about some children who've set themselves up in the hills. Do you know about them?'

He said 'We didn't expect you so early.'

'You didn't expect me at all.'

'Did you want one room or two?'

He had opened the registration book that was on the counter. He pushed it towards me. Then he came from behind the desk and went to the front door that I had left ajar and looked out onto the car-park.

I thought – He too thinks he knows who I am: this is one of those films in which there is a flip in a space-warp and suddenly you find yourself in someone else's story.

There was a girl (woman, girl) coming down the stairs into the hallway. She was young, not much more than twenty; she was in a dressing-gown. She had reddish curly hair, and wore no make-up. She came down the stairs slowly, as if she were an actress in a drama. She paid no attention to me or the man by the front door. She went behind the reception desk and struck one of those bells that go ping! to summon an attendant.

The man by the door turned and said 'He's not there.'

She said 'No he's here.'

'Have you been outside in that dressing-gown?'

'No I've been inside it.'

She was gazing ruminatively at the book in which I had signed my name. Her dressing-gown was padded; she had a small waist. The monkey inside me had begun to jump up and down; but then became still, as if it had become aware of some more potent presence in the forest.

I thought – But thank goodness Janice is not with me!

The man said 'I've told you a hundred times –'

She said 'And I've paid no attention.'

32

'Will you go upstairs –'

'Certainly.'

She had a soft lilting voice. She picked up my suitcase. I said 'No, I'll take it.' She murmured 'Rape!' She carried my suitcase to the bottom of the stairs. I went after her and took hold of the handle; she did not let go. We stood still with our hands interwined on the suitcase. She kept her eyes cast down. Then she said 'Would you like one room or two?'

I said 'One. What do you mean, two?'

I thought – You mean, you might really share a room with me?

She let go of the suitcase and went ahead of me up the stairs.

Within her dressing-gown there were those strange shapes that might represent, it seemed, the forces of the universe. I thought – This is not to do with the monkey scratching on the stump of the tree; it is more that here are roots from which that flower might grow from the top of the head –

When we were on the upper landing she said in a formal voice 'Did you have a good jouney?'

I said 'Yes, thank you.'

'The roads are quite clear at this time of morning.'

'Yes they are, aren't they.'

'Why are you on your own? I thought you were with a companion.'

'Why did you think that?'

'Perhaps she will come later.'

'I don't know.'

She opened one of the doors in the passage and went through. There was a somewhat nondescript bedroom with two beds and a door through to a bathroom. She went to a window and looked out onto the car-park. I put the suitcase on a chair and sat on a bed. I said 'This is the most extraordinary place. Everyone acts as if they know me.'

She said in her lilting voice. 'Perhaps they do. Do you find that gratifying?'

'I don't know.'

'But you are quite famous, aren't you?'

'Not that famous.'

'Well I'd never heard of you.' She turned away from the

window and came and stood in front of me. She said 'Though everyone likes a mystery.'

I thought – It's true I like the idea of your being in charge of this situation.

She said in her actressy voice 'Did you notice a man in the car-park, or on the beach, who drives around in a car like a pumpkin, with two frog-footmen like in "Cinderella"?'

I said 'Yes.'

'You did?'

'Yes. And he asked me to give a message to you.'

She seemed to blush. She said 'What was it?'

'That perhaps things are all right after all. That everything is for the best in the best of all possible worlds.'

'That's all?'

'Yes.'

'It's a quotation?'

'Yes.'

'Who from?'

'Leibniz, I think. And then Voltaire made fun of it.'

'Why? Yes I see why. Are they readable?'

'One is unreadable and interesting, and the other is readable and boring.'

'I am sure I can guess which is which.'

'Yes.'

There was the impression, with her standing in front of me, of her offering herself to me, but not for sex: perhaps rather for something to grow out of the top of the head.

She said 'You were asking about those children. I think it terribly important that you see them.'

I said 'You know them?'

'Yes. Their leader is Gaby. I think it terribly important that you talk to her, and hear what she says.'

There was a noise in the passage outside. The girl listened; then went to the door which I had left ajar and said 'Fuck off, Fred.'

A voice which seemed to be that of the bald man with spectacles said 'What are you doing?'

She said 'The usual, what do you think?'

'I want you downstairs in two minutes.'

'That should give us time.' She closed the door. She came back and sat on the bed beside me. She said 'He's supposed to be my father.'

'And is he?'

'No.' Then in her actress's voice – 'Though does one ever know!'

I said 'Sometimes.' Then – 'Does it matter?' Then – 'It depends what you make of it anyway.'

She lay back on her elbows on the bed. She was watching me. I thought – She is searching to make sure I might be the person that she requires.

She said 'Oh yes. Gaby originally came from Yugoslavia, did you know?'

I said 'No.'

'She came over as a refugee, some years ago, with her family. I don't think they were her family actually; but that's right, it doesn't matter.'

I said 'It was in Yugoslavia that some children said they'd seen the Virgin Mary.'

'Yes, you know –'

'Was it that that put the idea into Gaby's head?'

'I suppose so.'

'Did Gaby see a vision?'

'I don't know.' Then – 'But as you say, it depends on what she'd make of it, anyway.'

She had her legs slightly apart as she lay on the bed. I thought – God knows, these messages are ambiguous enough about what she requires –

I said 'Why did you think I'd have someone with me?'

She said 'People usually do, don't they?'

'What –'

'Or if they don't, they think of nothing else, like Fred.'

'Not always –'

'There's a group of men here like Bluebeard's Castle.' Then – 'No, not always.'

'Have this group got anything to do with the children?'

'Oh that, perhaps, yes.'

She got off the bed and went to the window. She raised the

bottom half of the sash and put her hands on the sill and lifted herself on her toes and arched her back. She seemed to be doing breathing exercises.

I said 'What more can you tell me?' And then when she didn't answer – 'And there was that scare this morning –'

She said 'Oh of course, we might all be dying of leukaemia!'

She left the window and came and stood in front of me again. She looked belligerent. She said 'But of course they'd never say.'

I said 'The people at the plant? The people like Fred?'

'They protect themselves.'

'Doesn't everyone?'

'Who?'

'Gaby and the children –'

'From what –'

'By not saying. I mean, are people afraid of what they might say?'

She began to clench and unclench her hands, and frown, as she stood in front of me. Then she murmured 'That's brilliant!' She began to walk around the room. She hit her hand against her thigh.

I said 'And that's the sort of hold you've got over Fred?'

She stopped in front of me again. She was taking deep breaths. I thought – It is not so much as if she is doing exercises, as that the air is exercising her. She said 'All right.' Then 'Will you help me out of that window?'

I said 'Yes.'

'That boring old fart will be waiting for me downstairs.'

I said 'And then you'll have some hold over me?'

She seemed to think about this. She became quite still. Then she took off her dressing-gown and handed it to me. Underneath she wore a T-shirt and shorts.

She said 'If you want to find the children, there's only one road up into the hills. You go about five miles, then there's a signpost on the left with its arms off; a track goes down to some farm buildings in the valley.'

I said 'Thanks.'

'You're welcome.'

'What's special about these children?'

'You think it's important to have a hold over people?'

'Sometimes.'

'When?'

'If you know what you want.'

'I don't think the children mind dying.'

'Do you?'

'No much.'

'Why not?'

She had gone to the window. She put one leg over the window-sill. Then she said 'I find this very difficult.'

I said 'Yes.'

'Will you give my love to Gaby?'

'I will.'

I had put my head out of the window beside her. There was still quite a drop. We waited. She said. 'Do you want breakfast?'

I said 'No. Yes. I think I'll sleep.'

'You can go through to the kitchen where there's coffee and bread and stuff. Charlie thinks he can fix Fred's computer, so probably he's got him out of the house.'

'Who's Charlie?'

'You met him on the beach.'

'How does he think he can fix Fred's computer?'

'I don't know.'

She got down on her stomach with her legs hanging out of the window. I got hold of her wrist. I said 'You've still got quite a drop.'

She said 'What's special about Janice?'

'Nothing special.'

'Is she pretty?'

'Yes.'

I was holding her arms just below the wrists. She let go of the sill of the window and hung from my arms. Looking up at me she said 'Why is Voltaire boring?' I said 'Perhaps he wouldn't see what's difficult.' I swung her outwards and let go . She landed on the grass at the edge of the driveway. She crouched for a moment, looked this way and that, then straightened and walked round the corner of the hotel.

I thought – Perhaps I can watch her from a window in the bathroom.

I went and lay on the bed.

I thought – How did she know about Janice? How did Charlie know me?

Then I slept.

Three

I was woken by the telephone. I had been dreaming. The dream was disappearing – there had been a group of people standing on a beach; they had been waiting for something to be dragged up from the sea – Oh don't lose it! don't go!

The telephone was like a wave of lava coming down from the land.

I said 'Hullo –'

'Hullo? It's me, Janice.'

'Janice!'

'You don't seem very pleased.'

'Oh but I am! I've been dreaming. But other people's dreams are so boring, don't you think?'

I had been with the girl who had taken off her dressing-gown. She had hung out of the window from my hands. This had not been a dream! She had gone on to the beach. The wave of lava had sent people tumbling into the sea –

Janice said 'Yes.'

'I drove all night. What time is it?'

'Half-past eight. I'm sorry if I've woken you. But something rather vital has been happening.'

'I know, I've had a terrible row with Melissa.'

'It's not that —'

'Why did you ring her?'

'Why didn't you wait?'

'How could I —'

'I know.'

'What do you know —'

'That you've had a row with Melissa. I've just rung her.'

I held the receiver away from my ear. I did not want to listen to any of this. The girl with the dressing-gown seemed to have known me for years. She had gone to find the young officer on the beach?

Janice was saying 'Jack says we've got to get on to it quickly.'

'Get on to what?'

'Have you been listening?'

'No.'

'Wake up.'

'How did you know I was here?'

Janice waited for a time and then said 'There's only one hotel. I booked a room last night. Didn't they tell you?'

I said 'No. Yes. No.' Then — 'I see.'

What did I see? That everything is a confusion; then you let your eyes relax, your mind relax, and shapes and figures appear quite clearly as if in one of those magic pictures you move away from your nose —

— and then you lose them again?

Janice was saying 'Jack says there's been a scare at the plant.'

I said 'Did you ask for one room or two?'

'Will you make sense —'

'Yes.'

'Look, I'm sorry if I made trouble with Melissa. But I thought I was doing it for the best.'

'You've spoken to her this morning?'

'Yes.' Then after a time — 'I thought you wanted me.'

'I do want you!' Then — 'Melissa was at home? She was all right?'

I had got off the bed and had carried the telephone to the window. There were a few more cars in the car-park. There was only my car in front of the hotel. I wondered if the cord of the telephone would stretch to the bathroom, where there should be a window that looked out over the sea.

Janice said 'Look, I'm coming up. How long does it take?'

'Five or six hours.'

'Well get going without me.'

'Janice —'

'Yes?'

'I don't really think there's been much of a scare.'

'Have you got a hangover?'

'No.'

'Well what is it?' Then the line went dead. I had been carrying the telephone through to the bathroom and I seemed to have broken some connection.

In the bathroom there was, yes, a window that looked out onto the beach. The tide was still out; there were no figures on the beach.

I came back into the bedroom and sat on the bed. Janice had rung the hotel last night so that was why they had been half-expecting me. But how had Charlie known this? The girl had gone out early in her dressing-gown to meet him?

But what was all that between Janice and Melissa? Possibilities hung above my head like a gross and smiling genie half out of its bottle.

I looked out into the passage. The hotel, as before, seemed to have no other guests in it. I went back to the bathroom and washed and shaved; then went down the stairs. There was no one at the reception desk or behind it in the office. I went along the passage to a kitchen at the back. Here there was, yes, a toaster and a machine for making coffee.

I set them to work and sat and tried to understand more of what was happening. Charlie, a security officer, would have behaved with more urgency if there had been a serious scare: would not have sent his message about the best of all possible worlds —

— I did not even know her name!

My dream had been of fire and brimstone coming down to the sea —

— This might be part of the story I had come for?

When I had gone out to Yugoslavia to do my follow-up on the

story of the children there I had visited the site of some graves on the other side of the hill from where they had seen their vision. Here, some forty years before, atrocities had been committed – women and children had been herded and buried alive. This was an area where it had become customary to commit such atrocities – by Croats on Serbs, by Serbs on Croats; by Fascists and Communists and Catholics and Orthodox Christians all taking turns, it seemed, to do to one another what appeared to come naturally to them – that is, for instance, burying women and children alive. On the other side of the hill was the area made smooth by people's knees; but this too seemed natural, and its crop of crosses like sprouting seeds. I had wondered – Is there some portent here; some message to be learned from the juxtaposition of corpses and seeds at the two sides of the hill. But I had not really been able to write about this; this was one of the several things I had not been able to write about at this time, anything that I said being able to be invalidated by a possible opposite. But if certain things are beyond language, then how are they to be looked at at all; how is one to know –

The coffee was boiling. The toast had popped up like hands with no fingers out of graves.

In Yugoslavia I had joined a party who were to attend a ceremony at one of the graves: bodies were being dug up so that they could be properly re-buried. The victims had been members of the Serbian Orthodox Church: the murderers had been Croat Roman Catholics. The killings had been a retaliation, it was said, for an earlier slaughter by Serbs of Croats; all these were forerunners of larger and more indiscriminate massacres of both Serbs and Croats by Communists. I had watched while a mechanical excavator went to work on the side of a hill: it scooped up earth out of what looked like a filled-in well; the excavator deposited rubble which men with picks and shovels then sifted carefully. Eventually they came across what seemed to be bones; the excavator stopped; the men with picks and shovels went down into the well. The group that I was with began intoning psalms – Oh God forgive us our iniquities, and so on. I thought – But we like our iniquities, what would we do without them; even though we expect retribution for them –

I was eating toast and drinking coffee in the kitchen of the hotel. I was thinking – Oh God, can you not just stop our iniquities; even though you know we like being punished –

By the graves there was a group of women from the village on the other side of the hill; they were waiting as if somewhat impatiently and not singing. Among them was a woman whom I had seen the day before by the polished stones where the children had seen their vision: she wore a pale blue uniform like that of a nurse or perhaps of a lay religious order. She had been standing rather than sitting or kneeling within the rocky patch of crosses; she had been crying but as if somewhat furiously crying: I had thought – Of course, she is like the Virgin Mary! Now, on the other side of the hill, she broke away from the group and went to where the men with picks were working and she picked up a handful of earth and threw it briskly into the well. The men stopped to watch her. She moved off past the rubble and the excavator and went down into the valley. I did not see her again. I had thought – These images emerge very clearly: I would not know what more to write.

I was in the kitchen. I was putting my mug and plate into the sink. I seemed to have had my toast and coffee.

I went through the hotel and out onto the circle in front. My car was where I had left it: I thought – I am surprised? I planned to do some shopping at the grocer's before I drove to the children in the hills; then I would arrive bearing gifts to them. There were still no other cars in front of the hotel. People at the edge of the town were beginning to go about their business.

My car was by some bushes of the solid thick-leaved kind that flourish by the sea. As I was unlocking the door a boy came out of the bushes: he was the boy, it seemed, that I had seen earlier on the beach – he had brushed-up fair hair and a freckled face. I was glad to see him. I thought that he must have been waiting for me because he wanted his shell, or perhaps some money: had I not offered to buy it? I said 'Hullo, do you want your shell?' I had it in my pocket: I held it out: he looked at it as if he did not recognise it. I thought – Surely he must be one of the children in the hills.

I said 'Look, I'm just going to get things in the grocer's across the road. Then I'm going up into the hills. You can come with me. Or wait for me in the car.'

I left the door of the car open and walked across the car-park. I thought − But why do I imagine he is one of those children: because of the other coincidences? It may simply seem that I am abducting him: are there not suspicions about this sort of thing in this place anyway −

− Or perhaps he just does not understand English?

The grocer was setting his wares out in front of his shop. He would have seen me with the boy. I said 'Good morning; you're open nice and early.'

He said 'What do you want?'

'Bread and butter and milk and eggs and cheese. And oh yes, orange-juice and chocolates.'

'I mean, what's your business?'

He went back into his shop. I saw that the boy had followed me: he was standing on the edge of the pavement watching. The grocer was inside rummaging behind his counter. I thought the boy might have followed me because I had not paid for his shell, so I held it out again and said 'I'll give you a pound.'

The grocer said 'It'll cost you more than that.'

'I was talking to the boy.'

'What boy?' The grocer had come to the door of the shop. He was carrying a broom. I thought − Perhaps it's true that the children are invisible to most people in this strange country.

The man brandished his broom at the boy and said 'Shoo!' The boy snatched one or two apples from the stand outside the shop and ran away.

I said to the grocer 'All right I've said I'll pay!'

The grocer came back into the shop. He began takings things I had mentioned from the shelves and putting them into a basket almost violently. I said 'What's wrong with this town? Everyone seems barmy.'

The grocer said 'There's nothing wrong with this town. It's only people like you who think there's something wrong with this town.'

'I want sugar and bacon and tea.'

'You come here to make trouble −'

'I make trouble? You know me?'

'Yes. This is a perfectly healthy town −'

'I wasn't talking about that.'

Through a door at the back of the shop, in what might be a sitting-room, I briefly saw a figure, half-listening and half-trying to keep out of sight, that I thought might, or might not, be the man called Fred.

The grocer was cramming the stuff that he and I had collected into a plastic bag. I took out my wallet. The grocer said 'You were offering him money.'

I thought – You mean, I really might be in trouble?

I paid the grocer and walked back across the road and the car-park to my car. I thought – I am becoming paranoid: I imagine myself being watched –

Then – But I had worked out, hadn't I, that the children might have some hold over people in this town?

When I reached my car there was no sign of the boy. I thought he might have set off up the road. I drove out of the car-park; the road went under a railway bridge. Just beyond this there was a bus-stop and by it, yes, the boy was waiting. I stopped the car, opened the passenger door and said 'Get in.' He did not seem to recognise or understand me. I thought – I should be getting used to this by now: or does he really think I am going to carry him off into the hills? I held out the shell again: and then a pound from my pocket. He looked at them, and at me, wonderingly. Then he climbed into the seat beside me and took the pound.

I said 'And now you can show me the way.'

When I was driving he turned the coin this way and that curiously as if he had not seen one before; then he raised his head and seemed to listen; then he turned and looked over the back of the front seat. Then he raised himself and leaned right across it with his behind in the air.

I thought – This is ridiculous.

Or – What if indeed this boy has nothing to do with the children in the hills?

Then he clambered right over the front seat and sat in the back. I could see his face in the driving-mirror, smiling.

The road wound up into the hills. We passed a group of walkers with back-packs; a clergyman pushing a bicycle. I thought – One or two escaping from the cities of the plain?

The boy in the back of the car had begun talking quietly in what seemed to be a foreign language. I thought – Well I don't see why this should be more odd than anything else. Then I looked in the driving-mirror and there appeared to be two of him seated side-by-side: I thought – Well surely this is odd! or it is the double vision that I sometimes get when I have been drinking? But I have not been drinking! So you mean – what – these are the two angels that visited the cities of the plain? The two manifestations of the boy seemed identical except that the hair of one was brushed up slightly higher than the other. I had a sensation of the hair slightly rising at the back of my own head. I was watching out for a lay-by in which I could stop and look back. I thought – Or one should not look back when leaving the cities of the plain –

I found a stopping-place and turned to the back of the car. There were indeed two boys seated side-by-side. They were watching me brightly. I thought – All right, they are twins: there is nothing so unusual about twins? One of them is the boy who came out of the bushes and the other is the boy by the bus-stop: one came to the grocer's and the other hid in the car; one or the other was on the beach earlier this morning: all this explains why from time to time they did not recognise me –

– all this makes sense?

I said 'Abracadabra!'

They spoke to one another briefly in the language I did not understand.

I drove on. There were clouds being blown by the wind; patches of sunlight swept across the landscape. I thought – All right, I do not know what is happening: I am ferrying these twin souls to where they might be born –

– What is the point of angels?

One of the boys tapped me on the shoulder. I jumped. There was a signpost on the left of the road from which the arms had been removed; a track went down towards the valley. I turned onto the track and stopped. There was a van or minibus blocking the way in front of me. A man was standing leaning against the side staring down into the valley. A young couple with back-packs were sitting on a hillock at the side of the track; they were gazing into the valley. It was, yes as if they might be at the site of some visitation. I looked in the driving-mirror and saw that the boys had ducked down behind the front seats. I thought – Of course, they do not want to be seen by the man beside the minibus.

I got out of my car and walked up to the man. In the valley, some three or four hundred yards away, there was a group of farm buildings round three sides of a yard: on the fourth and nearest side was a stone wall with a gateway. Towards this a car was moving slowly down the track with a man and a woman walking in front of it. I thought – They are officials: they are the sheriff and his men on their way to some showdown. Within the farmyard there were, yes, children. They were grouped around what looked like a telegraph pole or flagpole that was lying on the ground.

I stood by the man by the minibus. I said 'Good morning.' He did not answer. I said 'You've come to get the children?' He still said nothing.

I thought – Some people hear, some people don't, in this strange country.

I looked in through the window of the bus and saw that there were some official-looking papers on the front seat; they had headings which were to do, yes, with the Social Services.

When I looked at the man he had the grey chalky face of someone in the last stages of sickness or despair: his skin seemed to be turning to paper. I thought – There is after all some contamination here? and not just of radioactivity? I had been about to announce to the man my credentials as a journalist; but now I too said nothing. I thought – You might survive if you say nothing – escape from the cities of the plain.

It seemed I should get the bag of provisions out of my car, then walk with it down the track into the valley. And I could see what was happening with the boys. When I got to the car the back door was ajar; the boys were not there. I thought – They will be escaping into the hills? they will be trying to get down unseen to the farmyard? I looked up at the young couple who were seated on the hillock; they looked down at me blankly. I thought – They may think I am some official: or anyway, fellow agents do not recognise each other in hostile territory.

I took my bag of provisions and set off down the track. Ahead of me the car and the two people walking in front of it had reached the gateway into the farmyard. As I moved down the track my view of what was happening in the farmyard was cut off by the wall. There was no sign in the landscape of the two boys who had been in my car. I wondered – But if one both knows and knows that one does not know what is happening, does this make a proper outcome more likely to occur?

When I reached the gateway into the farmyard I could see again the scene within. The children – about a dozen of them, their ages between eight and twelve – had fastened ropes to the top end of the long pole that was lying on the ground. They had split into two groups: one, consisting of three girls, was standing by the base of the pole close to where a hole had been dug; the other and larger group, consisting mostly of younger boys, was backing away from the pole holding the unattached ends of the ropes. The boys were moving towards the wall to one side of the gateway. It was as if they were about to try to raise the pole with the ropes – an operation such as might be depicted in a children's encyclopaedia to show how ancient Egyptians had raised obelisks. It was as if the children were so intent on their task that they had hardly noticed the man and the woman and the car that had entered the courtyard. A second couple, a man and a woman, were getting out of the car; the four of them stood and watched the children. I had stopped in the gateway. I became aware – with the slightly demented sensation again as if not only the hairs but a bit of my skull were rising at the back of my head – that one of the boys holding the ends of the ropes was apparently one of the boys who had been in my car; he had the same brushed–up fair hair: but this was not possible! he would not have had time to get round to the farmyard from my car: I would have seen him: and anyway, he was wearing a short leather jacket while the others had been wearing just their white shirts. So he was a third boy: so all right, they were triplets: so what on earth were the odds against this sort of thing? I just did not want to think about this too much. And anyway, what was there to think about it? I remained in the gateway to the farmyard. The four grown-ups were observing the children as if the children might be putting on some show for their benefit. The boys holding the ends of the ropes were climbing up on to the top of the wall; they were balancing precariously. I thought – But they cannot possibly pull

the pole upright while they are standing on the wall, they will pull
themselves inwards, they will topple like clowns. Two of the girls
at the base of the pole had put their feet against it; they were
making a block against which the pole might be raised, and then
when the pole was upright it might be eased into the hole. I
thought – But it is too far from the hole! it is more likely that the
base will slip and will injure the girls. The third girl had stood back
and seemed to be in charge of the operation; but she was doing
nothing; she wore a white T-shirt and shorts; she had short fair hair
and a round face; she appeared to be the girl whose photograph I
had seen in the local paper; she was Gaby. The boys on the wall
were making no more than gestures of pulling on the ropes; they
began to lean forwards, then swayed back, waving their arms,
overbalancing. Then the one nearest to me – the boy with
brushed-up fair hair – dropped the end of his rope and looked
behind him and jumped back carefully onto the ground outside the
wall: it might have seemed, perhaps, that he had been falling. He
crouched: he looked at me as I stood in the gateway: I thought –
He has at least noticed me. Then he moved off, still crouching so
that he was out of sight from the farmyard, along the outside of the
wall to the corner of the farm buildings. The other boys who were,
or had been, on the wall, were doing likewise – letting go of their
ropes and making out they were overbalancing and then jumping
and crouching and scrambling outside the wall to where they
disappeared behind the buildings. Within the farmyard the two
girls had bent with their hands on the base of the pole; the two men
had gone to help them; the women were watching; they had their
backs to the boys who had been on the wall. The two girls stood
back and let the men take over; they went and joined Gaby. The
two men were managing to move the base of the pole nearer to the
hole; then they gestured to the women to come and help them.
The women put their feet against the base of the pole and the men
backed away and picked up two of the ropes; it was as if they were
about to demonstrate how the task should properly be done. The
two men, pulling, got the top of the pole some feet off the ground.
Gaby turned and looked at me.

I thought – All right, I am here; thank you for recognising me.
The women were trying with their hands and feet to guide the

base of the pole towards the hole. The pole was nearly upright when it begn to swing, slipped, and the base of it seemed to catch one of the women on the ankle. She sat down heavily. The men were hanging on to their ropes and were trying to keep the pole upright; but suddenly they were running round it as if it were a maypole or as if they were objects on the ends of strings that were about to be hurled outwards. The three girls were moving towards a doorway in the barn at the back of the farmyard. The men on the ends of the ropes seemed to lose all control; the pole whirled and crashed down on the bonnet of the car that was parked in the farmyard. The woman on the ground had rolled over and was holding her ankle; one of the men joined the other woman and they knelt down by her. The other man went to look at the car. The three girls had disappeared from the farmyard.

I thought – With one great leap – and you are out in the hills above the plain?

I thought I should go round the outside of the farm buildings and try to see where the boys had gone; and from here I might get round to the back of the barn into which, it seemed, Gaby and the girls had disappeared. On the outside of the buildings was an area of rubble and nettles and twisted iron; there was no sign of the boys; they had run away into the hills? they would regroup later? I walked with my hands up to keep clear of the nettles. It was as if I might say – I surrender! I will ask no more questions! I will watch, and listen, and one thing will happen after another.

Round the far corner of the buildings, at the back of the tall barn, was a high wide door similar to the one in front: through these loaded wagons of hay must once have passed. Beyond the two doors, past the darkness of the inside of the barn, I could see through to the farmyard in which one of the men and the other woman were helping the injured woman out towards the track; she was limping with her arms round the shoulders of the others. The second man had got the pole off the bonnet of the car and was pulling at the metalwork of a wing that seemed to be jammed against a wheel. Then he seemed to give up, and followed the others.

I had stepped into the barn and was keeping to the shadows. It was a fine old building with an oak-beamed roof: spars and struts interweaved like lacework. The floor was of concrete and had been swept. In the corner on the left was an area of floor over which straw had been laid; here the children might have slept. Against the end wall was a row of plastic bags neatly propped; a suitcase was on its end as if ready to be taken away. In the corner beyond there were cooking utensils and a paraffin stove and plates neatly stacked; it was as if the children had been ready to go, but not to wherever the men and the women had wanted to take them. I thought – This is some Noah's Ark; they have reached dry land?

At the far end of the barn – as I moved past the high wide doorway I saw how the man and the two women were struggling up the hill; they had been joined by the man who had been by the car; he was waving towards the man by the minibus at the top of the track – at the far end of the barn there was a high loft supported by a structure of props and beams; a ladder had been pulled up on to the platform just under the roof. On the ground in front of this structure, also precisely laid out, was an array of objects as if designed to be on show – *objects trouvés* as it were, of a kind that might have been picked up on a hillside or beach. There was a length of wood like the skull and horns of an antelope; there were stones with coloured stripes as if painted, strands of seaweed encrusted with small shells like jewels. And there were some larger shells, yes, one or two with double whorls or spirals like those of the one that the boy had handed to me. All the objects had something striking and similar about them; they were forms which had the appearance of being something else; natural structures that seemed more likely to be artefacts. There was the claw of a crab with a further claw growing out of it; the skull of maybe a sheep with a hole in the centre of its forehead. I had the impression that I had been to this place, or in this situation, before – but this is said to be a trick played by circuitry in the brain. I also had the impression that I was being watched from the roof.

In front of the array of objects, as if it were a row of sentry-boxes, was a line of plastic containers like the one that the boy had been carrying on the beach. I squatted down to examine these. They were semi-transparent with a plastic film over the top held in place by a rubber band: stuck to the bottom was a disc of some thicker plastic. I thought – Yes I know where I have seen something like this before! in a television programme I was involved with about radioactivity. Such containers are a primitive means of testing for a certain form of radiation which is registered in specks on the plastic disc at the bottom. You set the containers out here and there on the ground –

I looked up towards the ceiling. There were cross-beams running just below the apex of the roof. Resting on one of these with her arms like folded wings – I had seen somewhere the beams of a church ceiling like this on which was carved the faces of angels – was a figure lying flat with her head on her hands: this was Gaby. She was gazing down at me. I still held my plastic bag of provisions. I thought – I am glad I have some offering.

For a time she did nothing. Then she twisted her body over the side of the beam and hung for a moment from her hands; then let go with one hand and caught an upright spar and swung herself down like this from hand to hand on the structure that supported the loft. She was like some gymnast, but without showing off; just performing a necessary task quickly. She landed on the concrete with her feet together, her arms held behind her for a moment again like wings. Then she looked at my plastic bag. I said 'I've brought you some food.'

She said 'Thank you.'

'I've come from the hotel. Someone there sent you her love, I don't know her name.'

'Ellen.'

'Yes Ellen.'

I was looking for somewhere to put my bag. I thought I should place it in some formal relationship with the array of objects set out on the ground. I said 'I'm a writer for a newspaper. I came to do a story about you, but I don't know what to ask or what to say.'

I set down the plastic bag. She went to the high doorway into the farmyard and looked out. The two men and the woman on the track were reaching the top of the slope. I thought – Their minibus may not be able to get past my car.

I said 'Did you see a vision?'

She left the doorway and went to the far end of the barn; she moved with a strong strutting walk like that of a dancer. She picked up the suitcase that was on its end and she carried it back towards me. She did not look at me.

I said 'Were those Social Services people coming to get you?'

She opened the suitcase, which was empty, and squatted by the row of plastic jars. She began to pick them up and put them carefully one by one into the suitcase.

I said 'Have you had any other sort of trouble with them, or with your family?'

I thought – But of course she will not answer: and now I have had my three questions, or riddles, like the man in the fairy-story. So what will happen next: do I get my head chopped off?

She looked to the far end of the barn. She went there and picked up some straw and came back with it and squatted down and packed the jars firmly with it in the suitcase. Then she said 'Do you come from London?'

I said 'Yes.'

'Do you have children?'

'Yes.'

'How many?'

'One.'

'A girl or boy?'

'A boy.'

'How old is he?'

'Twelve.'

'Can I come to London and help look after him?'

She spoke in a flat voice with only a slight foreign accent. When I did not immediately answer her last question she looked up at me with pale blue eyes that seemed to have some hurt behind them.

I said 'I don't think he needs much looking after.'

She said 'You don't think so?'

She looked away. I thought – But it is as if I have some hurting behind my eyes. She went on packing the suitcase, and then closed it.

She said 'Will you take this to Mrs Ferguson?'

I said 'Who's Mrs Ferguson?'

'She's the lady who owns these buildings. She helps us.'

'You need help?'

'She lives in the big house on the left just up the road.'

'I didn't know.'

I thought – Of course children need help; from anyone who will help them.

She left the suitcase on its end and went again and looked out of the doorway into the farmyard.

I said 'I don't know what my wife will say. I'll ask her.'

She said 'Mrs Ferguson says she'll pay.'

'Pay for what?'

'My schooling.'

'You want to go to school in London?'

'Yes.'

'You want to stay with us while you go to school in London?'

She watched me. I thought – There is the pain that wants to get out as if from graves behind the eyes.

I said 'Look, I must ask you some questions'

She said 'I'll answer if it won't do any harm.'

'You originally came from Yugoslavia?

'Yes.'

'How long have you been here?'

'Four years.'

'You came with your parents?'

'No.'

'Who with?'

'My uncle.'

'Why did you say you'd seen a vision?'

'I didn't.'

'Who did?'

'My uncle.'

'You didn't deny it?'

'No.'

'Why not?'

'Why should I?'

'Why did your uncle say it –'

'Ask him.'

She looked at me belligerently. I thought – She is like Ellen, yes: and I have known, haven't I, that these children should be fighting?

I said 'All right, no questions about your family or the Social Services people.'

She said 'They don't matter.'

'But will they let you come to London?' Then – 'All right, what do you want to do at school in London?'

'Physics and biology.'

'You know where to go? I mean, Mrs Ferguson knows what school you can go to?'

'I think so, yes.'

I looked at the objects spread out on the ground that were like seeds, like fossils. I thought – And they can stay here; and be dug up after a thousand years –

I said 'All right, I'll take the suitcase to Mrs Ferguson.'

'Thank you.'

'You know what's in those jars?'

'Yes.'

'What?'

'Bits and pieces.'

'Of what?'

'Light.'

'You're testing –'

'Yes.'

'For Mrs Ferguson?'

'Yes.'

'What else does she do?'

'We set the jars out for her. We collect them.'

She seemed suddenly to be in a state of anxiety, or embarrass-ment. She clenched and unclenched her hands; she moved from foot to foot. I thought – This is, again, like Ellen: she's acting, she is not acting? she is doing this for my benefit? There was the sound of someone running in the farmyard. I thought – Of course, it is the Social Services people come back to get her.

I said 'Will you come with me to Mrs Ferguson?'

She said 'No.' Then – 'I'm not sure.'

I said 'How can you be so sure that they'll let you come to London?'

She said 'I'll have to see, won't I.'

I went to the doorway of the barn and looked out. There was a man standing at the side of the battered car: he was the grey-faced man who had been by the minibus at the top of the track. He was peering round the farmyard as if searching for someone – for Gaby – for the cause, perhaps, of his despair. Or cure? When I looked back Gaby was standing with the heel of one foot slotted against the instep of the other: it was as if she were a dancer expressing due preparation before emerging on to a stage. I wanted to say – Be careful! you think you can handle them?

Then she picked up my bag of provisions and walked out of the barn.

I stood back from the door and watched. The man gazed at Gaby as she approached him, as if he were seeing a vision. Gaby went up to him and spoke to him and turned and looked at the barn. I did not know if he could see me: I did not know what she might be telling him. I thought – Of course, it might be in her interests to tell him that she has told me – anything! Gaby went round to the far side of the car and opened the door and got into the passenger-seat. I thought – But the car will not move! The man got into the driving-seat and started the car and it lurched off making a terrible grinding noise where the tyre was rubbing against the metalwork of the wing. I watched it while it shuddered round the farmyard and towards the gate. I thought – But Gaby will know where to find me – in this strange country? I picked up the suitcase and went out into the yard. It was as if Gaby had known that the man would be coming for her: as if he had known that she would get into the car. I thought – And by this, she thinks she might get to London? I was walking up the track: the car ahead of me had almost reached the top of the slope. I thought – The tyre may cause the car to catch fire: it may become its own Sodom and Gomorrah. The couple who had been watching the scene had gone from their place on the hill; the car with Gaby went out of sight. When I reached my car I found it had been manhandled slightly off the track and there was a handwritten notice on the windscreen saying that I would be considered for prosecution on account of having caused an obstruction.

Four

Perhaps it was because I had had so little sleep that the day and the outside world assumed a style in which it seemed pointless to ask even to myself too many questions: the world went on its way; questions only diverted attention from what was happening. On the beach that morning I had had the impression of modes of perception beyond those of our blinkered world; of possibilities opening out if one watched and listened. Blinkers were structured by our conditioning: without them we might feel lost, but we might also be free; might be in touch, even, with such forces as might nudge the world on its way.

I had got into my car. I was sitting looking down at the now deserted valley.

I had done stories on the problem of perception other than the one to do with the helmet that was clamped over one's head like the neocortex of a brain: in a sense one always wore one's helmet – that functioning which contrived that one should see things just as one was accustomed to and in no other way. Light, sensations, impressions, entered the brain and were transformed by it into – what? – a landscape, farm buildings, the bonnet of a car. But what of that part of the brain that could see that this was so; that could watch and listen for what might be the effect of this understanding on what it saw –

One story I had become involved in was to do with those particles of light, radiation, whatever, that were picked up by an amateur device such as the one that the boy had carried on the beach and those that had been put into the suitcase by Gaby. The discs of plastic in the bottom of these containers registered particles of radiation: these marks could be studied under a microscope; they could be analysed, quantified, set up in a system of statistics: but what was the aim of these operations? It was known that these particles – alpha particles in particular – could damage cells; might knock bits and pieces out of the genetic code; might cause leukaemia for instance, or sterility. But this was known because this was what was being tested – this was what people wanted to know about in the present world – mechanisms concerning impotence and sterility. I had asked one of the so-called experts in this field what else it might be conjectured that these particles could be doing, and he had said – Almost anything. I had said – You don't know? He had said – We only know what we set out to know; that is, what we are given the money to know.

I had said – You mean, you are given the money to find out about death: what about life?

He had said – Who would give us money to find out about life? Then – I mean, it is easy to ask questions about death, you know what it is. Who knows what life is?

I had turned my car round and was facing the road. I could not exactly remember doing this. I had said to the person who was an expert in radiation – But shouldn't we be trying to find out more about evolution, change, or we will be for ever stuck like monkeys sitting on the stumps of trees –

He had said – What do you look for when you want to find out about evolution, change? Mutation happens when and where you don't look.

I had said – So you call it chance?

– You don't see light: you see that on which it has fallen; what has occurred.

I had tried to follow up this story. There were experiments being done to try to show that in certain conditions mutations might be said to be directed; that is, mutation in bacteria occurred that might be to the bacteria's advantage. But for every finding that seemed to show this, there could be one that showed the opposite. I had thought – But it is when you are looking or not looking that an advantageous mutation might occur –

– Would it be possible to devise an experiment at which one could be looking without exactly looking?

I was driving up the road into the hills. I had lost my train of thought: indeed it was difficult in this line of questioning not to wander off the road. It seemed in fact that I was in danger of falling asleep. I should look for a place to pull up off the road and rest. There was a space just before a bridge: I stopped. Then other memories came in like random seeds; like a fall of leaves.

I had been driving some years ago on the borders of Hungary and Czechoslovakia: I had been doing a story on the industrial pollution in this area – the smog, the poisoned rivers, the acid rain that was killing forests. I had wanted to say – Look, this is a more insidious threat to the planet than the nuclear threat because people have become so accustomed to it; their blinkers concerning this are such that they cannot see a way to anything different. And so, in such conditions, how can there be change? I had come in my journey to a landscape of denuded trees that was, yes, like a battlefield; I drove past a town where dragon-like factories belched black smoke and ramshackle houses nestled against them like piglets. I went on to a village where the road ended in mud. Beyond this was a lake which was said to have died: all life had gone from it, the villagers were sick and deformed. I got out of the car and walked along planks of wood that had been laid at the side of the road; looking down, it was as if I might see faces in the mud like those of the damned in Dante's hell. There were one or two old women visible through the doors of hovels; they tended to fires whose smoke seemed to add to the poison in the air; there was not much other life. I had become dissatisfied with what I had planned to write: what was the point of just giving one more doleful warning like those of the Virgin Mary – Children, children, I know you are sick and starving; but how about just one more effort to mend your ways. Better, perhaps, just to say – For God's sake, why not become a bit worse and get the whole thing over quicker; and then perhaps some new species can begin again. Or perhaps by saying this children might be stirred to mend their ways? I came to a place in the village where there was a group of children crossing the road; they were heading down a side-street in the direction of the lake. They were pushing a miniature cart or float within which there was what appeared to be a doll; it was wrapped in sacking and had a cap on its head. I could see the lake at the end of the side-street — a dark and sodden mudflat and then an expanse like oil. I thought — The land and the water have become one: there is no distinction anymore beneath the firmament. It seemed that the children might be going to make some offering to the dead or dying lake with this doll, like fishermen do in France or Spain when they push an image of their local saint out on the sea. But what good would this do them — what good does it do to the fishermen — except to comfort them in their inability to think of anything different.

I followed the children; they reached the edge of the lake; they were unloading the figure from its float. They were unwrapping it and taking off its cap. I saw then that it was human and it was alive. It had a shining head and a bright fair face. I saw also that it had no arms or legs — or rather it had small flippers for arms, and something like feet or fins but no legs. The children were carrying this child to the water in their arms; it seemed that they might be about to drown it. I thought I should shout — No! But had I not been wondering that just this might have to happen to sick members of the tribe? Then the children laid the figure gently in the water. It was still looking up at them brightly. Then it swam off busily, using its flippers as fins, using its feet almost as some sort of propeller — it was like some energetic motor-boat with which children might play on a pond. The children clapped and cheered: I thought I might cry. I had not looked closely at the children till now — it was often difficult to look closely at children in such places at this time, so often did they seem to be victims of want or atrocity. These children might be either boys or girls; they had shaved heads; I thought — But they are more like images of creatures from another planet. The child that was in the water went round in a circle; came back to land. The children caught it, had some communication with it, then set it off again on its circuit. It seemed that this was one of the children born deformed as a result of pollution; but now it was swimming so busily! and its companions were taking such care of it; there was such a determination for life! I watched while it completed two or three circuits. Then the children lifted it from the water and dried it and wrapped it in its sacking; they set it on its float again and pulled it back towards the village. As it went past me it seemed so triumphant! I thought I might exult or howl. But how long would they be able to look after it? How long would it stay alive?

I was in my car by the wood. I had been remembering the dead lake. I had perhaps fallen asleep. I had dreamed that bits of cloud like burning paper had come down: then the air cleared.

I was parked just short of the bridge over a stream. It seemed that I should go for a short walk to clear my head. Then I could go on to Mrs Ferguson's.

There was a path into the wood along the side of the stream; the stream ran so busily! There was all this activity going on – the water fed the trees, the trees were like lungs that breathed, they created and preserved the air – how – by turning carbon dioxide into oxygen? by maintaining the ozone layer without which we should all be burned up by the sun? And the air contained clouds by which the trees and the earth might be watered: and the whole apparatus worked, this was the miracle; this was the mechanism that went on as it were off-stage – that one could not exactly see by looking. I had once written a piece saying it was quite sensible for humans to talk to plants and trees: this was a way of showing some recognition of what they were doing.

I came to a place in my walk where the wood on the other side of the stream opened out and there was a field of corn. The corn was high but not yet quite ripe; there were two narrow tracks leading to the centre of the field of the kind that are made by the wheels of agricultural machinery. My remarks about plants and trees had been in the course of an article on the curious phenomena known as crop-circles – those meticulously cut-out shapes in fields of standing corn that had been appearing in various parts of the world at that time but especially in southern England. At first it had been thought these were caused by meteorological disturbances; then when the patterns had become too elaborate for this explanation to make sense it was supposed they must be hoaxes – what they must not be, so reasonable people insisted, was anything to do with the paranormal. Then, however, the occurrences became so complex and so frequent that the idea that people could be organising and secretly synchronising such enormously laborious hoaxes seemed itself to suggest something paranormal; and so it became easiest not to think about the phenomena at all.

My editor, Jack, had said to me – Then what is your explanation?

I had said – I have no explanation. I think the explanation is that they are bits of information to show that there are some things about which it is not the point to look for an explanation.

– But bits of information promulgated by whom?

– But the point is there is no answer to that question.

I was standing on the bank of the stream looking across at the field of corn. I had visited two or three of these circles and they had indeed been mysterious with shapes and paths curling to and from them like the fronds of ferns, and at the perimeter meticulously interwoven but not crushed stems of corn. And it was true I had felt wonder rather than the need for explanation; and would have liked to come across such phenomena again.

I could not see into the centre of the field. But I could jump the stream and walk along one of the tracks that had been made by machinery and then perhaps – I could do no harm – I might come across, walking with my hands up, one foot in front of the other –

I jumped the stream, I tip-toed through the corn. The stems were so upright! they grew thus because of gravity? But what was gravity, except something that one experienced, could measure, but for which there was no explanation –

I was indeed coming, yes, to a space in the middle of the field that seemed to have been carved out, flattened: I had not really expected this (and so it had happened? You do not ask questions!). The shape was not quite a circle: it was more like a heart. (I thought – But is it really possible not to ask questions?) The edge of the shape was precisely defined and had a narrow line of stalks going in the opposite direction to the rest of those that were flattened – this was the phenomenon that I had seen before: it was one of the complexities that had made hoaxes seem unlikely. I walked to the centre of the shape and stood there. I felt, as I had felt before, something quite potent about being within such a form; this was likely, of course, to be no more than self-suggestion. It had been claimed by some experimenters that within such circles there was sometimes a higher-than-usual level of radioactivity; it had been claimed by others that this could be a purely natural local phenomenon. Nothing could be quite proved; what experiment could be set up to establish the difference? Or indeed what experiment could be set up that would show anything different from what it was designed to measure –

I sat down within the circle. It seemed that there was simply too much light coming in – to my mind, my imagination – this was what had happened to me on the hillside in Yugoslavia: there I had seen the lady in blue on the smoothed-out rocks, and later by the graves –

– A white light being a matter rather of objects than connections:

– A light that travels in darkness being an expression of the whole –

– Opening up a world of possibilities, from which this or that can be chosen.

I thought I should go on.

I did not want to go back to my car. From a map I had looked at before I started on my walk it had seemed that I might be quite close to Mrs Ferguson's house; there had been a shaded area with dots beyond the stream that might denote parkland and a house. There were further track-marks going on from the far side of the heart-shape in the field. I thought that by going down these I might approach, unseen, the house where Mrs Ferguson lived; and thus – what – myself appear like something paranormal? someone from a space-ship, with a message? I went on down one of the further tracks. I thought – It is as if the heart-shape had been pierced by an arrow: or rather, as if the arrow were here first and then the heart came down to give it meaning.

Coming into sight just beyond the far end of the field – the ground over which I walked was slightly convex – was what turned out, after a few more steps, to be a caravan – one of those elaborately carved and painted gypsy caravans standing on high spoked wheels; it was within a grass compound at the edge of the field. Its shafts were resting on the ground at the end closest to me; between them had been built a wooden ramp that led up to the door. On the side facing me was a window, and within it there was the head of a woman, or rather what was almost more like the portrait of a woman – one of those surrealist paintings in which the frame of a picture surrounds what there might be in reality. She was a woman with long fair hair and of indeterminate age – anything, I guessed wonderingly, from seventeen to seventy. She might be Mrs Ferguson? She might be, like a crop-circle, some phenomenon essentially without an explanation.

I had stopped when I saw her: I went on. I thought – But of course she is not a painting: it is just that she has the stillness of a painting; and she had eyes that without moving seem to follow you when you move –

I reached the end of the corn where there was a small ditch before the grassy clearing. I stopped again. It seemed that the ditch might represent some barrier, some need for caution, like the stream that had run across the beach –

The woman in the window said 'Did you do that thing in the field?'

I said 'No.'

'Well who did?'

'I don't know.'

Her head disappeared from the window. She seemed to glide backwards and to one side without rising or taking steps. I waited. I thought – Perhaps she is indeed a witch.

She re-appeared in the open doorway of the caravan. She was in a wheelchair: I thought – So there is that much explanation! She said 'I've got instruments in that field.'

I said 'What sort of instruments?'

'Recordings. But I've turned them off. Nothing ever happens when they're there.'

She pushed herself back into the interior of the caravan. I stepped over the ditch and went to the bottom of the ramp so that I could see inside. The caravan seemed to have been fitted out as some sort of makeshift laboratory: there was a shelf beneath the window with a microscope and plastic trays; some jars of the kind that Gaby had put into the suitcase.

I said 'The presence of instruments stops anything happening?'
She said 'Yes.'

'Couldn't you get some experiment to show that this is what is happening? I mean to show that if anything is to stay as a potential – to show potentiality – then of course it can't be observed, measured, or it would become actual.'

She said 'Oh yes, of course, you know about such things.'

She was looking down at one of the trays. The window above the tray faced onto the cornfield. The trays were those used by biologists to contain what is called a culture – living formations and perhaps transformations of cells.

I said 'Gaby asked me to bring you a suitcase of those jars that she and the children have collected. But I'm afraid I've left it in my car. I didn't know I'd come across you.'

She pushed herself from the shelf. She leaned back in her chair with her eyes closed. She said 'You've seen Gaby?'

'Yes.'

'In the barn?'

'Yes.'

'And what were they doing – '

'There were some Social Services people who I think had come to fetch them. But they got away.'

'Where to – '

'I don't know. Then Gaby went off in a car with a man who seemed to have come back for her –'

'She'll kill him!' Then – 'I sometimes think she might –'

'I don't know.'

She wheeled herself along the central passageway of the caravan looking into the trays. I wondered – They contain some liquid, some culture, that might or might not be able to produce whatever is to their advantage –

She said 'What have you come here for?'

I said 'I'm writing a story.'

'How far have you got?'

'I haven't begun.'

'If you do write it, then won't there be an end to potentialities?'

She said this as if amused. But when she looked at me it was as if

there were some hurting behind the eyes as there had been with
Ellen and Gaby.

I climbed to the top of the ramp. Within the trays there were,
yes, liquids and encrustations; small islands between sea and land.

I said 'Not necessarily, no.'

'Why not?'

'It depends on the type of story.' Then – 'What are you doing
here?'

'Experiments.'

'What on?'

'The same as you.'

'Particles? Radiation?'

'Yes.'

'Bacteria?'

'Yes.'

'And what do you find?'

'What's suited to the experiment.'

'And so you can affect it –'

'What –'

'What happens –'

'By choosing the experiment?'

'Yes.'

'Or the experiment of having no experiment –'

'That's what I've been wondering!'

'Yes, it's possible to set or not set the conditions.'

She wheeled herself towards me again. She faced me with her
expression of somewhat fierce and controlled amusement. She said
'You see, I read what you write. I follow you. I even read your
piece about the children in Yugoslavia.'

I said 'But that was years ago!'

'Yes.'

'I didn't think anyone read that magazine –'

'One or two.'

'But how did you know me now?'

'They sometimes print a little photograph above the pieces that
you write.'

'People here seem to have been expecting me.'

'So there's nothing all that mysterious.'

'You don't think so?'

'If you like.'

She had pushed herself to the top of the ramp. It was as if she might be waiting for me to help her down. I did not want to leave the caravan. I said 'But these experiments: you collect those jars: you mean what they contain, show, might affect what you've got in the trays?'

She said 'The jars show alpha particles —'

'Yes I know.'

'These can knock bits out of the genetic code. They can affect cells, structure, brain —'

'Causing death —'

'Causing break-up, stress —'

'And then?'

'Cells more likely to mutate when they are under stress.'

'Yes I know.'

'That which preserves their status quo gets broken up —'

'When they are in need? threatened?'

'Yes.'

'They can find what will feed them? what is to their advantage?'

'Not exactly find —'

'If they produce more mutations, then these will naturally include more mutations that might be to their advantage —'

'Yes.'

'And these will be chosen —'

'Not chosen —'

'May survive —'

'If you like.'

I had moved round behind her. I was standing with my hands on the handles of her chair. I thought I might say — And you are finding that here there are conditions suitable for mutations? So there are some that might be advantageous for humans — for the cells, heart, brain?

She said 'Gaby and the children were in some danger. They were taken in for tests.'

I said 'They played on the beach? in the stream?'

'Yes.'

'They were allowed —'

'It was useful to have tests.'

'And you let them?'

'How could I not? And they are extraordinary children, don't you think?'

I was easing her wheelchair down the ramp. I thought – One false move, and we might fly off out of control.

Then – This is the sort of experiment one might look at without looking?

I said 'You think these particles might affect possibilities; what goes on in the mind, in the brain –'

She said 'No one knows.'

'With these children –'

'No one knows.'

'But here they are –'

We had reached the bottom of the ramp. I let go of the handles of her chair. She said suddenly 'You're making me very tired.' She set off pushing herself rapidly along a path that led away from the cornfield. I thought I might say – I'm making myself very tired! Then she stopped and I caught up with her. She said 'You write very well.'

I said 'Thank you.'

'Does anyone pay any attention to you?'

'You do apparently.'

'Will you be looking after Gaby?'

'I don't know, should I?'

'I don't know, has she asked you?'

'Yes.'

'Then I expect you will.'

We went on along the path through the wood. She still pushed herself; I trotted along half beside her and half behind her. Coming into view were the gables and and turrets of a large country house with lawns and gravelled paths. On a driveway was a car parked with two men standing beside it. I thought – They are the Social Services people: they have come again after Gaby. Or they are police: the Social Services people have already got Gaby.

I said to Mrs Ferguson 'What about these things that Gaby won't talk about?'

She said 'Her family? The locals?' Then — 'Haven't you written somewhere about that?'

'Have I?'

'The things that can work only if you don't talk about them —'

'Gaby's had trouble with the Social Services people? She's got a hold over them?'

'Well I wouldn't talk about it, would I.'

Mrs Ferguson had stopped. She was watching the two men by the car. We were still half in the cover of the wood. The men had seen us. It suddenly seemed important that I should not be detained and questioned by them: but also that I should not be seen to run away.

I said 'Do you live here on your own?'

She said 'My son is sometimes with me.'

'I'll bring you that suitcase.'

'Yes please do that.'

She pushed herself on towards the house. I went with her. I thought — Now indeed there may be some experiment of the kind we do not quite know what we are looking for.

We had left the wood and were moving across a lawn towards the gravelled drive. I thought — Those men are not the ones who were in the farmyard: though how can you tell with this strange tribe. They would not know that I had been in the farmyard: they would be coming to see Mrs Ferguson about the children? I was walking behind Mrs Ferguson and I put my hands lightly on the back of her chair: I might indeed be someone hired to push her to and fro. The men had round, rather flat faces like clamps on the wheels of cars; they were surely, yes, plain-clothes policemen. The shorter one said 'Good morning, Mrs Ferguson, or should I say good afternoon?' I thought — Good heavens, can it be afternoon? I was in fact asleep in the car? I looked at my wrist; I had not got my watch; I might have left it in the bathroom of the hotel. I looked up at the sun. I could not see the sun. I thought — Perhaps the policemen will think I am a lunatic, on parole to push Mrs Ferguson to and fro and to look up at the sun.

Mrs Ferguson was saying 'What do you want now, I thought you'd got what you wanted —'

One of the men was saying 'It isn't that, Mrs Ferguson.'

I was thinking – I must get back to the hotel and ring Melissa: I should do this before Janice arrives: what on earth will I do with Janice? I mean, what about Ellen. And indeed, about Gaby –

One of the men was saying 'Can we have a word in private, Mrs Ferguson?'

Mrs Ferguson was saying 'What have you got to hide?'

'Nothing to hide, Mrs Ferguson –'

'This gentleman may be interested in what you have to say.'

They were not looking at me: it was as if by this I might not be there. I thought – The police may be in with the Social Services people? they may be frightened, and want to hurt Gaby too?

– Mrs Ferguson may want them to know I'm a newspaper person?

One of the men said 'One of our colleagues has been injured in a car.'

'One of your colleagues?'

'Yes.'

'Then you were in the business too?'

I was trying not to forget my conversation with Mrs Ferguson in the caravan: I needed to get somewhere to write it down. – In conditions of stress there was an increase of mutations: cells starved of their usual nutrients might produce variations which could survive on what was available –

But one of the Social Services men had been injured in a car? this was the man who had been driving Gaby? The wheel had caught fire; the fire had spread –

– Bits and pieces were knocked out of the genetic code –

But they would have said if Gaby had been hurt?

Mrs Ferguson was saying 'He's not dead? Are you saying he's dead?'

I felt it vital that I should get back to my car. I could look on the road for any sign of Gaby. I thought – Indeed, we are all under a certain stress –

One of the men was saying 'He'd been to the farm buildings. We thought he might have been coming on to see you.'

Mrs Ferguson said 'Are you afraid he'll talk?'

I thought I had done all I could with Mrs Ferguson: I could still represent some threat to these men. One of the men was murmuring 'It would be denied.' I thought – But I should find out more?

I said 'I was at the farmyard this morning. What happened to the child?'

They were still acting as if they had not heard me. I looked up again as if to get direction from the sun. I thought – If we none of us know what is really going on, it might be quite sensible to look up at the sun.

After a time one of the men said 'What child?'

Mrs Ferguson said 'Gaby was in the car?'

I thought – I told you she was in the car! Then – Oh I see.

The second man said 'No, Gaby was not in the car.'

Mrs Ferguson said 'Where is she then?'

I thought – Did Mrs Ferguson really say: She'll kill him?

Mrs Ferguson began to wheel herself violently towards the house. One of the men called after her – 'Mrs Ferguson, it looks as if the car was driven deliberately off the road –'

She stopped. She had her back to us. I thought – She is stage-managing this: she thinks she might set up a situation in which she gets what she wants?

She said 'So will that get you on or off the hook?'

I thought – But Gaby must be all right!

I had to get back to the hotel. Or was there still something of a chance to find out –

I said 'Was that a scare at the site this morning?'

One of the men said 'Why did you think Gaby was in the car?'

The other man was saying 'So you see it might be a health hazard, Mrs Ferguson –'

Mrs Ferguson was saying 'That's a useful way of putting it –'

The men were beginning to climb into their car. I thought – That's enough, now go –

I said to Mrs Ferguson 'I'll bring you that suitcase.'

One of the men said 'What suitcase?' He began climbing out of the car again.

I thought – Oh damn!

Mrs Ferguson said 'Oh hadn't he got it with him?'

I set off walking across the driveway in what I thought must be the direction of the road. I was thinking – What suitcase? That suitcase? Then – So patterns of mind are broken up, are they, to produce confusion; stress: or indeed – a health hazard! Had we stage-managed it correctly, Mrs Ferguson and I – not knowing quite what was happening or what we wanted. I wondered if one of the men was coming after me: there had to be some risk. I was coming to a ditch; beyond it was an area of parkland, then a line of trees and beyond this there should be the road. On this, at some distance, my car would be parked. So what was the nature of this experiment: to see who would or would not survive? But of course this could hardly be put into words. Gaby had been with the grey-faced man as they drove off in the damaged car; the man had seemed to be on the point of death anyway; had Gaby jumped out of the car just before it went into the ditch? I was making this up: what else was there to do? Or perhaps the injured man was nothing to do with the man with Gaby in the car. I had jumped over the ditch. I was walking across parkland.

Gaby had known what she was doing when she climbed into the man's car? I had her suitcase, surely, in the boot of my car –

I had come to the line of trees beyond which was a wall. I knew how to jump over walls: you put your hand on top and then swung your legs like a pendulum –

– You were guided by gravity –

– That which controlled, kept together and kept apart, all the bits and pieces that were flying about in the mind, in the universe –

– like seeds, like bullets –

– like a code.

I was walking up the road towards my car. I thought I might go and look at the reprocessing-plant and power-station: on my way I might meet Gaby? They had taken Gaby in for tests? They had used the children as guinea-pigs?

– Did I really want to go back to the hotel, where Janice might be waiting –

Gaby might really come with me to London? Perhaps I should not ring up Melissa just yet –

One could be taken like a tourist round the site of the reprocessing-plant like Virgil and Dante round heaven or hell?

When I had travelled in Eastern Europe doing my story about pollution I had got permission to go to the area that had been contaminated by the nuclear disaster at Chernobyl. I travelled with a guide: there was a huge fenced-off area from within which farms and a small township had been evacuated; the flat landscape was peaceful in the way indeed of being an area to which few humans could now come. We were allowed to drive right up to the site of the vast burned-out reactor that stood like a ruined monument or tomb. One other reactor on the site was still working: in spite of the pronouncements about continuing danger the countryside needed the electricity. It was as if the authorities were playing some game with statements about what might be dangerous and what might not – using whatever might be to their advantage. My guide and I were made to put on white cotton masks and caps; my guide was a pretty dark-haired woman who got the giggles as we put on our masks. There was a soldier at the barrier beyond which we could not go who did not wear a mask; he carried a radiation detector on a pole which he moved to and fro like someone sweeping up leaves – as if he were putting on some sort of show for us. He announced to my guide various readings that he said he was getting on his detector, my guide translated these to me still half-giggling as she lifted a corner of her mask. I thought – She is flirting: but in this sort of predicament we are all playing a game? We went on to the evacuated township where there were apartment blocks still in the state in which they had been left. My guide explained – but I had stopped paying much attention to what she explained: she would be telling me what she had been instructed to tell, and indeed how else were facts and figures chosen. In some of the buildings I could see a few figures moving as if trying to keep out of sight: my guide did say – Yes, some old people had been allowed to return: why? well, who could stop them; and this was supposed to be an area of research, wasn't it? Then she acted as if this was something she should not have said – putting her hand up jokingly as if it were a mask over her mouth. I wondered what I might be able to do that evening with my guide. I noticed a water-tower at the edge of the township on which some storks were building their nest.

On the road in Cumbria I had come to my car. I had climbed in and was sitting in the driving-seat: I again hardly remembered doing this. I thought – But those people at Chernobyl, they knew nothing at first except what people told them – and this was in response to clicks or pointers on a screen. The light or darkness was invisible. People had lived or died.

I had asked if I could be taken to a nearby hospital in the Ukraine: there were said to be still some victims of the explosion – also some of the children who had later been born deformed. It was about these in particular that I wanted to learn. There seemed to be some doubt about whether I would be allowed to do this: my guide went off to telephone. When she returned she said that such children had been moved, they were at another hospital undergoing further tests. Eventually I was taken to a hospital in which there was a ward of sick children, several of whom had deformities like those of the child I had seen swimming in the dead and oily lake. I was told that these deformities had been caused by the radiation from the explosion and of course this was probably true; but there were many other possible causes and by this time I was not necessarily believing anything anyone said. I thought – These people sometimes want to exaggerate the effects of the disaster so that they will continue to get foreign aid; sometimes they wish to minimise the effects simply in order to be able to continue providing electricity; and so indeed they move from one attitude to another –

And I can go back to the possibilities of what I might do with my guide in the evening.

I was in my car in Cumbria. I was driving down the road towards the sea. There were the four huge cooling-towers of the power-station and reprocessing-plant in front of me. I thought – All right, the function of this ogre's castle, this genie half in and half out of its bottle, is perhaps to provide a circumstance of crack-up within which some humans may be able to uncover what will work to their advantage –

– Being on the look-out for mutations that might be favourable in their dire need –

– Or of course to find themselves in an environment in which humans can no longer exist.

Five

'Hullo, Ellen.'

'Hullo.'

'I gave your love to Gaby.'

'You've had two messages. One from your wife, and the other from Miss Stevens.'

'Where did Miss Stevens ring from?'

'She didn't ring, she's here.'

Miss Stevens was Janice. I had come into the hotel and found Ellen behind the reception desk. I had visited the site of the power-station and reprocessing-plant: I had looked for a burned-out car on the road.

I said 'What time is it —'

'Half-past six.'

'Half-past six!'

'Your watch is in your bathroom.'

'Thanks, Ellen.'

'I didn't think she was so pretty.'

In the hotel there were a group of men with their heads together in a corner of the bar. One of them was Fred; another was the grocer I had seen in the town that morning.

I said 'What was the message from Janice – I mean Miss Stevens?'

'She seemed uncertain where to put her bag.'

'And what did you say?'

'*Moi, j'ai dit*, did she really want me to tell her.'

'Ellen, all right, and where is Miss Stevens now?'

'She went out; I expect for a quickie on the beach.'

As before with Ellen, I got the impression of something significant happening without having much idea what it was. She was sitting in front of the computer and watching the screen and tapping keys. On the screen were rows of figures. I thought – She is pretending to be jealous of Janice: but not because of me?

I said 'I think I'd better have a drink.'

'I think you'd better had.'

'What did my wife say?'

'She said could you ring her. It was rather urgent.'

'Was that all?'

'And, oh yes, she asked if Miss Stevens had arrived.'

'And what did you say?'

'I said I didn't think she had much to worry about with Miss Stevens.'

'You didn't!'

'No I didn't.'

'Then what did –'

'I said I thought Miss Stevens might have gone to meet someone on the beach.'

The man called Fred was coming up to us from the bar. He saw Ellen sitting in front of his computer. He said 'What are you doing?'

She said 'Summoning up Doctor Whiplash and the Belgian Schoolgirls.'

Fred stretched over the counter and pressed one of the keys. The screen went blank. He said 'I need that information!'

Ellen said 'We're about to go critical, do you think?'

She stood and came round from behind the desk. Fred took her place in front of the computer. He tapped at the keys. Ellen said to me 'What would you like to drink?'

I said 'A large whisky and soda please.'

'Shall I bring it up to your room?'

'Oh Ellen, would you?'

'I told you this place was like Bluebeard's Castle.'

I waited by the bar while Ellen went behind it to get me my drink. The men round the table in the corner had stopped talking; they watched her. I thought – They are the group like Bluebeard's Castle: they deal in pornographic videos?

When Ellen brought me my drink she said 'I thought you were supposed to have laid off drinking.'

I said 'Ellen, I know you know everything, will you please shut up?'

I carried my drink up to my room. There a suitcase was standing on its end in the middle of the floor. I thought – That is Janice's suitcase? the suitcase from the back of my car? the suitcase that the men by Mrs Ferguson's house seemed to be interested in?

– Janice would not have told Ellen about my drinking? Melissa?

I picked up the telephone. I had no idea what to say to Melissa. I found it difficult to remember the last scene between Melissa and me: it was such a long time ago: not even a day? I had gone up the stairs: I had hit her? But was this like some pornographic video: you only remembered such things when you liked –

I stood holding the telephone by the window. Here I had held Ellen as she climbed out –

I said 'Melissa?'

Melissa said 'Oh thank God, I've been trying to find you.'

'Why, what's happened?'

'Have you been out?'

'Yes. How did you know where I was?'

'Is Janice with you?'

'No, but I suppose I'm expecting her.'

'Billy's gone missing.'

From where I was standing by the window I could see coming into the car-park in front of the hotel the Land-Rover I had seen that morning on the beach. It was being driven by the young officer that I had understood from Ellen was called Charlie. There was a woman beside him on the front seat.

I said 'What do you mean, Billy's gone missing?'

'He was supposed to spend last night with the Armstrongs, it was their turn to take the children to school. Then when I went to pick him up he wasn't there.'

'Where?'

'At school.'

'What time was this?'

'Half-past four.'

'Then perhaps he went back to the Armstrongs –'

'No, I've rung them, they thought he and Jenny were spending the night with us.'

The Land-Rover was stopping in front of the hotel. The woman getting out of the front seat was Janice. She gave the young officer called Charlie a rapid peck on the cheek. Then she ran into the hotel. I thought – You mean, Ellen was serious, she really might have gone for a quickie on the beach?

I said 'But were they at school today?'

'Yes.'

'They were?'

'Yes.'

'Then they've probably cooked up some plan. They'll turn up later. You know what they're like.'

'Is that all you can say?'

'I think so.'

'Billy doesn't want to come home –'

'Melissa –'

'Can you blame him?'

I was trying to work out – Janice bumped into Charlie in the Land-Rover? Janice knew Charlie before? Then after all it might not be Charlie and Ellen who are in love –

Then there was the image of Billy running out into the road.

I said 'Melissa, look, I'm sorry, but this is nothing terrible yet. It's only half past six.'

'It isn't.'

'What is it then?'

'Ten to seven. And I've got a black eye.'

'Have you? I didn't think you had.'

'Well I have.'

'I expect Billy just wanted to be on his own with Jenny Armstrong.'

'Is that all you can think of?'

I thought I might say – That sort of thing. Not really. No. Yes.

Janice had appeared in the doorway of the bedroom. She stood there like some tragic actress playing a woman betrayed. I had sat on the bed with the telephone. I did not think she could have seen my looking out of the window.

I held my hand over the mouthpiece and whispered 'I'm talking to Melissa!'

Melissa said 'Who are you talking to?'

I said 'Janice. She's just come in.'

'How are you getting along with Janice?'

'Not very well, actually.'

Janice had tip-toed to the centre of the room and was picking up her suitcase. She moved back with it to the door. I put my hand over the mouthpiece and whispered 'Billy's gone missing!'

Janice paused by the door. Then she went out, leaving it ajar. I stood and looked out of the window again. Charlie was leaning with his arm on the windscreen of the Land-Rover.

Melissa said 'So what do you want to do?'

I said 'What do you mean? I don't know. I don't want to do anything much really. I want Billy to be all right. I want to do a story about these children in the hills.'

'I thought you were supposed to be doing a story about radioactivity.'

'Who told you that?'

'I thought you told me that.'

'No. Did Jack tell you?'

'Oh Jack, Jack, why is it always Jack?'

I thought I might say – Who else is it then?

In the circle in front of the hotel Charlie was looking at his watch: then he sat in the Land-Rover. I thought – Janice will now appear with her suitcase? Ellen might come up to my room? I felt, as I had done before, that there was too much white light coming in: I needed darkness.

I said 'Then how did you know where I was?'

The line had gone dead. It seemed that Melissa had rung off. I thought – But of course she had to ring me about Billy: and why should not Janice have told Jack, and indeed Jack have told Melissa, where I was –

Then – But which was the night that Billy was supposed to be with us; or with the Armstrongs?

I sat on the bed. I thought I would sit for a time doing nothing. Then I might try to ring Jack. Then I might ring back Melissa. Or I might go and see what had happened to Janice – or to Charlie. If Charlie had known Janice before, had known she was coming up here to see him, this might explain – everything? It did not seem much to matter. Except now – I might have a chance with Ellen?

The telephone rang. I picked up the receiver. Melissa said 'And who is that fucking girl who answers the telephone?'

I said 'Oh yes, she's called Ellen.'

'She seemed to think she knows me.'

'Everyone seems to think they know everyone around here –'

'I expect you've told them –'

'Told them what?'

'Told them you've got a wife who's off her trolley –'

'Are you? I thought it was you who'd told them about my drinking –'

Melissa seemed to have rung off again.

I thought – But Melissa, we are all, who cares, half on and half off our trolleys –

I had been trying to decide what to do. Then I had done nothing. Perhaps I should see what had happened to Janice. Perhaps she and Ellen were having a confrontation on the stairs. Somewhere or other there might be some exact understanding of what was happening.

Janice was in the passage sitting on her suitcase with her head in her hands. I said 'Janice, what's happening?'

She said 'Nothing.' Then – 'You didn't want me!'

'I did!'

'You don't want me now.'

I was thinking of trying to sit beside her on her suitcase. But it might collapse and crush all those little jars – oh no, that was another suitcase. I knelt on the floor and put my arm around Janice. I said. 'I'm so sorry, but look, I'm worried about Billy.'

'Poor Billy!'

80

'I had this row with Melissa —'

'Is she back?'

'What?'

'They've given us separate rooms.'

'Have they?'

'Did you want that?'

'What do you mean, is Melissa back?'

'Who's that girl who seems to think she knows everything about me?'

I thought — If she does, she's the only one —

Then — What were you doing with Charlie?

I said 'Look, come back to the room.'

She said 'I did say I would, didn't I?'

She stood and I picked up her suitcase and we went back into the bedroom. I thought — You said you would do what? Then — You mean, now, we might make love?

I said 'What were you doing with Charlie?'

She said 'Charlie?'

'The man in the Land-Rover who dropped you off at the hotel.'

'Oh Charles, yes. He's the security officer at the plant.'

'I know.'

'I thought I'd get on with the job.'

I thought I might say — What job?

I said 'Did you know him before?' I didn't think it would be to my advantage to add — Is that why you came up here?

She went through into the bathroom and left the door ajar. She seemed to be undressing. I thought — Well, good heavens, one takes advantage of what turns up —

She said 'And what have you been doing?'

I said 'Oh not very much.'

'Who have you seen? Charles said he'd seen you —'

'Yes. And I've bumped into the Social Services people. And the police. But I don't think really that's the story —'

'No, Jack says that's not the story —'

'But I don't think there's been much of a scare either —'

Janice came back from the bathroom. She had taken off her shirt and trousers and was in her underclothes. She stood in the doorway and struck a pose. She looked remarkable. I thought – But this is no good: what about Billy; what, now, about Melissa –

– Or what about Ellen?

Janice said 'So what is the story?'

I said 'For God's sake, Janice –'

She came and knelt on the floor and rummaged in her suitcase. She produced a small spongebag from which she took one of those small packets like a tea-bag: she held this delicately, by one corner, between finger and thumb. I seemed to have become paralysed. I thought – I can make out it is because of Billy.

After a time Janice said 'Look, I've got some people coming downstairs in twenty minutes.'

I said 'What people?'

'Charles says there's a group of people here like the Ku-Klux-Klan.'

I thought I might say – I thought they were Bluebeard's Castle.

I said 'Look, Janice, this is very good of you –'

'But you don't want to –'

'I do!'

She sat on the bed and put an arm around me. She said again 'Poor Billy!'

I thought I might say again – But what was it that you meant about Melissa being back?

– There was something that you knew about Melissa, in the pub?

She said 'Look, you've been driving all night, you're tired.'

She got off the bed and went into the bathroom. I thought – Well I would have liked to be in a four-star hotel in the hills with Janice –

– But Billy, are you all right?

Janice came back from the bathroom. She had put on some clothes. She said 'I'll just go down and see these people.'

'Yes, you do that.'

'Look, I did want to be here with you, really.'

'It doesn't matter –'

'But you do believe that?'

'Yes.'

'Look, you're worried about Billy. And I didn't know you cared all that much about Melissa.'

I had lain back on the bed. I thought – Once Janice has gone perhaps that blessed darkness will come down: perhaps I will sleep; perhaps I will be able to follow some trail in my head –

Once Melissa and I had been at a party and there had been a man with pointed eyebrows like a devil. Melissa had said – Oh yes, I find him attractive. He had been in pursuit of Melissa; Melissa had been flattered; we had all been drunk. Then it became apparent towards the end of the party that he was one of those men who suggested – not in so many words: this is one of the things that only work if you do not quite put them into words – why did we not both go home with him and we could all go to bed together. And part of me had wanted to do this – the strange hidden part that wants to be bisexual, or a pimp, or whatever – and part of Melissa had wanted to go: what is the point of being drunk if one is not ready to look into the corners inside oneself where there are snakes and toads and dragons? But when we were with the man in his home he was such a sad old devil: he made us cups of tea and Melissa said – I'm so sorry, so sorry. And he had said – Please don't worry at all. And so we went home; and we found Billy standing up in his cot looking down at the baby-sitter who had passed out drunk on the floor – and so where is this trail in my head going – what does one do about those snakes and vultures in corners? If one does nothing do they not eat out your heart, guts, balls –

The telephone rang. I had been sleeping. I was in the bedroom of the hotel. I picked up the receiver. A voice said 'Dad?'

I said 'Billy!'

Billy said 'I thought I'd call you.'

'Where are you?'

'Mum said would I call you –'

'Are you at home?'

'Mum had to go out.'

I was struggling upright. Janice had gone. And I had not made love to Janice! I wanted to say – Where did Mum go, do you know?

'Dad –'

'Yes? Where were you last night –'

83

'With the Armstrongs.'

'They said you were with us.'

'No, that was tonight.'

'Oh I see. But you're all right?'

It seemed suddenly that I should not ask too many questions, even to Billy, or he would be driven into a corner —

He said 'Yes, Dad, are you all right?'

'Yes, I'll be coming back tomorrow, or the day after, I'll see you then. I've been doing a story on some children here who've set up on their own —'

'Yes, I know, Mum told me —'

'But where did Mum go to, do you know?'

There was a silence at the other end of the line. I thought — But I have to show that I care!

'Dad —'

'Yes?'

'Do you think Mum's all right?'

'Why.'

'I don't know.'

There were the noises of people talking downstairs. There were the noises of cars arriving or starting up in the circle outside the hotel.

I thought — But one should not put these burdens onto children.

I said again 'But Billy, you're all right —'

'Yes.'

'You'll get to school tomorrow —'

'Tomorrow's Sunday.'

'Oh yes. But Mum will be back?'

I thought — But if tomorrow's Sunday, then there wouldn't have been any school today —

Billy said 'Dad, it's all right. Jenny's with me.'

I said 'But Mum said she went to pick you up at school today —'

After a time Billy said 'There was a rehearsal of the play.'

I said 'Yes, all right, Billy.' Then — 'I'll ring Mum later.'

Billy said 'Yes, Dad, take care.'

I rang off. I thought — There's no way in which parents can stop putting burdens onto children —

— They can let them know they know this?

The noises that were coming from downstairs were like those of a party in progress. Janice's suitcase was still in the middle of the floor. I thought – Why should not Melissa have gone wherever it is that she has gone –

– I can ring Jack later?

I realised I was very hungry. I had not eaten since – when – my coffee and bun in the service-station in the middle of the night? my coffee and toast for breakfast? I needed a drink. What had happened to the glass of whisky that Ellen had given me: I had carried it up myself to the room: I had finished it?

I did not remember finishing it.

On the way downstairs I thought – It is the hypocrisies of grown-ups that destroy children –

– If these are out in the open, ordinary human machinations –

– Then children can learn?

There was quite a crowd in the hallway of the hotel; they seemed on the point of being ushered out of the front door by Fred. When they saw me they stopped. I thought – They are like frogs in a pond which become silent when one passes them by.

Still seated in the bar was the group of men round a table. They too were silent: they seemed to be watching, and perhaps trying to listen to, the only other group in the bar, which consisted of a man and two women and Janice. One of these women had a foot up on a chair and a bandage round her ankle: I recognised her as the woman who had been injured in the farmyard. The other woman was dark and exotic and wore a very short skirt. The man was also dark and had a ring through his ear. It seemed that Janice was taking over the business of interviewing the people that I should have been interviewing. I thought – I really imagine that one only obscures things by talking?

I went to find Ellen to ask if I could have some food. Ellen was standing with her back to the wall behind the reception desk. I whispered to her, as if we might be playing some children's game of hiding from the grown-ups – 'I'm hungry!'

She put a finger to her lips. She looked round cautiously, as if to see whether the crowd in the hallway had gone out of the front door. When she saw that they had, she whispered. 'I'll get you some supper.'

'Thank you.'

'It'll be in the kitchen.'

I moved back to the hallway and then to the bar. I went up to the group that was around Janice. I thought – Thank goodness Janice is doing my job for me: perhaps this is what she wanted to come up here for?

She said 'Hullo. This is Mrs Wilton, this is Mr Kempinski, and this is Miss Simmons.'

I said 'Hullo hullo hullo.' I thought – In some other reincarnation Miss Simmons would have been good for a dark night in the woodshed –

Janice said 'Mrs Wilton was telling me about the scene in the farmyard this morning. And then the tragedy.'

Mrs Wilton said 'He was not an elderly man.'

I said 'Oh yes I'm sorry, the tragedy.' I thought – The man in the car?

The man with the earring, Mr Kempinski, was peering round at the group in the corner as if to see if they were listening. They looked away. He said 'I was telling Mrs Wilton I only knew him slightly –'

Janice said 'This is Gaby's father. You know Gaby?'

The man said 'Not father, uncle –'

The woman in short skirt, Miss Simmons, said 'I'm afraid I was responsible for saying he was Gaby's father –'

The man said 'He came to see me once.'

The woman in the short skirt said 'But the editor and I never meant to suggest that it was anything to do with Mrs Wilton.'

The woman with her foot up on a chair, Mrs Wilton, was not paying much attention to the group immediately around her. She was gazing into the distance and chewing the insides of her lips. She had iron-grey hair and a grey face: she seemed sick, like the man who had been in the car with Gaby that morning.

Janice had turned her attention away from us too. Charlie had come into the hallway. He was leaning against a pillar and lighting a cigarette; Janice was watching him and pretending not to watch him. I thought – This is like an opera, in which people stand behind pillars and other people sing at the tops of their voices and pretend not to notice them.

86

I said to Miss Simmons 'You're the one who wrote those pieces in the local paper?'

She said 'Yes.'

'I thought they were very well done.'

'Why thank you!' She flashed her eyes at me.

I thought – But this really isn't the time for any of this!

The man with the earring, Mr Kempinski, was saying 'I never felt it was up to me. Gaby has always gone her own way.'

Janice said 'But you said she'd seen a vision?'

Mr Kempinski said 'No, I never said that.'

Miss Simmons said 'He said that she was behaving as if she had seen a vision.' Mr Kempinski put a hand on her knee.

Mrs Wilton said 'Oh I'm not accusing you!'

Miss Simmons said 'Of what?'

Mr Kempinski said 'There are one or two things I could be accused of!'

Miss Simmons said 'He thought it would stop the talk.'

Ellen was coming out from behind the reception desk. She went up to Charlie and took the cigarette out of his mouth. Janice was watching. I thought – It really doesn't matter about Mr Kempinski and Miss Simmons –

Janice was saying 'Well it didn't, did it.'

Mrs Wilton said 'Well it will now.'

Miss Simmons said 'They say his steering broke.'

Mr Kempinski said 'I only saw him once or twice.'

I thought – Perhaps it really doesn't matter about the man who went off the road?

Janice was trying to drag her attention away from Charlie and Ellen. Charlie was taking another cigarette from out of a pack. Ellen took a quick puff from his first cigarette, then stubbed it out in an ashtray. I thought – But does this matter?

Janice was saying 'And when did you come over?'

Mr Kempinski said 'I left in nineteen eighty-eight, but I knew I was leaving behind a time-bomb.'

Janice said to me 'Mr Kempinski was working on a nuclear installation in Yugoslavia.'

I said 'And that's what you're doing here?'

He said 'Only as a builder, of course.'

Miss Simmons said 'But he knows enough!'

Mrs Wilton said 'But I do know that Gaby hasn't been affected.'

I said 'By what –'

Miss Simmons said 'By the contamination, of course.'

Fred had come back in through the front door. He was carrying an instrument like a small radio with a wire attached to a rod. I thought – He is like that soldier at Chernobyl, who seemed to be sweeping up leaves; but that soldier did not even trouble to wear a mask. Fred made a gesture to the men who were in a corner of the bar and they got up and joined him in the hall. Fred poked his rod about in the corner as if it were a hoover. Charlie and Ellen paid no attention to him, behind or beside their pillar.

Miss Simmons said 'I don't think we should stay any longer in here.'

Janice said 'You think there's a danger?' Then to me – 'There was a scare this morning.'

I said 'You know I know there was a scare –'

'But you won't take it seriously –'

'No.'

'Why not –'

'Charlie said –'

'Do you believe everything Charlie says?'

There was a telephone ringing at the reception desk. Ellen left Charlie and went to it: Fred and the group of men with him went too. I thought – There will be news of – what – some disaster like that at Chernobyl? Then we can all use it as a diversion –

I said to Mr Kempinski 'When you say you left behind a time-bomb, you mean, in what was Yugoslavia, you thought there'd be a crack-up, some disaster?'

He said 'Well there has been, hasn't there –'

Janice said 'That's not what he meant.'

Mr Kempinski said 'I know what he meant.' Then – 'Yes, sooner or later.'

Miss Simmons said 'Don't you think there's been enough already?'

Mrs Wilton said 'I agree. I don't think we should stay here any longer than we have to.'

Ellen was coming from behind the reception desk. I thought –

She walks, yes, like some sort of dancer. She said to me 'Your wife is on the telephone.'

I said 'Oh thank you.'

'You can take it down here, if you don't mind everybody listening.'

I followed Ellen to the reception desk. The group with Fred were leaning over the counter. They were watching a piece of paper that was emerging from the printer of the computer. I murmured to Ellen 'These are the Ku-Klux-Klan?'

She said 'What?' Then – 'Oh yes.' I thought – But it was Janice who called them the Ku-Klux-Klan! Ellen called them Bluebeard's Castle.

I took the receiver. I said 'Hullo?'

Melissa said 'I just thought I'd ring to tell you that everything's all right.'

'I know, Billy rang me.'

'Billy rang you?'

'Yes.'

'How did he know where you were?'

I closed my eyes and rested my head against a wall. There was the white light coming down again: I thought – Or perhaps indeed it is radioactivity. I opened my eyes and looked around: Fred had taken the piece of paper from the computer and was moving with the group of men around him back across the hall. One of the men was carrying a map which he held as if it were a sail to catch the wind –

Melissa said 'Hullo?'

I said 'Hullo? I thought you'd told him my number.'

'No.'

'Look, just make sure Billy's all right. I'll be back tomorrow, or as soon as I can.'

'Why can't you be the one who makes sure Billy's all right?'

'For God's sake, Melissa –'

'Perhaps he got your number from my answering–machine –'

'Yes. Yes. All right.' Then – 'How did it get on your answering–machine?'

'I was just ringing you to say everything was all right –'

'Yes. Yes. Melissa.'

Fred and his group were moving towards the front door. They were carrying their piece of paper, their map, and their instrument that was a geiger-counter. On their way out they paused and the man carrying the instrument pointed it at a corner of the doorway. They gathered round. I thought – Perhaps it is registering the sand from my shoes –

Melissa was saying 'None of this matters.'

I said 'That's right, Melissa.'

'Then what does.' She rang off.

Ellen had been with me when I had gone to the telephone. Now I could not see her. She had gone to the kitchen? Janice and Miss Simmons and Mr Kempinski were helping Mrs Wilton to her feet. I went to Charlie who was now sitting on the bottom step of the stairs. I said 'Should we go?' He said 'There's no need.' Then – 'No, you stay.'

I thought – I meant, is it safe –

– He knows what I meant!

– But still, one of us might die?

The group with Fred had gone out of the front door: the group around Mrs Wilton were following them. Janice broke away and came over to Charlie and me and said 'I'll pack.' I did not know which one of us she was saying this to. This did not seem to matter.

Charlie said 'I haven't got the Land-Rover.'

Janice said 'I've got my car.'

I thought I should go and see what was happening outside. In the circle in front of the hotel Mr Kempinski and Miss Simmons and Mrs Wilton were tottering towards a car. Fred and his group were zig-zagging here and there with their geiger-counter as if they were looking for a bunch of keys in the dark. I thought – And it is, thank God, nearly dark.

Charlie and Janice had remained in the hotel. I thought I would go round to the back and look through a window to see if I could see Ellen.

At the side of the hotel that looked out onto the beach there were the lighted windows of the bar: this and the hallway were now empty. I did not know where Janice and Charlie might have gone. I had the curious impression one sometimes has when looking through the windows of a lighted room, that by standing outside one might see more of what is happening than if one had been inside. A light came on in a room upstairs: this must be my bathroom. I thought – Oh yes, Janice has gone to pack: but she never unpacked – only her spongebag with her condoms in it. The lower sash of the window was raised and Janice looked out. I retreated behind some bushes. I thought – She is looking for me? she is checking on how to avoid me? Downstairs, in the hallway, Charlie appeared; he had come from upstairs? he had been having what Ellen had called a quickie with Janice? Then he went off down the passage to the back. I thought – And now he is looking for Ellen. A light came on from behind a frosted window on the ground floor. I tried to remember the lay-out of the hotel: on the way to the kitchen there were offices, or store-rooms; beyond the kitchen there was a back door to a yard? Another light came on in what might be the kitchen; by the light of this a figure could be seen, moving, crouching, along the outside wall of the hotel, as if trying to keep out of sight from the lighted windows. This was Ellen. I thought – Now stay quite still. Above, Janice had disappeared from the window of my bathroom. From the back door by the kitchen a light and then shadow appeared as if a door was opening and than there was Charlie's voice saying – 'Ellen?' Ellen was standing motionless with her back against the outside wall between two lighted windows: she was looking in my direction: I did not know if she could see me: I thought – But this is all right. The light in my bathroom went out; then the light and shadow at the back of the kitchen swung as if the door were closing. Then the lights in the kitchen and the store-room went out. I thought – And so, yes, one can construct the story. Charlie re-appeared in the hallway: he was just in time to meet Janice and take her suitcase as she arrived at the bottom of the stairs. Janice put her arm round Charlie's neck and kissed him. She and Charlie went towards the front door. Charlie turned out the lights in the bar. After that there was darkness. Then one's eyes began to become accustomed to the twilight.

There was a moon that was more than half full; it was quite high in the sky. There was the sound of a car starting up and driving away in the car-park.

I thought – So all right! Now people have gone. And Ellen and I may be the last two people left on earth –

– We will not mind dying?

Ellen was moving from the wall of the hotel. She came up to me and said 'Now I'll get some supper.'

I said 'That would be lovely.'

'Will you get the others?'

I thought I would not ask – What others?

She said 'They're down on the beach.'

I set off down through the sand-dunes towards the sea. The moonlight was hard and glittering: I thought – Like radioactivity? Then – There is some sort of immortality, I suppose, if one does not mind dying.

Down by the water's edge – the tide was once more far out – there were some figures standing. They were facing the sea; they might be, yes, the children. I thought – They are waiting for something to come up onto the land: or they are like gods that have come down to watch? I was walking over the pebbles and onto the huge stretch of sand; this was when things seemed not to get closer nor further away; you were forever in the present, with the moonlight like the darkness that was the nature of light itself. The figures by the water's edge were indeed those of children; the one towards whom I was walking, standing with her ankles just in the water, might be – then was – Gaby. She had her hands on her hips; she was wearing a T-shirt, or vest, which came down to the top of her thighs. There are figures like this in the unconscious; that stand by the edge of the sea; that might be of a race that has yet to be born. Gaby was watching some of the other children who had gone out up to their waists and then up to their shoulders in the water; there was one, a girl, some twenty yards out – the water at this sort of tide remained very shallow – and then two or three children even further out, their heads above the water like buoys. It seemed that they were the three boys with brushed-up hair, the triplets: they were carrying some burden on their shoulders that was like a snake. I thought – They are making some offering to the sea? it will it be like the child with no arms and no legs? Then – But I know what they are doing! I have seen this sort of thing before: it is a way of going fishing in the sea. You take out at low tide a long narrow net and there are floats along the top of it and weights at the bottom; you pull it in a huge semi-circle and then drag it in by ropes at either end; and within it, if you are lucky, there are fish; and always seaweed and stones and crabs. Standing at some distance to the left along the beach was another girl as if ready to receive the ropes at the end of the net being pulled round by the three boys – their heads now disappearing and reappearing against the lines of gentle waves. I thought – They are walking on the bottom of the sea; it is as if they are walking on water. Gaby and the girl in front of her were waiting for the boys to complete their circuit; then they too would pull on their ends of the ropes. I thought – But they will never be able to land the net on their own! it will be too heavy; I know because I have done this; you need a vehicle, or a much larger team. I had reached the edge of the sea; I was standing by Gaby; I could at least help with one of the ropes. I thought I might say to Gaby – Or what trick will you produce this time; like the miraculous draught of fishes? The three boys were coming in towards the shore; they were already beginning to struggle; they were letting the main part of the net stay in the sea and were coming into the beach, paying the ropes out behind them. The girl on the left went to help them; Gaby and the girl in front of Gaby and myself had picked up our ends of the ropes; we were pulling hard; we were managing at least to keep the net in its shape, but we had not the strength to get it in. Gaby looked round.

There was a vehicle coming down through the sand-dunes from the direction of the hotel; it was moving without lights, bouncing, roaring slightly; it was like what had seemed a mirage on the beach that morning; it was like some animal coming to claim its rights by the sea. It slithered across pebbles and then came smoothly across sand: I was afraid that the children might now have to run: I thought – How can I protect them? But the children did not seem to be startled by the apparition; they were keeping up the tension on the net. The vehicle came up, turned, pointed the other way; then backed to a place between where the ends of the ropes were being held. The vehicle was a Land-Rover; it was Charlie's Land-Rover; I thought – But I should have known something would turn up! Then – But Charlie is not here? The Land-Rover had stopped and a young man got out. He began to undress. He took off his shirt and trousers and threw them in the Land-Rover, then he did a short wild dance with his arms in the air. Then he went to the ends of the ropes held by the three boys and the girl and he dragged the ropes to the back of the Land-Rover and knotted them around the tow-bar. Then he came over to Gaby and the other girl and me. He said to me 'Hullo.' I said 'Hullo.' He said 'A Perfect Day for Banana Fish.' I thought I might say – Oh yes, I see. He was a young man, probably in his early twenties, with a bright round face and fair curly hair. He took the ends of the ropes that Gaby and the girl and I had been holding and he dragged them and tied them to the tow-bar; then he got into the Land-Rover and put it in gear and drove it slowly up the beach. The net, in its loop, was pulled out of the sea. I and the children stood outside it and watched. I thought – But 'A Perfect Day for Banana Fish' was a story in which a young man chose to die.

The net emerged as if indeed there was occurring some birth: water swirled sluggishly over the top; seaweed and one or two small fish went with it. As the apex of the loop came into the land there became visible a dark struggling mass shot through with flashes of silver. I thought – Oh indeed, an illustration of the creation of darkness and light! When the whole of the net was clear of the sea the Land-Rover stopped; the young man jumped out and untied the ropes from the tow-bar. The girls opened out the two sides of the net; within it amongst the seaweed and sand there were several bass, yes, and four or five sole; and small and scurrying crabs. I thought – There are constellations that appear thus in the night sky. The boys stepped into the net and went after the fish; the young man jumped in and joined them; the children were naked. They plunged and caught the fish which slithered about in their hands. Gaby had taken off her shirt and was knotting it so that it formed a bag; she held it so that the boys and the young man could put their fish into it. The other girls had taken off their shirts and were knotting them; Gaby put some of the fish into their bags. The boys picked up crabs by their shells and watched their claws waving; then they let them go and watched them scuttle back towards the sea. The young man dragged the net clear of the seaweed and straightened it, and then with the boys folded it neatly. He ran and plunged into the sea and splashed and washed himself; the two other girls fastened their bags and put them over their shoulders. They set off along the beach in the direction of the town. Gaby was helping the boys load the net onto their shoulders: I gathered up a bundle of the boys' clothes. I thought – Perhaps one day I will have learned this language in which you do not speak and know just what to do – one thing after another.

The young man came out of the water and put on his clothes and waved at me briefly. He said 'How to stay alive!' Then he got in the Land-Rover and drove off across the sand.

I thought – This has been some baptism in the sea?

Six

As we walked up the beach towards the hotel it was as if we might indeed be figures in some mythological representation – a frieze on a temple architrave; a shadow-play on a screen. Or might we not rather be the originals behind the screen? The three boys went in front; they were still naked; they carried the folded net like a trophy over their shoulders: as shadows, might they not appear as chained prisoners? Gaby followed with her bundle of fish; she was a pilgrim on her way to salvation. And I – what was I? – the person from the audience who finds himself for a moment behind the screen? in the world of things-as-they-are; with the beings that cast the shadows.

Or could we be envoys from another planet with a job to do: to infiltrate the enemy lines, as it were; would we ever return, did we have our suicide pills, or would we learn to live in the world in which we found ourselves.

There were no lights on in the main part of the hotel; the cars had gone from the circle at the front. From the back there was the shaft of light from the kitchen door that was like a ramp that we might walk up. I thought – Or this is our space-ship? we might even be going home.

Ellen appeared at the back door with the light behind her; she seemed somewhat larger than life – the original for an apparition. The three boys went to an outhouse at the back and deposited the net; Gaby went up to Ellen and handed her the bundle of fish. Ellen went into the hotel with it and Gaby and the boys followed; I came behind with my bundle of the boys' wet and dirty clothes. The kitchen was warm with its huge oil-fired range and pots and pans hanging above it; they were like the cymbals and gongs and bells that accompany an Eastern theatrical presentation. Ellen tipped the fish from Gaby's bundle onto a slab; Gaby took off her remaining piece of clothing and handed it to Ellen; I gave Ellen my bundle of clothes. Ellen looked at my slightly wet shirt and trousers, and smiled. She took the clothes through to a scullery where there was a washing-machine. I sat at the end of the long wooden table at which I had had coffee that morning. Gaby had begun to gut and clean the fish expertly: the boys were getting plates and cutlery and laying the table. Ellen came back and took the fish from Gaby and put three of the bass on a baking tray and sprinkled herbs and wrapped them in silver foil and put them in the oven. The boys were cutting slices from a loaf and they put these on the table. No one spoke. I thought – You mean, old God, we are building that tower to heaven; and if we are quiet enough no one will hear us? Gaby came to the other end of the table and poured out glasses of milk; then she sat with her head resting on her arms. The three boys sat in a line on a bench at the side of the table facing the stove. Ellen leaned with her back to the stove and her hands on the rail behind her. I thought – This is what is meant to be human means of communication?

Gaby said 'Tell us a story.'

Ellen said 'I've told you all my stories.'

One of the boys said something in the language I did not understand.

Gaby said 'Tell us the story of the great king.'

One of the boys said something further.

Gaby said 'The king who did not know what was his dream.'

Ellen looked briefly into the oven. The boys took some slices of bread and spread them with butter. Gaby watched with her head on her arms. Ellen stood with her back against the stove; she was wearing her white dressing-gown.

Ellen said 'Once upon a time there was a great king who was called Nebuchadnezzar. He had a dream, and when he woke up it seemed there had been all the answers to everything in the world in his dream, but he could not remember what it was. He reached for it, he lay and waited for it, but it would not come back.'

As she spoke Ellen mimed something of her story – resting her cheek against her hand, reaching out towards the light that hung from the ceiling, gazing at the boys as they so carefully watched her. I thought – They have the dream, even if they do not exactly understand what she is saying.

Ellen went on –

'King Nebuchadnezzar sent for all the wisest men of his land and he ordered them to interpret his dream: he said he would load them with riches if they would tell him his dream's meaning – for thus he would know all the secrets of the universe. But the wise men said – Great King, how can we interpret your dream if you cannot remember it; if you cannot tell us what it is we have to interpret? And they thought – You bloody old fool.'

Ellen went to the door of the kitchen and looked out into the passage. Then she came back.

'But the Great King was very angry that the wise men could not interpret his dream. He thought – What are wise men for, if they cannot interpret things unless they know what they are? What is the world coming to? Off with their heads!'

Ellen opened the oven door and looked inside for a moment. She drew back as if flames were coming out.

She went on – 'But there was one child, call her Daniel, who had become known as an interpreter of dreams. And she had three friends, three boys, who all looked the same, with bristly hair, and who stank of fish –'

The three boys began to roll about on the bench. Then they became still. I thought – They know this story? But what on earth is it, anyway –

Ellen moved to and fro in front of the stove as if she were creating, or searching for, the story as she went along.

'And Daniel said unto her three friends – For God's sake, boys, if we don't watch out this old fool of a king will have us in the oven, because he knows we have been fishing in the sea, and he thinks we should know his dream. And he has a point, doesn't he, because of course we can say we know his dream! that is, if he can't remember it, and no one else is saying that they know it.'

Ellen stood and stared at the boys. It was as if suddenly she were saying something in silence; and that was the rest of the story.

Gaby said 'But what was the dream –'

Ellen said 'The fish will be ready in five minutes.' Then she went out of the kitchen.

We sat round the table. I was trying to remember – What in fact was the end of that story? The children were put in the fiery furnace? They survived?

– Some sort of fire and brimstone?

Ellen came back into the kitchen and said 'Can they have a bath in your room?'

I said 'Yes.'

'And sleep there?'

'Yes.'

'Then it will just look as if you had gone berserk.' She smiled.

She went to the stove and took the tray out of the oven. She unwrapped the silver foil and put the fish onto a platter. She brought this to the table and doled out the fish. We began to eat ravenously.

Gaby said 'Then Daniel and the three boys went to the king and said – We can tell you your dream. And he said – What? And they said – You dreamed you were a great king and you saw everything had a meaning; but because you thought you should be able to say what it was, a great mountain came down and smashed you to pieces; and these were scattered, and became loaves and fishes, which are what we are eating now.'

Ellen said 'You'd say that?'

Gaby said 'Yes.'

'They'd pop you in the oven.'

I thought I'd say – You'd survive.

I had begun to feel extraordinarily sleepy. I was not quite sure if I had spoken out loud. I thought – Perhaps I am that king and I am dreaming I am being shown all the secrets of the universe: I will not try to say what they are. I will say – All right, children; this is not a dream; this is what things are –

Ellen was standing over me. She said 'Shall we go up then?'

I said 'I've been asleep.'

I wanted to say – And where will you sleep?

She said 'I'll just tidy up in the kitchen.'

We set off along the passage to the hallway in our procession: the boys in front, pretending to wrestle, bumping off one another, pretending to fall asleep; Gaby following; myself coming behind. Gaby, naked, was like something not so much human as a form of which philosophers speak. The boys went up the stairs. It seemed more than ever that there was no one else in the hotel. The boys waited outside the door of my room: I thought – They know this room? they have been here before? Gaby went in and turned on the lights; Janice's suitcase was no longer there. Gaby drew the curtains. I thought – They have come to have baths here as well as to feed? Then – This is why there is a fear of contamination? The boys went into the bathroom; I could hear them turning on the taps. Gaby lay on one of the beds; she reclined with her head propped on an arm. I thought – If she is a model, I could paint her: she is that which is to be discovered within the canvas; within the mind? On her stomach there was a mark as if she had been burned: I had not noticed this before. It was as if the canvas of a painting had been attacked by a madman to get at what might be beyond. I said 'How did you get that?' She said 'I was burned.' I thought – She does not want to say more. Or – You flew too close to the sun?

I went through to the bathroom. The boys were playing with the taps, squirting each other and splashing. I sat on the seat of the lavatory; the boys tumbled into the bath. There was a welter of limbs, protuberances, joints, clefts, orifices; after a time they settled down in a row. I thought – Of course they are like those three, what were their names? who were put in the fiery furnace: there are paintings like this – the three as if in a cooking–pot, their heads just showing above the rim. The boys watched me brightly. I thought – You expect me to wash you? Well I won't. Or you mean – What do you mean? I went back into the bedroom.

Gaby was lying on her side with her head on her forearm as if she were asleep. I sat on the bed beside her.

I had once done a story about a home for delinquent or retarded children. There had been some scandal; children were said to have been abused; I was shown a video film of an eleven-year-old boy who was epileptic and was apt to become obstreperous and then had to be restrained. He was a strikingly beautiful boy. It was as if those handling him and trying to undress him to put him to bed were being led on some trail by him; he became limp and yet recalcitrant; he was half-watching his handlers out of the corner of his eye as he was pushed and pulled; it was as if he were inviting or provoking manipulation – as if by this he might gain some identity, even authority. The handlers were doing not much more than their job. I had thought – Why are you showing me this? It is the job of those in authority to take risks with the weaker members of the tribe? Then the weaker members can blame you? Those showing me the film had said – You see? I had thought – But will it really help you, if I try to explain this –

I was sitting in the bedroom on the bed next to Gaby. I took off my jacket and rolled up my sleeves. I went back into the bathroom. I said 'All right, come on, I'll wash you.' I thought – We are so frightened of children: of course they are not only clay but fragile china in our hands.

In films of people handling radioactive material they put their hands into protective gloves that poke through a screen; they manipulate whatever it is through the screen; they need to be out of touch with what they are doing. I thought – I have no screen; who cares; this is the point – what does it mean, does it matter, if children are like radioactive material? The boys giggled as I washed them; they twisted themselves into this or that position; put their heads down, legs up; pretended to slip over and be drowning. I held them under and scrubbed their heads: I made them stand up and turn around. I thought – Oh well this is quite pleasurable, is it not? of course people are frightened of getting pleasure with children. They may get millstones round their necks and be cast into the sea. But what if there are pearls of great price at the bottom?

I went back into the bedroom. Gaby was watching me with one eye open. I thought I might say to her – Won't you be having a bath?

I sat down again for a moment to think. What was, after all, the point of the story of Nebuchadnezzar's dream? That things were in your power: you could make of them what you liked? But you had to know, or to find, what you liked: this was what was hidden in the flesh; in the stone –

I must have fallen asleep again. Gaby had gone from the bed beside me. I thought – But I have not lost my dream?

I went back into the bathroom. Gaby had climbed into the bath with the boys. She was lying with her head against the top of the back of the bath. Two of the boys were lying alongside her and half on top of her; she had her arms around them; their heads were resting on her shoulders, their mouths were close to her just-growing breasts. They appeared to be sleeping. The third boy was doubled up at the far end of the bath with his face down in the water by Gaby's groin. I thought – Well, if you have to go, what a way to do it! Or – These are bodies of the righteous waiting for the day of resurrection. The boy with his head under water raised it for a moment to let his breath out and take another in; then he laid his face under water again. I thought – Come on angels: you still need help to get out of the egg.

I got my arms underneath the boy with his face under water and lifted him; he was quite light. I wrapped him in a towel and carried him through to the bedroom. There I sat on a bed and dried him. He was pretending to be asleep. There are children's games like this in which the child pretends to be asleep and so can be tickled and manoeuvred; thus he can feel he is in the hands of some old God again, before birth or just after, when he was picked up and dangled and dried and sent out under the sun. The boy was smiling. I laid him on the bed with his head on a pillow. He was on his back. There are drawings by old draughtsmen like this of the perfect proportions of the human body – arms and legs spread out as if these also represented the structure of the universe. The boy had a small erection. I thought – The frail peg on which the universe rotates.

I pulled the bedcover over him. I thought – Grown-ups like to think that is a peg to which they can be tethered?

I went back into the bathroom and got my arms under the nearest of the boys who were lying on Gaby; I carried him through to the bedroom. I thought – But it is not too difficult to imagine the background to taboos; indeed this is like walking with bare feet across hot coals. This boy was quieter than the first as I dried him: I thought – I do see there is an instinct to hurt children: their coherence and their composure is such a threat! of course we are tempted to make them as disorganised as ourselves – they who will supplant us. What do they expect us to do – go down without fighting? Have we not told them that even love is some sort of fight? I had to be more rough with this boy to dry him: but he too was smiling. I laid him beside his brother. He too had a small erection. I thought – Or we want to devour such fruits; as if they were deadly nightshade in the Garden of Eden.

I went back into the bathroom. Gaby and the remaining boy were side by side in the bath. I got my arms underneath the boy and I slipped and almost fell on top of them. Gaby smiled. I thought – She has never been sleeping.

I carried the third boy through to the bedroom. There was almost no discernible difference between the three boys. I thought – Things, in order to have form, have to go in threes: three Gods or gods; three modes for perception: that which is, that which knows, and that which goes between. It is we who try to tell children that things are all-of-a-piece. But we should know of ourselves that we are not. It must have come down to earth, somewhere, this form of understanding?

I laid the third boy on the bed beside the other two. The one on the outside was falling off. I pulled the bedcover over them and tucked it in. They wriggled and moved their arms and slotted into one another.

I went back to Gaby in the bathroom: she lay with her eyes closed. I thought – She knows that I know she is not asleep. I watched her. There is the story of a hunter who watched the Greek goddess Artemis when she bathed: she set his own dogs onto him which tore him to pieces. Or there was Circe who turned men into pigs – they could be protected only by a magic herb which is found on a mountain. But what this herb was no one knew – except Odysseus. This was like Nebuchadnezzar's dream: you could find and say what you liked, if you liked –

I leaned over and tried to get my arms underneath Gaby: she was surprisingly heavy: indeed we might go headlong into the pit! She raised one arm and put it around my neck. I thought – And then how long before resurrection?

I carried Gaby through to the bedroom and sat with her on my lap on the bed. We were then indeed in the position of some *pietà*. But was she not now laughing? I was conscious of my old root going down into the earth: might it now at least flower above the top of my head? Adam must have taken with him one or two seeds or cuttings from the Garden: oh yes, there were those stones from the Tree of Knowledge of Good and Evil; they must have come out in his shit –

But what of the Tree of Life?

Gaby was stirring from her position as part of a *pietà*; she twisted and leaned back and swung her leg that was nearest to me up and over my head so that she was then facing me sitting with her legs astride my knees. In doing so she opened up what indeed might be seen as her wound made for cuttings, her repository for seeds, her secret garden. There is the idea in Tantra that if two people can use sexual attraction to confront one another, touch one another, even embrace one another, yet maintain their identity and distance – holding back from the business of invasion, possession, fusion, annihilation – then a field of energy is created and held in between, within which whatever seeds are formed of creation or procreation will not be used as it were by a hungry spider to feed off the paralysed body of a wasp; rather the seeds, energy, will be of the nature of those which have created and held together the universe – which ensure what is rather than what is not. And by the experience of this force created within and between there will be not only the distinction but an end to distinction between the one and the other – the knower and the known; the individual and the whole. And then you will have the reality rather than a dream in which you understand exactly what things are. There are glimpses of this at moments like a white light coming down; but now it is like a snake growing up your spine and then there it is, yes, bursting out of the top of your head. So that it is indeed as if you were once more in the Garden but now are the branches and flowers of that tree: and you are looking for that old God who once made you so ashamed: and if you find him you can surely say – Come along, old

Godadaddy, you need not be ashamed! this is not your silly old Tree of the Knowledge of Good and Evil: this is the Tree of Life.

Gaby was sitting on my knees. I had not bothered to be drying her. She had drawn up her knees into the position of a foetus – or indeed of someone climbing the smooth trunk of a tree, to get to what unimaginable delicacies at the top. I had my arms around her. I thought – Oh there is the tail of that old snake, yes, rootling about at the foot of the tree: but it is also that force, hold still, by which we might get to the top. Is that not so, Gaby? She pulled her head back and looked into my eyes. I thought – No need to go further: we are at home. We are the needle held upright on its point by gravity –

How quiet the old place had become! And there were no weeds growing. You do not call them weeds, you call them flowers. There was our comfortable cave in the rocks; that was where we had hidden when the Roman soldiers went past. The tomb had been broken into: that other old tree had fallen across the roof. And there was old Godadaddy as if collapsed with his back against the roots –

I was sitting with Gaby on my knees. I was looking into her eyes. I thought – All right, but how do we come down to earth before we set off on that journey?

I became aware that Ellen was coming into the room. She was in the doorway struggling with what seemed to be a huge stone slab. I thought – Now don't overdo it! Or do we not come down to earth? we know there are angels –

– But don't we have to get the earth, old Godadaddy, up to the top of the tree?

What Ellen seemed to be struggling with was an enormous double mattress: she was holding this in front of her as if it were a screen. It seemed about to topple and to crush her or expose her. I thought – She is the like the lady in blue on that hillside who did not want too much to be seen. Gaby had turned to watch Ellen: she was still in the position of someone about to be born or giving birth: or, yes, like someone about to climb down a tree. I thought – Or it is the seeds that drop to earth?

Ellen had got the mattress into the room where it eventually collapsed with her on top of it. She lay there rather ostentatiously with her arms out in a cross. Gaby said 'Has anyone come back yet?'

Ellen said 'No.'

Gaby said 'That's all right then.' She climbed off my knees.

It was as if I were not having to remember my vision, my dream, because it was now in the room with us. We had gone back to our old homestead; the animals had gone; the branch had fallen across the roof: we could not stay, but we could spend a night here. Ellen had picked herself up and had gone from the room and was coming back with a bundle of pillows and blankets. Gaby was helping her to arrange these on the mattress. I thought – Of course, God must have found it difficult to be a single-parent family –

– So you mean, what of Billy and Melissa?

– But only one night!

It seemed I should go and have a bath: I could at last get my clothes off. Or in so far as I might be the snake I could shed my skin: but without the snake how could anything have been possible? I sat on the edge of the bath and let the dirty water run out. At Lourdes, they offer you a cup of the dirty water to drink after lepers have bathed in it; no one has been poisoned. You do not have to believe; only do it –

– We did not eat of the Tree of Life because no one told us not to?

– We are all growing up, Godadaddy.

I ran some more water in the bath and undressed and climbed in. I sat there as if I were in a cooking-pot of my own choosing. I wondered – I will be eaten? I will not need to be eaten –

Ellen came and stood in the doorway. She said 'Shall I wash your clothes?'

I said 'Yes please.'

'They'll be ready by morning.'

I thought – You mean, you will be spending the night here?

I had a vision of a girl in a white smock riding on a black horse across a battlefield. She was picking up bodies as if to take them to Valhalla; she was sticking them on the end of her lance as if they were bits of paper. I thought – But this is the dream that is over –

I had been walking in a wood one day with Melissa and Billy. Billy had said – Why isn't God happy?

I had said – Isn't he happy?

Billy had said – He's always so grumbly.

Melissa had said – Perhaps he didn't have someone to love him as a baby.

Ellen was standing in the doorway again. She said 'Do you want some cocoa?'

I said 'Yes please.'

'I'll put it by the mattress.'

I thought – I'll be sleeping on the mattress?

I climbed out of my bath. I thought – But yes, what we never got quite right is the coming together and being a part of a family.

In the bedroom the boys were tucked up in their bed with their heads side by side on a pillow and over them the cover that made it seem as if their bodies might be one. I thought – A theological problem. Gaby was sitting on the other bed with her hands round her knees. Ellen was on the mattress brushing her hair. I remembered – What was the story of Lot and his daughters –

– After the destruction of Sodom and Gomorrah Lot's daughters thought that their father might be the last man alive on earth, so they made him drunk in order to sleep with him –

– But I am not drunk –

– That is the difference?

Gaby said 'I don't want to be alone.'

Ellen said 'Then don't be.'

There was a cup of cocoa on the floor by the mattress: I stood with a towel wrapped round me. I thought – I shall sit on the mattress by Ellen and drink my cocoa; then I shall attend to whatever turns up. Things have to be done in due order, do they not, to find out what they are. I drank my cocoa. I thought – And you will learn what I learn, will you not, my wife and children –

– This is happening?

I had lain down. Ellen was pulling a blanket over me. Then she turned off the lights. She was climbing under the blanket beside me.

I turned to Ellen and put my arms around her. I thought – Well, gods are human: but then, what are gods? It seemed I was about to make love to Ellen: I was at an edge of the known world and falling over. I thought – This is destruction or self-destruction; or I will fly. Then – Well, he was a bird, wasn't he, that old god, when he flew out of that tree? I was about to go inside Ellen – she seemed to be quite ready – when I became aware that Gaby was climbing under the blanket behind me. At least I was sure it was Gaby; who else could it be? she put her arms around me. And so she was riding on my back like a child on the back of a dolphin even as I was the dolphin riding on the sea. I was inside Ellen but as we took off there was no invasion, possession – with the child at my back holding me. I thought – I see! We are no longer lonely scavengers bearing trophies to Valhalla; we are two of us carrying a third to where it will be free. Oh this is supposed to be a terror to children, is it? But hold on, hold on, Gaby! it is you who will fly with us now beyond this tree; and we will be not so much a dolphin and the sea as the winged horse Pegasus as it rises like the sun.

Seven

When we left the hotel in the morning – not hurrying though wondering perhaps if we might be caught as we came out into the light –

– Ellen having brought us our clothes washed and dried; having brought to the bar downstairs mugs of coffee and tea which we drank warming our hands around them as if it might be cold outside –

– which it was not, though it was quiet and still; no one being about at the edge of the town that early just as there had still been no one else in the hotel –

– it being Sunday morning? but what had really happened that other Sunday morning –

– There had been very few people about, coming out into the light?

And now we, after our night, could be free to go on our journey?

Ellen stood in the doorway of the hotel. She was in her white dressing-gown: she looked like – all right, I need not say any more! I said 'You're not coming?' She said 'No.' I thought – But she will know where we go.

I had the suitcase of plastic containers in the boot of my car: I could now take these to Mrs Ferguson: I could also take Gaby and the children – what else should I be doing? I had imagined that the young man who had turned up on the beach the previous evening was Mrs Ferguson's son: had he not said – I could not remember – but he would be seeing us? Was it necessary to remember? Things were happing one after the other in this bright dark light.

Ellen remained in the doorway of the hotel. It suddenly seemed unbearable that I might not see her again. But what was unbearable or bearable in this strange world? Of course something unique had happened, and so should not happen again –

I said 'Thank you.'

She said 'Oh that's all right.'

Gaby and myself and the three boys went to my car: the boys were not banging about now; Gaby herded them briskly. It seemed that they at least knew where they were going. They did not look back at Ellen: I thought – They know they will see her again?

I drove with Gaby and the boys into the hills. This was where myself and two of the boys had come the day before: what was it that had happened since then. You do not exactly make yourself remember: images come and go in your head. There had been a scare about radioactivity; this had been picked up by people with instruments in the hotel. But it could not have been much of a scare; there was no official reaction. Charlie was said to be able to fix Fred's computer? But this had been a joke? Charlie, however, had wanted to go off not with Ellen but with Janice. Janice had known Charlie before, this was why she had wanted to come up here: she had needed me as an excuse, or to make Charlie jealous – and so on and so on. Ellen might have wanted to make Charlie jealous – with me? Oh that would not have been a joke! But that was surely not, God knows, what had happened. People perhaps had left the hotel because of contamination that someone had picked up on the beach: and thus we had had our night in the hotel. And that had not been a joke. And the group round Fred were like members of Bluebeard's Castle or the Ku-Klux-Klan – that was hardly a joke – but by using them, the children had been able to get some power – as over devils. I could not dwell on this easily: the images became convoluted in my head. I thought – Give them up, or let them run freely – this is what I have learned? Here we are, in the early morning.

We were on the road into the hills. This was where we had passed the clergyman pushing his bicycle: this was where the young couple had sat on their hillock looking down into the valley. And here we were now, myself and the boys and Gaby. We might pray – Let things happen in the past and future in such order and with such luck as they offer now.

When I had gone to Russia to do my story on the aftermath of the Chernobyl disaster and had expected to find cover-ups and instead had found almost an exaggeration of its effects, I had seen that there were practical reasons for this – the chance of a diversion from the crack-up of Communism; a chance of procuring aid from the West. But also there had seemed to be a compulsive need to dwell on disaster without a concomitant view of the hope this might carry with it: for had not the failure of trust in technology indeed been a symbol, a symptom, of the failure of all systems dependent on mere manipulation? And should not such a failure in some sense be greeted? But of course there was little aptitude for saying – How grand that there should be such a disaster! in order that, of course, something new might grow. Oh yes, in a disaster people die; but do not people die anyway? I had somewhat lost my nerve when I came to write this story. I had said to Jack, my editor – There have been these wandering clouds of dust all over Eastern Europe; they break things up: but you cannot quite say to people – How lucky to be broken up! Jack had said – No, you cannot say that. I had said to my clergyman friend – he to whom I had talked about the appearances of the Virgin Mary – But God could say that? He had said – Well he sometimes seems to, doesn't he?

I thought – I can imagine I am referring to myself being broken up? in this particularly wonderful early morning.

We were coming to the bridge where I had parked my car and had slept: this was on the way to the circle in the field which might or more probably might not have something to do with radioactivity. In a fairy story, what would have happened while I had slept? Fingers would have come down from the clouds like waves, like particles: would have effected some transformation.

When I had come back from Russia I had tried to find out more about the effects of radioactivity – about why some people were affected with sickness and death while others with similar exposures were not. Scientists did not seem to be at home with this question: all they could be sure about were the statistics. Within individuals it could be seen that radiation particles caused damage to cells: such cells usually died before further damage was done. But cancer cells were damaged cells that did not die: they went on proliferating until the whole organism died: they came up against no mechanism that might say – Stop! But what this mechanism was, it did not seem possible to pin down. It seemed that life depended on some intricate working of a whole; a balancing between what should die and what should not. One reason why this could not be measured was because any effort to do so would itself affect the intricate working of the whole –

I had said to my clergyman friend – You mean, life may be something you have to understand as a matter of faith, because if you try to understand it in any other way then this invalidates what you are trying to find –

He had said – Oh but you can see when it works, can't you?

We were coming to gates with stone pillars at the left of the road. I turned into a driveway. I had not been at this side of the house before. Set back from the drive, against the background of a wood, were the ruins of a Gothic abbey: there was the stonework of the windows of the choir and one huge arch of the chancel and then pillars of descending height in the nave. The whole thing was like a skeleton of a dinosaur. I thought – Indeed this might be a setting for the Ku-Klux-Klan or indeed the Hellfire Club. Then – But it is out of these old bones that something new might grow? Did Gaby come this way: like a girl on a black horse on a battlefield? I drove on. On the gravel in front of the house where I had stood the day before with Mrs Ferguson and the two policemen, there was the fair-haired young man who had come onto the beach the night before. I thought – So he is Mrs Ferguson's son: everything is in due order. As we approached he bent down and peered through the windscreen of the car. I slowed and stopped. When he saw who we were he started running past us to the side of the house where there was an archway through to a courtyard that seemed to contain outhouses and stables. The boys piled out of the car and went in pursuit of him; it was as if this were some game that they had played before. The young man went running round the inside of the courtyard; the boys ran after him; it was not as if they were trying to catch him, it was more as if this were some exercise of almost military precision. Gaby and I had got out of the car; we went to the archway and watched. As the young man and the boys ran round the courtyard a flock of pigeons or doves flew out of and up from a building at the far end; in the gable of this building were the holes of an elaborate dovecote. The openings were in the pattern of the triangular shape of the gable; underneath each hole was a number on a tile set into the stonework; the numbers ranged from 1, on its own at the top, down through six more lines to number 28 at the right-hand bottom of the triangle. The young man and the boys made a complete circuit of the yard and now stood with their backs to the house staring up at the dovecote. The pigeons had flown around and had settled on neighbouring rooftops; the young man and the boys seemed to be waiting for them to come back to their holes. This, after a time, they did – landing in ones or twos on ledges in front of this or that hole and then waddling off into the darkness. The boys murmured to themselves or to each other: the young man watched them: then he turned to me and said 'Good morning.'

I said 'Good morning.'

He said 'This contraption was built by my great-great-great-grandfather or whatever in the eighteenth century. The triangle of numbers is supposed to be magical, I can't remember why, except that twenty-eight is what is called a perfect number, because its factors or divisors, or whatever, add up to itself: which anyone would want to do, God knows. And my great-great-grandfather, or whatever, thought that doves, or pigeons, were the representative of the Holy Ghost; and so by this device, and by watching what holes the doves came out of and went into, he thought that God, the Holy Ghost, might have a chance of getting his message across to humans: which otherwise he seemed to be finding it notoriously difficult to do, God knows.'

I said 'I see.'

'I mean my great-grandfather, or whatever, having taken note of the numbers of the holes that the pigeons went into and came out of, then could work out whatever mathematical correlations he liked; but all this gave him a chance to imagine that what he liked might be to do with the Holy Ghost –'

I said 'Like the *I Ching*.'

'Yes, like the *I Ching*.'

'But birds do have that capacity –'

'What –'

'For coming home.'

Gaby had gone to the boot of the car and was taking out the suitcase that contained the plastic jars. The boys had followed her and were competing for who would take the suitcase from her and carry it to a side-door into the house. The young man and I followed them. He said 'But occasionally they'd go into an unexpected hole –'

I said 'And that's what he'd be looking for?'

The boys had gone into the house and were setting off down a long stone corridor. Gaby followed with myself and the young man. He said 'It's a means of breaking up old patterns, in the mind, so you might see something other than your own manipulations –'

I said 'Connections.'

'But still you wouldn't know what –'

'But you might find them.'

At the far end of the corridor there was a door into what might be a lift. There was a button beside it which one of the boys pressed. A mechanism began to churn and grind. I thought – Of course the children have been here before: it's a sort of home to them?

They young man said 'Oh yes, they'd be there.'

The boys were talking quietly among themselves in the language I did not understand. Gaby was listening. Then after a time she said 'Fifteen and nine and eleven and four.'

The young man said 'And what does that mean?'

The boys went on murmuring. The lift was taking a long time to come. Then Gaby said 'Fifteen times nine is a hundred and thirty-five, minus eleven is a hundred and twenty-four, multiplied by four is four hundred and ninety-six.'

The young man said 'And that doesn't mean anything.'

I said 'Four hundred and ninety-six is the next perfect number.'

The young man said 'Good God!' He made a face.

The boys looked at him and laughed.

Gaby said 'And what does that mean?'

The grinding and juddering noise ceased and the door sprang open. There was a small lift with a notice displayed prominently – Maximum Three Persons. The others squeezed into the lift with the suitcase. I made as if to stay outside, but the young man made room for me; he said 'That notice is a theological statement.' I squeezed in with them and the door clanged shut and we stood pressed together with our arms by our sides. The young man said 'Now pray to St Christopher.' The lift was not moving: the three boys took deep breaths and held them and Gaby jumped once up and down on the floor. The lift began to grind upwards. The boys seemed to be struggling to hold their breaths and the young man was making funny faces as if to make them laugh. I thought – This is praying?

The lift stopped and the door clanged open: the boys bundled out and Gaby and I and the young man followed. We emerged directly into a long panelled room that might once have been a picture gallery or one of those spaces in a large country house where the inmates used to stroll up and down to take exercise in bad weather. One end was furnished as a sitting-room or library with shelves of books to the ceiling, and armchairs and a sofa facing a huge open fireplace; the other end had been fitted out as a laboratory or workshop of a more elaborate and permanent kind than that which had been set up as an outpost in the caravan. There was electronic equipment stacked along an inner wall, a long table on which there were trays and retorts and test-tubes in racks, two microscopes including one of the kind that produces an enlarged or constructed image on a screen. At a separate table were three computers with keyboards and screens in a row. The three boys went to these without any prompting and sat on stools in front of them and tapped on the keyboards and watched the screens. Gaby had carried the suitcase from the lift and she went with it to the far end of the room where Mrs Ferguson, in a quilted dressing-gown, was in her wheelchair watching the screen that seemed to be connected to the microscope. The young man said. 'We get some extraordinary results with them.'

I said 'With the boys.'

'Yes.'

'Because they're triplets?'

'I don't know.'

He went and sat with his feet up on the sofa. I followed and perched on the arm of one of the chairs. I thought – We go tapping around in our minds for what might be connections –

I said 'What do they do?'

He said 'They make models.'

'Of what?'

'Of complex systems. Of reality.'

He was watching Gaby at the far end of the room. She was unpacking the suitcase and putting the plastic containers onto the long table by Mrs Ferguson.

I said 'They don't manipulate?'

'What –'

'The possibilities.'

He jumped up and walked to and fro in front of the fireplace. He said 'I'm sorry to assume you want me to go on like this, but I've read quite a bit of your stuff, you see –'

'What bits –'

'– Scientists get what they look for, so what goes on that they don't see –'

'– So how can you see what you don't see – ?'

'Yes.' He stopped and looked at the children and Mrs Ferguson at the far end of the room. He said 'My name's Peter.'

'I said 'You're Mrs Ferguson's son?'

'Ellen said you were surprised when we knew you –'

'Well I would be, wouldn't I.'

'You didn't seem to be.'

'No, I see.'

Gaby was coming back from the far end of the room. She went to the sofa and lay and put her feet up. I thought – She is doing what Peter did: she has loved Peter? we make connections.

I said 'But what exactly is your mother doing now?'

He said 'Oh – there's radiation that damages cells, causing death; but sometimes it doesn't. So what is it that does or does not do this?

Can we even look for this, if looking's part of what does or does not do it? You've written about this.'

'Yes.'

'– Reality is a function of the experimental condition – a butterfly's wingbeat in Brazil can cause a hurricane in California – and so on and so on.'

'Yes. So can you fix the experimental condition? Cause the butterfly's wingbeat?'

'No. Yes. No.'

'You wouldn't know –'

'But if it's chance –'

'You can make chances more likely.'

Gaby seemed only half to be paying attention to what we were saying; as if she might have heard it all before, and was waiting for us to finish.

Peter said 'But still, when something unusual comes in, you can either kill it or use it –'

'Or let it use you –'

'Exactly.'

At the far end of the room the boys had stopped tapping at their keyboards and were sitting back and watching as if to let the computers work on their own. Mrs Ferguson had left the screen that was connected to the microscope and was pushing herself over to join the boys at their table.

I said 'But that, you can choose?'

Peter said 'Choose what –'

'To allow things to happen –'

'That might effect change?'

'You can watch them.'

Peter had sat down on the floor by the sofa next to Gaby. He put his arm across her, his head on her knee. I thought – Perhaps it is he who has made love to Gaby. So – A butterfly's wingbeat –

Peter said 'And so by this you might learn about assimilation, adaption; instead of fighting, killing?'

I said 'Oh, the bad things too –'

'Making use of them? Letting them make use of you?'

'You might see what they are and so come to an end of them.'

Peter had turned his face and pressed it against Gaby's leg. Gaby lay with her eyes closed.

He said 'That would be the experiment?'

I thought – This is an experiment –

I said 'And see what survives.'

Peter sat up. Gaby opened her eyes and looked at me. Peter said 'Has Gaby told you of her vision?'

I said 'You did see a vision?'

Gaby said 'I've told you –'

'What –'

'I knew you had a son called Billy.'

Peter was looking away toward Mrs Ferguson and the boys at the far end of the room. They were murmuring in the language that I did not understand. I thought – You mean: I don't know what you mean –

I said 'No, you didn't tell me.'

She said 'I did, in the barn.'

'I told you I had a son. You could have found out he was called Billy.'

'How –'

'People here knew me.'

'They didn't know Billy.'

'No.'

Peter said 'She rang him up.'

I said 'You rang up Billy?'

Peter said 'So perhaps after all it is just a matter of electronic communication –'

He clambered to his feet. Mrs Ferguson was coming wheeling down the room. As she approached, Peter sprang to one side as if he had only just noticed her. I thought – You mean: I still don't know what you mean: it is easier for us to act as if we were computers –

– But since we know this, we know we are not computers?

Mrs Ferguson was saying to me 'Can you stay till this evening?'

I said 'Yes.'

'Gaby may be in trouble.'

'I know.'

'We should know by this evening.'

'About that man?'

'Yes, did you hear —'

'He won't say anything.'

'We don't know.'

Mrs Ferguson pushed herself to one of the long mullioned windows that looked out across the park. There were some thunderclouds forming as if for a storm. I had put out of mind about Gaby and the man in the car: he might be injured; he might be dead. I thought — You mean, we might make it one thing or another; if we do not think we know?

I followed Mrs Ferguson to the window. I said 'Those experiments you are doing with cells —'

She said 'Yes —'

'They're cells without a nucleus —'

'Yes.'

'The ones that under conditions of starvation, stress, increase their production of mutations, some of which will be those which can feed on what is available —'

'Yes.'

'And these cells have some inbuilt means of communication one to another: can share information, I mean, as if they were not separate but parts of a whole —'

'They can transfer, share, DNA —'

'And even a nucleus is simply one cell that has been assimilated by another —'

'That is contentious —'

'But the cells of the brain —'

'What —'

'Have components that work on that level?'

She was looking out of the window. I thought suddenly — What was it that put her into a wheelchair?

She said 'What all this is leading up to, what you're really asking is — What is it that makes the world of possibilities that exist on the quantum level turn into this or that.'

I said 'Yes.'

'Well what is it?'

'Consciousness? You give it your attention?' Then — 'Don't we know that —'

Mrs Ferguson had turned and was watching where Gaby was kneeling in front of the fire trying to light it. There was a metal basket in the fireplace with logs and kindling-wood and paper, the paper suddenly flared. I thought – Talk like this suddenly flares: bits and pieces drift about the universe.

Mrs Ferguson said 'Are we talking physics or biology?'

I said 'Both.'

Peter called out 'We're talking about God –'

Mrs Ferguson said 'I knew you'd say that.'

She wheeled herself to the fireplace where Gaby had succeeded in lighting the fire. Gaby crawled and leaned with her head against Mrs Ferguson's knees. I thought – But can I write about this?

Peter said 'You're asking what's the mechanism by which knowing can change possibilities into this or that –'

I said 'Yes. But I can't write about it.'

Mrs Ferguson said 'Why not?'

I thought I might say – Can the brain look at itself, or look at itself looking at itself –

Peter said 'You can write about what's here.'

I thought – You mean, you'll find the connections?

Mrs Ferguson was stroking Gaby's hair. Peter was standing over them. I thought – But I know almost nothing of these people: does this matter? Then – And why is Ellen not with us? Mrs Ferguson suddenly pushed herself almost violently away from Gaby and Peter: she went wheeling to the far end of the room. Peter began to go after her, then stopped. Gaby was on all fours on the carpet. I thought – But I do know these people: what is happening is what is here.

I sat on the sofa by Gaby. I said 'Why did you go with that man in the car?'

Gaby said 'I had to.'

'Why?'

'He had some tapes.'

'What of?'

'Some of me.'

Peter called out from half-way down the room – 'And of the Virgin Mary!'

Gaby had her back to him. She called out – 'That was just the tape!'

I said to Gaby 'And what happened to these tapes?'

'He said he'd destroyed them.'

'And had he?'

'No.' Then she called out – 'Had he!'

Peter called – 'I don't know!'

I said 'And what happened to the car –'

Gaby said 'He crashed it.'

'And how did you get out?'

'I'd already got out.'

'And what happened to the tapes.'

'I told him I'd got them.'

'And had you?'

Gaby was looking at Peter. Peter was standing half-way down the room. I thought suddenly – But none of this matters: one does not want to be like that man in the car –

– This is a dead end. Leave it.

It seemed I might go and join the boys by their computers at the far end of the room. Mrs Ferguson had gone back to her trays of liquids. As I passed Peter I tried to think of something to say to him: I smiled and made a face: he followed me.

On one of the screens of the computers there was the diagram of a square being formed and growing by increasing in a spiral – a thickness winding round it like a snake growing out of its own head. This went on till the formation filled the screen: coloured lights were flashing on and off in the squares within the square apparently at random; then they settled and formed a pattern, a new shape. I stood by Peter. The boys had left the computers and were looking at the trays of liquids and encrustations that were on the long table by Mrs Ferguson. I thought – You mean, there are connections between the trays and what is happening on the screens –

– You make them?

Peter was standing beside me. I said. 'What's happening?'

He said 'What's understanding –'

'That's the question?'

'That's the experiment.'

On another of the screens there began to appear and disappear and reappear in slightly different forms immensely complex patterns of fronds and curls and spirals; these were like structures in nature but almost more elaborate; they were like blueprints, templates, for what might be in nature – structures like ferns and flowers or perhaps claws and fins and shells. Each manifestation was apparently being increasingly magnified or seen at greater depth: so that it was just as if what was being demonstrated was that there was no end to the formation of complexity, there was just the level at which you chose to look. Or it was the looking that created them? I had seen photographs of such images; I had not before seen them forming and being re-formed on a screen. They were the images that computers came up with when you fed in instructions that designs which led to infinity should be expressed in a finite shape. The result was – not chaos, disintegration, but rather – transformation, beauty. With the connection of the finite and the infinite, this was just how the system worked –

I said to Peter 'But what did you start with?'

He said 'Those little dots that you collected.'

'In the containers?'

'Yes.'

'But they might refer to anything. This is a mathematical problem, or activity –'

'We had a map. A plan of where they came from –'

'Which you fed in –'

'Yes.'

'But that might refer to anything –'

'Yes. But isn't that the point?'

'What? What were the instructions –'

'Find the connections.'

'What connections?'

'They know the rules –'

'What are rules? They're assumptions –'

'That there are such things as connections.'

The images on the screen seemed to be rising up like sea-horses from the floor of the ocean; then riding away above tree-tops to the light –

I thought – All right, I have these images –

– They are in the brain –

– But the outside world?

I said 'But you're not finding out about the outside world –'

He said 'Oh yes you are.'

'What –'

'That it's beautiful.'

'And that's what you want?'

'Don't you?'

I thought – Oh yes, yes: and those bits and pieces of light, like bullets, are beautiful?

I moved to the trays of fluids and encrustations that were on the long table. Peter followed. There were coloured shapes like those of a relief model of an archipelago, banks and rocks and islands rising from the sea, shallows and mudflats like settings for precious stones. I thought – We are looking at life, all right: and what is formation without death: and that is beautiful?

Peter said 'Have you thought why we choose images like a butterfly's wingbeat, and not the toe of a frog –'

I said 'But the toe of a frog would be beautiful –'

'Oh yes, that's right.'

I thought – But still, we have the ability to make what's beautiful?

Mrs Ferguson had left us and gone back to the computers. The images on the screens had not moved for some time. My mind, like they, seemed to have fused. I thought – I have lost all track; the white light has become solid: what do we make, what do we break up: what is reality?

Then Mrs Ferguson pressed a switch and the images on the screens disappeared. There was a flickering for a time, and then darkness.

Mrs Ferguson said 'Why don't you ask Gaby.'

I said 'Ask Gaby what?'

'What is the recognition that makes things what they are: that makes them all right –'

'I have asked Gaby.'

'She's coming to stay with you, isn't she?'

I went back down the room to Gaby. She was sitting on the floor by the sofa. I thought – You mean, she really did have some vision?

123

I sat down beside her. I said 'Why did you say you'd seen the Virgin Mary?'

She said 'Because I had to.'

'Why?'

'Because then what she said might be happening.'

'What did she say? I mean what did you say she said –'

'I said she said that things would have to get worse before they got better.'

'Why did you say that?'

'Because I felt it. And that's what she usually says, isn't it?'

'And where did you say you'd seen her?'

'Not by the Abbey. In the cornfield.'

'But you made it up –'

'I said that she'd told me to say I'd made it up.'

'And she hadn't –'

'What do you mean?'

I thought – But I have known this from the beginning, haven't I?

I said 'What did she look like? I mean –'

'She wore a blue dress.'

'And what else did she say – I mean what did you say she said –'

'She asked me to give a message.'

'Who to?'

'To someone called Billy –'

'Why Billy –'

'That was a name that came into my head –'

'And you didn't make that up –'

'No. I mean, I did make up the name Billy. That was what came into my head.'

'And what was the message –'

'I've told you –'

'What did you tell me? You wanted to come and stay –'

'Yes.'

She twisted her head and stared at me. I thought – All right, all right; that's all: you want to come to London: you know I have a son called Billy.

I said 'But I must go home first. To tell them you're coming.'

I tried to think of what had been going on at home. Billy had not

124

been there and then he had been: or had he been there all the time. Melissa had been away, but I did not know where, or did I? I could not remember. Gaby had rung up Billy, or had she made that up: had I in fact told her about Billy? All these shapes, complexities, were there: then faded into darkness.

Gaby was standing in front of me holding out her hand. She was saying 'Come on, I'll show you –'

I said 'Show me what?'

She laughed and said 'The tapes! Or another message, if you'd rather.'

Peter said 'You know where they are?'

Mrs Ferguson said 'They were looking for them yesterday.'

I took Gaby's hand. Peter went ahead of us to the lift. He said 'Do you know, I feel liberated – I don't know why.'

Gaby said 'Don't you?'

Gaby continued to hold my hand in the lift. Peter was staring at the notice which said – Maximum Three Persons. I thought I might ask – And what will happen to the three boys? Peter said 'And we can change the past too, can we?'

On the ground floor Peter led the way along a passage to the front door. The main rooms of the house seemed to be deserted. We went out onto the gravelled drive: Peter turned to the left and went towards the Abbey. Gaby stood and watched him. Peter stopped and said 'I thought you said they hadn't found them.' Gaby said. 'They found the stuff in the Abbey.'

Gaby set off in the other direction across the lawn towards the wood through which I had come with Mrs Ferguson the day before. I followed with Peter. I thought – All right, one thing happens after another. But I must get home: why did I say I would stay till evening? Because Gaby might be taken in for questioning? and I, as a reporter, might be useful for bargaining? But this still doesn't seem to be quite what matters. Peter was saying 'They found the suitcase?' Gaby was saying 'What suitcase?' Peter was saying 'I don't know everything, do I?'

We were coming to the end of the path through the wood to where there was the field of corn. Gaby went to Mrs Ferguson's caravan and climbed up the ramp; Peter followed and stood on tiptoe at the top of the ramp and looked out towards the centre of the field. He said 'Good God, who did that?' Gaby reappeared from inside the caravan holding a small plastic pack of the kind that hold tapes for video recordings. Peter said 'I hope you managed to get the stalks at the perimeter going the other way from the rest.' Gaby came down the ramp behind Peter and she handed him the packet: Peter handed it on to me. He said 'And now you have the power to bind or to loose us in your hands.' I thought – You mean, people will be concerned to think I have got these? Then – And perhaps I can have a quick look in the evenings. I put the packet in my pocket. Peter stepped over the ditch and set off along the narrow track towards the centre of the field. Gaby and I followed. I thought – A moral situation.

Peter stopped in the shape like a heart in the centre of the field and looked around. He said 'Definitely a hoax for political purposes in the first or second centuries.'

I thought I might say to Gaby – This was where you said you'd seen the Virgin Mary?

Gaby said to Peter 'You're going to see Ellen?'

Peter said 'Yes.' Then to me – 'There's nothing on those tapes.'

I said 'Oh yes, your mother said she was making some recordings in this field.'

Gaby said 'Give our love to Ellen.'

Peter set off along the track at the far side of the circle. Gaby sat down cross-legged on the ground. I thought – And now I will lay down on my back, and close my eyes, and perhaps we can remain in this other world till evening.

The dark thunderclouds had gone from overhead. There were drops on the ground like bits and pieces of light. I thought – There must have been some showers, or a wingbeat.

Gaby had moved herself round behind me and was lifting my head and laying it on her crossed legs. I thought I might say – Thank you. She said 'I want to thank you.' There was a warmth coming into my head as if there were poles at either side of it: I knew what this was – Gaby had placed the palms of her hands at either side of my head and was holding them there just not touching me. I thought – So this is a message?

It was perhaps as if we were again within that tree or looking down from it on to a vast and rocky landscape – and down on myself, also, on this plain. I was together with that lady in blue, was it, whom I had seen on the hillside where the children had seen their vision and later by the dug-up grave. This lady and I were sitting side by side by a stream: we had travelled far and were resting. And, oh yes, I was also in the cornfield where Gaby had said she had seen her. And Billy and Melissa and I had once had a picnic like this, by a high and rocky stream. I was aware of Gaby with her hands on either side of my head in the cornfield. These images were coming together: it was as if they were all held within the branches of the tree. I thought – Yes, I can stay here till nightfall.

Eight

Driving back from the countryside of hills at night – hills that were like chrysalids from which new life might emerge; where I had lived and moved for two days and a night (had it been no more? an infinity perhaps in the world of possibilities), the second day being an intensification of the present and thus containing imitations of both past and future: if you make yourself empty, might not then something other than yourself come in –

– a phoenix's wingbeat, a horse flying above tree-tops; a landscape over which you can take soundings.

We had lingered in the circle in the field of corn, Gaby and I; had walked back through the wood; had visited the Abbey and sat on fallen stones. Here rituals had once been performed by men in black cloaks trying to empty their hearts and minds so that God might come in; they had abased themselves with incantation and drama: had God come in? Bodies had become humbled and littered as if around a stage: there was not much expectation of resurrection till after the final curtain.

I had said I would stay till nightfall: this was not difficult, with particles of recognition and light glittering like dew on the landscape.

We had gone back to the house, Gaby and I: one or two pigeons were perched on ledges outside their holes; they seemed to observe us without watching. The kitchen in Mrs Ferguson's house was not so different from the one in the hotel. Here we sat; Gaby set out food; such ceremonies are repeated. I thought – What is it about this strange world? You are bumps on a continuum –

– a web, a network; junction-points slung between mountains.

I had had some communication with the boys: I had learned that arrangements were being made for them to go to some specialist college in America. I had thought – We are like some cell: Gaby, the boys, Mrs Ferguson, Peter, myself – also Ellen, Melissa, Billy. Things transmute; you see the effects; you do not see what makes these –

You call it chance: the unheard music?

Driving back into the flatland of the motorway at night – there was the service-station where I had tried to sleep: that was the person that I had been before –

– You do not step into the same river twice –

– In this river you take soundings?

Arriving back at the city just when it was becoming light: the streets quite empty, yes; the roofs of the houses seeming quite low on the ground; as if they might be encrustations in one of Mrs Ferguson's trays –

– Once there was a gorgon above rooftops –

Now, coming back as if from the dead, the air is clear?

In the hall of my house there was the usual jumble of coats, shoes, bicycle, carrier-bags, unopened letters. So what had my wife and child been doing while I was away: attending to their own reorganisation of the universe? I could say – But you do see, don't you, that the light and darkness are one, when they make patterns. It seemed I should try to get to bed without disturbing Melissa – though she might perhaps be with her lover: and would even that be a pattern? I left my suitcase in the hall and went up the stairs. Here a couple of days ago Melissa had stood and I had put my arms around her, she had spat in my face: thus I had been able to set off on my journey – and now had come back from around the world? And she? The door of Billy's room was ajar. So he still was not here? he was staying with his friends? I had some fear. But I could get him back – that was what I had been learning. I pushed against the door of Billy's room. Light from a street-lamp came through flimsy curtains; there was a shape, two shapes, in the bed; two heads were lying side by side on the pillow. I thought – They are like the heads of the boys on the pillow in Cumbria. Then – All right, I do see. One of the heads was Billy's: the other was that of a young girl – it was Billy's friend, yes, Jenny. Billy's face was towards me; Jenny was hanging onto him from the back. Or they were like Gaby and myself on the mattress on the floor in Cumbria – a girl on the back of a dolphin and the dolphin riding on the sea. So what, here, was the sea: my knowledge; my memory –

– Of a winged horse flying above roof-tops –

– Of seeds that managed to grow on stony ground?

I thought I should not disturb them. Perhaps we could build a shelter for them, Melissa and I, as they lay curled up at the bottom of their tree –

– Hot coals and brimstone for warmth –

– There would be enough rain for water?

I went into Melissa's and my room, Melissa was not there. The bed had not been slept in. I thought – But I have been prepared for this: you make use of what either is or is not there –

I took off my shoes and some clothes and got under the bedcover. At least now I would be able to get some sleep. And it was wrong of Melissa to have left Billy and Jenny on their own – but now I need not feel guilty?

After a time I had the impression that Billy was in the doorway watching me. I had been dreaming of some explosion – on a beach there were children running, running; debris was falling. I was standing with Ellen in the shadows of the hotel: I wanted to see what would happen. I did not want to come back into the light –

I became aware that there was whispering going on on the landing. This must be between Billy and the girl called Jenny. But I would not wish them to have to hide as if from an ogre in his castle, so I said 'Come in, Billy.'

Billy was in the doorway. He was holding a cricket bat. He was naked except for a towel around his middle. I thought – He is like someone about to set off on a pilgrimage.

He said 'I thought you were a burglar.'

I said 'I might have been. How are you, Billy?'

'When did you get back?'

'Last night. No, early this morning.'

'I didn't hear you.'

'No, I didn't want to wake you.'

'You saw I was here?'

'Yes.'

I was trying to work out – What is it that is different? I am that old God who might now be shut out of the garden: but I am no longer jealous of the two of you curled up beneath that tree –

Billy said 'I think it's time for school.'

I said 'But you are all right, Billy?'

'Yes.'

'Mum's not back?'

'No.'

'Do you know where she is?'

'I was going to ask you.'

The girl called Jenny was lurking behind Billy on the landing. She wore a white T-shirt down to the top of her thighs. I thought – Oh yes, this sort of image I suppose might spread underground secretly –

– Or it is when you go fishing in the sea?

I said 'Hi.'

Jenny said 'Hi.'

'You're going to school too?'

'Yes.'

'I'll take you.'

Billy said 'Mum said she'd be back.'

'Did she leave a number?'

'Yes. No. I don't know –'

'That's all right, Billy.'

'Did you hear that explosion?'

'Was it? I thought it was in my dream –'

'No, I think it was a bomb –'

'Well, we seem to be all right.'

'Do you think Mum is all right?'

I had sat up on the edge of the bed. I was looking for my trousers: I wondered if I should put them on in front of Jenny. I thought –

We all walked about without any clothes on in Cumbria. Then – It would have done that old God the world of good to have been caught without his trousers.

I said 'What time is it?'

'Ten past eight.'

'What time is school?'

'We have to be there at nine. It's the last day.'

I said 'Mum will be all right.'

I went into the bathrom. Melissa had not taken any of her things: I thought – So that's all right. And downstairs the kitchen was tidy; things were still in their places, on the shelves; they had not flown away.

When Billy and Jenny appeared in the kitchen they were wearing jeans and white shirts. I thought – And this too is some regulation dress: we do not have to speak much; what shall I do – tell them a story?

I said 'I've been at this place in Cumbria where there's a nuclear power-station and what's called a reprocessing-plant, and there have been scares about radioactive leaks from time to time but no one quite knows what the effects are because no one quite knows just what to look for. I mean, often what you look for is what you find –'

Jenny said 'Is that where you met those children?'

'Yes, did Billy tell you? Or I told Melissa, yes.'

Billy said 'How are they doing? Are they managing on their own?'

'They did for a time. Then I think they needed to find people to help them.'

Billy and Jenny were eating cereals from bowls. I thought – They are wondering about themselves; and thinking – who are these people; what's the difference –

Billy said 'And one of them is the one that wants to come down here –'

I said 'Did I tell you that?' I wondered if I should say – Is it true that Gaby rang you? But I did not want to say too much.

Billy said 'I think Mum told me.'

Jenny said 'Who is it that's helping to look after them?'

'I said 'There's an old lady who lives in a big house in the hills. And someone called Ellen, who works in the hotel.'

It was as if Billy and Jenny glanced at one another quickly. I thought – But you don't mean, do you, that you might know about Ellen?

Billy said 'Dad, this is Parents' Day at school. You're supposed to bring things in the morning, and then there's a sale in the afternoon.'

I said 'What sort of things?'

'Oh that's all right. Mum said she'd do it.'

'You think she'll be there?'

'Oh I think so, don't you?'

Billy and Jenny carried their bowls and spoons and mugs to the sink and stacked them neatly. I thought – The reason I can't ask more questions about what Billy and Jenny and Melissa have been doing is because this might interfere with what is happening?

Jenny said 'Thank you for having me to stay.'

I said 'Oh that's all right.'

Billy said 'Do you think Jenny can come back here tonight?'

I said 'Of course, if you like.'

We went into the hall. Billy and Jenny put books and bits of paper into rucksacks. I thought – What happens happens: and then, you mean, you know when it is evidently right?

In the car and driving to school we were in the situation of herds of parents and children at this hour, doing what we were doing without much knowing quite what we were doing: so what with us was the difference? that we so obviously knew we did not quite know what we were doing –

Billy said 'Mum must have got held up in the traffic.'

I said 'Yes the traffic's bad.'

Jenny said 'Perhaps we won't be able to get to school.'

Billy said 'Jenny doesn't want to meet her parents.'

I said 'Why?'

Jenny said 'I don't quite know.'

We had come to a halt in the traffic. It seemed that there might indeed be an accident, or a fire: or did people just accept this as being normal at this time of the morning.

Billy said 'I said it was a bomb!'

Jenny said 'With any luck.'

I said 'Can I be of help with your parents? I mean, talk to them.'

Jenny said 'Well, thank you –'

Billy said 'Was it like this in Cumbria?'

There was a side-street I could turn down. The road was clear for a distance, then it was blocked again before it rejoined the main road. At the T-junction policemen in yellow jackets were handling festoons of yellow tape. I thought – So it was a bomb. Then – And what happens now.

I said 'We might go on foot.'

Billy was saying to Jenny 'They can't do anything to you –'

Jenny was saying 'I must get the timing right.'

I was backing the car into a space half on the pavement. I was thinking – Because there's a bomb, there's less chance of its being clamped or towed away –

Or – You mean, Jenny might have got some hold over her parents?

We set off on foot along the pavement past the line of blocked cars – myself leading followed by Billy and Jenny. At the T-junction there were flashing lights and people in uniform standing around: I thought – What do they do, where do they go, when there is no disaster? I might go up to a policeman and say – I am a press reporter; can you let us through? But then he might not, and we would have lost freedom of action. I wanted to see Melissa; it was unlikely that Melissa would be at the school, but still –

One of the cars jammed in the line just short of the T-junction was an estate car with the rear portion wired off as a cage for dogs: within this were three or four Rottweilers or mastiffs or whatever: these were slavering and writhing as if they were snakes in hell. Jenny had stopped by this car and was talking through the window to a woman in the driving-seat; she called to Billy, who went back to her. I had stopped by the T-junction and was wondering what to do. I wanted to find Melissa and say – But what we have worried about is all rubbish, you see: you perhaps with your probably non-existent lover and me with my old monkey sitting on the stump of a tree: these are just dogs writhing like roots in hell. I went back to Billy and Jenny who were talking to the woman in the car. Billy said 'Mrs Melhuish wants us to meet her grandchild who is arriving at the station.' I said 'Mrs Melhuish wants you to meet her grandchild who is arriving at the station?' Jenny said 'She doesn't think she can leave the dogs on their own in the car.' Billy said 'I do see that, don't you?' I said 'Yes.' Jenny said 'I'll go.' I thought – You mean, then you needn't meet your parents? This is one of the things that happen after another? The woman was giving Jenny instructions about where to meet her grandchild. I thought I might say – You knew Mrs Melhuish? But of course people seemed to know each other in this strange world. I said to the woman in the car 'Do you know if there's a back way round to the school?' Mrs Melhuish said 'Yes, you go straight on when Jenny turns off, and then you'll come to the fence by the back.' Billy said 'I know it.' I said 'Thanks.' Jenny had already set off back down the road. Billy and I followed. Jenny went down a side-street. I thought – I suppose I should be getting used to this sort of thing: or is there always some wonder? Jenny said 'I turn off here.' I said 'You know where to go?' She said 'Yes, platform four.' I said 'Well we'll see you at the school.' Billy said 'This bomb may have been quite useful, really.'

Billy and I went down an alleyway between the back-yards of houses. I thought – And this is quite like treading on hot coals? Billy said 'When you see Mum, you won't be angry with her, will you?'

I said 'No.'

'She didn't want to go.'

'Where?' Then – 'I see.'

'And tell her I'm all right, will you?'

I thought – Why, where will you be going?

We were coming to another alleyway at the far end of which was the wire fence that was, it seemed, the one around the back playground of Billy's school. There was a path alongside this which would presumably lead round to the front entrance by the main road. I said 'Billy, last night, where was –' He said 'She gets very lonely, you know.' I had been going to say – But I must know where! I said 'Yes I know.' Billy had stopped by a section of the wire fence that was sagging; it was as if people might be using it to climb over as a back way into the school. Billy had a hand on the fence: he said 'There's a path round to the front.' I said 'Yes.' I thought – You mean you don't want to meet Mum just now? You think it is better if I meet her on my own? I said again 'You think she'll be there?' He said 'Oh sooner or later, yes.' He began to clamber over the fence into the playground. I thought – So I don't ask him, do I, why is he doing this? He might now know anyway?

I walked along the path along the outside of the fence. I thought I might say – But you do know that if you have been liberated, my children –

– We, your parents or your children, have been part of this?

The front gates of the school were set back from the main road. There was a narrow space for pedestrians between the fence and where the road was cordoned off. Behind the fence and the school building was an open area almost as large as the playground at the back; within this an assortment of parents had been herded, or had taken refuge, as if they were colonialists at a time of civic unrest. Some were carrying trays of foodstuffs or plants or brick-à-brac which presumably they had brought with their children for the sale that afternoon: or were they belongings that they had managed to salvage from their past. I was searching among the parents for Melissa; but why on earth should she be here? She might not yet need to see me. Among the crowd within the gates of the school were two tall, gaunt figures I felt I should know; they appeared to be wondering whether or not they knew me: the woman was carrying a potted plant; the man looked as if he might be selling matches. I went up to them and said 'Aren't you Jenny's parents?' The man say 'Yes.' I said 'I'm Billy's father.' The woman said 'Oh thank God, of course we know Melissa.' The man said 'Were they with you last night?' I said 'Yes.' The woman said 'Oh thank God, they were supposed to be with us.' I thought I might say – But wasn't that the previous night? Or – Oh were they really? The man said 'We couldn't get an answer.' The woman said 'Why couldn't you have let us know?' I said 'I thought you knew.' The man said 'No.' The woman said 'But where's Melissa?' I thought – Yes, indeed, where is Melissa. I said 'Haven't you seen her?' The man said 'What?' I said 'I mean, isn't she here?' I was looking around the playground. I thought – Perhaps after all it is better if Melissa is not here, then I may be able to deal with Jenny's parents. The woman said 'But where are Jenny and Billy now?' I said 'Jenny's gone to meet someone at the station.' The man said 'Gone to meet someone at the station?' I said 'Mrs Melhuish's child, or grand-child.' I thought – I suppose you can reduce everything to chaos: then parents are distracted from going on about their children. Billy had appeared at the side of the school building; he had got round from the back and was trying to keep out of sight and to watch where I was talking to Jenny's parents. I wondered if I could get a message through to him – this is not going too badly. The woman was saying 'We were thinking of calling the police.' The man said 'We didn't want to call the police.' I said 'It's all right, she's as likely to be as safe at the station as she would be here.' The woman said 'What do you mean?' The man said 'Why, what has she been saying?' I said 'I mean, now this bomb has gone off.' I thought – This is becoming too difficult Then – You mean, her parents really might have been up to no good with Jenny? The woman was saying 'You know, at that age, they'll say anything.' I thought – But Jenny will have learned that it is best to say nothing?

Billy had disappeared from the side of the school building: he might have got whatever information he had required. I thought – How right parents are to be frightened of children –

– But from this they can learn too?

Jenny was coming through the front gates of the school holding a small child by the hand. It did not seem that she could have had enough time to meet the child at the station: and such a small child could hardly have started off on its own –

– So, you mean, Jenny just needed some distraction or protection when she confronted her parents?

Jenny came up holding the small child by the hand. She gazed at her parents belligerently. I thought – With her lower lip stuck out she is quite like Gaby. Her mother said 'Where have you been?' Her father said 'Couldn't you have let us know?' Jenny said 'I did.' Her mother said 'When?' Jenny said 'What did you want me to say.' Billy was approaching with another boy of his own age from the direction of the school buildings: the boy was making faces and flapping his arms at the small child who was hanging onto Jenny's hand. Jenny was saying 'Someone was already taking her from the station; it was lucky I turned up.' I was saying 'Well done, you found her all right!' The small child was trying to hide behind Jenny's legs; the boy who had come up with Billy was dodging to

and fro behind Mr and Mrs Armstrong as if he were playing a game.
I thought – This is like the routine with the flagpole in the
farmyard. Jenny said 'Mrs Melhuish is still stuck in the car with her
dogs.' The boy who was making faces said 'Jesus whelped.' Billy
said 'We'd better get along.' Then – 'See you later, Dad.' I said
'Yes, what time?' Billy said 'Two o'clock.' I said 'Perhaps Mum
will be here by then.' I thought – How good of him to say: See you
later, Dad! Billy and Jenny and the boy who had now taken the
small child by the hand went off towards the school building. As
they went the boy murmured 'See you later, kiddos.' I thought –
That's what they call us, is it – kiddos? I mean, that's what they call
Mr and Mrs Armstrong and other parents – and myself?

Mr Armstrong said 'What was all that about?'

I said 'I don't know.'

Mrs Armstrong said 'Why couldn't she have taken that girl
straight to Mrs Melhuish in the car?'

Mr Armstrong said 'Because she had the dogs.'

I said 'Yes, that's right.'

I was wondering – But was it last night, or the night before, or
the night before that, that Billy and Jenny were supposed to be
staying with you – or with us – or whatever –

– Where were they then?

The parents were being ushered out through a side-gate in the
playground; they had left their trays of offerings on a trestle-table in
front of the building. I went out with Mr and Mrs Armstrong. I
thought – But anyway, if you let one thing just happen after
another –

– Looking back, at least, you might find out where you have
been going?

In a side-road, on the opposite side of the school to the one
where I had left my car, Mr Armstrong said 'Which way are you
going?' I said 'To my office, it's down by the river.' He said 'We
can take you there.' I said 'Oh don't bother.' He said 'No bother,
our car's just here.' I thought – All right then –

– He wants to find out what I have heard about them from
Jenny?

I sat in the back of the Armstrongs' car. Mr and Mrs Armstrong
were in front. I thought – I am now in the position of those two

boys in my car in Cumbria: perhaps I can make the hairs begin to stand at the backs of Mr and Mrs Armstrong's heads –

Mrs Armstrong turned round. She said 'But Melissa will be coming back?'

I said 'I hope so.'

Mr Armstrong said 'Jenny gave us the impression that she was there when she rang us.'

I thought – Those two boys in the back of my car, they were fighters?

I said 'I think children take it for granted that the grown-up world is mad. This isn't difficult when they see the world that's run by grown-ups. But children often see themselves as responsible; and now they're beginning to work out what to do.'

After a time Mr Armstrong said 'They seem very fond of one another.'

Mrs Armstrong said 'Yes they do.'

I was trying to work out – It was the day before yesterday that Melissa had rung me and had said that Billy had not come home: that was referring to that evening, and Billy had come home. It was the night before she had said he was staying with the Armstrongs –

Mrs Armstrong said 'Is it really all right if Jenny comes and stays with you?'

I said 'Yes of course.'

'Arthur has to go to South America and I don't like him to travel alone.'

'Yes I see.'

'We have discussed this with Melissa.'

We were coming to the one-way system that went round the back of the heavy concrete building which contained the newspaper offices where I worked: this building was known as The Bunker. I said 'You can let me out here.' Mr Armstrong drove on. He was saying 'I don't think children come to much harm if one tries to be honest with them.' Mrs Armstrong said 'But I feel so guilty.' I thought – They may never let me out of the car if they feel guilty; they may go round and round; they may take me to a bit of waste ground and dump me in the river. Mr Armstrong said 'She could always stay with my sister.' Mrs Armstrong said 'Now don't start that again.' I thought – Or I can throw myself out of the car as

139

people do in films and roll over and over. I said 'Here! This will do! Here!'

At the entrance to The Bunker there were extra security men. I thought – They will guard me. Or will they test me with a geiger-counter and find I am radioactive –

On the first floor was the huge room where I had my cubicle and my desk to which I hardly ever came. Jack had a secretary called Madeleine who sat outside his inner door. She said 'What's happened, you're looking very fit.' I thought I might say – This tan is just before the skin comes off. I said 'Is Jack around?' I thought – We make jokes to prevent awkward questions. Madeleine said 'He's expecting you.'

Jack was looking tired. He had rings under his eyes. What was it I was supposed to remember? Oh yes, he might be having an affair with Melissa.

I said 'Jack, I want to go out to Bosnia, Croatia, Yugoslavia, wherever –'

He said 'There's a price on your head in Cumbria.'

'I know there's been too much done on shock-horror, on the senselessness of destruction and self-destruction. But I want to say, since everyone loves it, the sooner we get on with it and get it over with the better.'

'Have you seen Janice?'

'No.'

'She's bereft, or aggrieved, I don't know which.'

'She buggered off with a security guard.'

'I don't blame her, do you?'

'No.'

When I got closer to Jack it seemed that what had looked like rings under his eyes might be one black eye. I thought – Melissa caught him with a back-hander at the top of the stairs?

Jack said 'Are you clean, uncontaminated, safe, Aids-free?'

I said 'I don't think there was a proper scare –'

'Janice said –'

'You remember my piece on Chernobyl? Even there people were using statistics, records to make out what they liked. For the most part they wanted to make things even worse than they were: they wanted scapegoats, victims –'

'Don't we all –'

'Have you seen Melissa?'

'I'm not going to talk about Melissa.'

'Do you know where she is? All right, I'm talking about myself –'

'I'm not having an affair with her, if that's what you mean.'

I sat in a chair facing Jack across his desk. Jack was a neat man with finely wrought features. I thought – But the fact that he and I in some sense trust one another does not necessarily mean that I believe what he says.

I said 'There were these children in Cumbria who were in some trouble with the authorities. The people in charge had been up to no good with the children, or the children could say they had been, so the children had some hold over them. But they could only exercise this hold so long as the story didn't get out; I mean there was the threat. At least that's my story.'

Jack said 'Blackmail? Guilt?'

'One of the Social Services men drove himself into a level-crossing.'

'Was that the train that was carrying nuclear material?'

'Good heavens, I don't know.'

'It might have been a protest?'

'I don't know.'

I thought – I never really imagined that Jack was having an affair with Melissa? Or did I? Or what –

– Does one ever know?

Jack said 'Have you been home yet?'

'Yes.'

'And Melissa wasn't there –'

'No.'

'So what are you going to do?'

I thought – How do I know what I am going to do. People really think they know what they are going to do?

Then – You're really thinking of running a story about some anti-nuclear protest?

I said 'There's a rich old woman called Mrs Ferguson who lives with her son in the hills in a house the size of an aircraft-carrier. They're sort of mad amateur scientists, I don't know how mad, she's a biologist and her son's at Cambridge: they're doing experiments on the effects of radiation on the environment. Also on the nature of what is called chance, but what is chance, has it anything to do with consciousness, but what is consciousness? You can't do experiments about this because the way you set up the experiment is what you find; or want to find. But then these people are conscious of this. I suppose it needs a trick – to be both conscious and not conscious of what you're doing at the same time –'

Jack said 'Melissa's going to leave you, do you know?'

I said '– then at least things may happen in due order.' Then – 'No.'

'I think she wanted me to tell you.'

'Well, that's different.'

'Why –'

I thought – Haven't you been listening to what I've been saying?

Jack and I were facing but not quite looking at each other. I thought – Whatever it is that has been the experiment these three days, there has been some consciousness of trust in that of which we are not concious –

I said 'There was a Zen master who whenever any news was brought to him, splendid or calamitous, just said – Oh is that so!'

Jack said 'So you want to go to Yugoslavia.'

'Yes. Some of the children came from there.'

'You've got this obsession about these children –'

'Yes.'

'Have you seen Billy?'

'Yes.' Then – 'There are connections if you see them.'

Jack looked sad. I thought – But I have loved Jack: I can remember this.

He said 'I know your theory – what is it – that there's a transcendent world of possibilities from which we make actual this or that by observation; by choice –'

I thought – By knowing we have a choice: or –

– By knowing it's a possibility.

I said 'There was a scare, I mean a radiation scare, but the danger didn't seem to come from the power-station or the plant, it seemed to be being recorded on their instruments just because those particular instruments were there.'

Jack said 'Then where was it coming from?'

'They might not have known. Or they wouldn't say.'

'And you want to write about that?'

'I know a bit about what's happening in Yugoslavia.'

Jack stood up and walked to and fro behind his desk. I thought – He is going through the motions of having a choice – whether or not to send me out to some dangerous situation in Yugoslavia: as if he were King David and I were, what was his name, Uriah –

Jack said 'What you said about Chernobyl was that it happened to be followed by the crack-up of the entire Communist system. But there's no way except in sociological and political terms to connect one set of events with the other.'

I said 'And there was some sort of preview in 1956 –'

'What happened in 1956? I thought that nuclear disaster was in 1957 –'

'– And there was a crack-up in Yugoslavia as early as 1958.' Then – 'These nuclear effects can it seems be retroactive.'

Jack sat down behind his desk. It was as if he had come to some decision. I thought – And perhaps I will die – on that rocky landscape, by a stream, which was the vision I had in Cumbria.

Jack said 'You're tired.'

'Yes.'

'Go home.'

'You're joking.'

'Talk to Melissa.'

I said 'There are these crack-ups of nuclear installations in Eastern Europe. There's the trade in plutonium. There's worse: there are the spin-offs from the biological warfare establishments –'

Jack said 'You never followed up that story?'

'Not at the time. Everyone was saying what they liked.'

'And you let that stop you?'

I stood up. It seemed suddenly that I was on the point of falling asleep again. I said 'Well, I can do it now.'

Jack came to the door with me. I thought – He might think he has to stop me going to Bosnia – because of Melissa or guilt about Melissa? He said 'You'll be seeing Melissa?'

I said 'What does Melissa want?'
'She wants a home for Billy.'
'But she's got a home for Billy.'
'She says he doesn't like being there –'
'But he does –'
'He does?'
'Yes.'
'She says he likes being with friends.'
I thought I might say – But you make friends.

Nine

The story I had become involved with about the smuggling of radioactive material in Eastern Europe had come my way when I had gone out to report on the early stages of the war in Yugoslavia. I had wanted not so much to report on the horrors of war – many others were doing that – as to look for what might be at the back of this apparently so arbitrary fighting: at the way in which so many people seemed to feel just what fun war was. I had gone to a town some distance behind the lines – not that there were exactly any 'lines': some of the excitement lay in the chance that fighting might break out at any place at any time. But this town was a place to which politicians might with comparative safety but still with some bravado come – they could put on flak jackets and helmets and walk down the centre of streets while cameramen backed in front of them like courtiers obsequiously bowing out of an audience chamber. The town was a staging-post for relief organisations and then for United Nations troops; in the wake of these had come a horde of racketeers, traders, arms dealers, receivers and purveyors of stolen goods – who are in a symbiotic relationship with relief-workers and soldiers as are cameramen with politicians. Gangs purloined or took their cut from the supplies that poured into and overflowed from the bottleneck of the town, there was a flourishing market in other stolen goods, especially cars, brought in from other parts of Europe. Thus even those people who were in the area for the more reputable aspects of war could pick up bargains. But the big-time deals were with arms and drugs – those modern equivalents of gold and diamonds. Through such trade professionals could become millionaires and even amateurs could make small fortunes – with no questions asked. So that often it seemed that the supplies arriving for the relief organisations and so-called peace-keeping forces were in fact prolonging both the hardship and the war; for without the huge amounts that were hijacked and stolen, how could the fighters have obtained their necessary supplies and indeed how could war have been such fun.

I did not, on this trip, go to such places as might be seen as the front line – the outlying villages in which there was evidence of atrocities such as there often are in this kind of war, and particularly in this part of the world in recent history; the half-burned and mutilated bodies of women and children, either not buried at all or thrown often half-alive into open graves. It seemed to me that reports on these things had reached a level of saturation at which the images had lost meaning. What I wanted to look at was why to the perpetrators such atrocities seemed enjoyable; and indeed why others seemed to be gratified by reports of such things.

One of my ostensible tasks was to report on the politicians and local warlords who came to this town for the purposes of discussing peace. But to every observer there occurred at moments the question – In whose interests, God knows, would it be to achieve peace? These warlords were like princes: in peace, power would drift back to the stultifying hands of bureaucrats; how could there be a free flow of supplies and excitement if there was peace? Even those refugees who flooded into the town from outlying villages – in what sense would they want peace? They wanted revenge – revenge on those who had killed and mutilated their loved ones – no matter how much they knew that after revenge their enemies would want revenge on them. But for the sake of appearances, of providing a *raison d'être* for their jobs, politicians and diplomats had of course to say they were looking for peace: this was just one of the rules of the game in which they could travel around Europe like mediaeval prelates; staying in four-star hotels and looking pious when journalists and film crews poked microphones under their noses as if they were acolytes demanding that their objects should be sanctified.

Also in the wake of diplomats and racketeers and journalists had naturally come the further parasites of war – the rubberneckers, the adventurers, the tourists, the pimps and prostitutes of war – coming to escape the boredom of a forty-year-old European peace, having heard news not just of excitement but of sex and revelry. (I sometimes wondered – might I not be in such a category myself?) There was a flourishing night-life in the town I had come to. Almost the only good aspect of war is that it is a release from social restraints of class and money – a condition in which power is able to be in the hands of the adventurous and brave. In this respect might there after all be something not wholly despicable in the idea of virtue or even fun in war –

– But surely for this one should confine oneself to a private and personal form of war?

Amongst the politicians who had come to the town at this time was a Junior Minister from our Foreign Office with whom I had once been briefly acquainted; he had come on a fact-finding mission to the town. He was being pursued by a greater than usual flock of journalists not because of his role as a diplomat, but because he happened to be a central figure in one of the currently ubiquitous sex-scandals at home. The Minister was known as a notorious philanderer, and one of his mistresses had recently sold her story to a magazine. (The details hardly matter: they are usually made up or touched up to suit taste.) The Minister had been called on to resign; he had not resigned; he had come out to this town to try to deal with the apparently more reputable titillations of war. A flock of journalists had used the occasion to come too.

The circumstances in which I had made the acquaintance of the Minister a few years previously were as follows.

We had met in the sitting-room of a notorious young woman – an ex-debutante, a budding actress, a model, or whatever – who lived with her mother in a flat in Chelsea and was being groomed, preserved, promoted, both by her mother and herself eventually to make as advantageous a marriage as possible. While she waited it was helpful to her to give the appearance of being immensely sought after by a variety of suitable admirers: the Junior Minister came obviously into this category; I had recently published one of my controversial pieces and so might squeeze in myself as a makeweight three-days' wonder. We had met, the Minister and I, in her small sitting-room that was indeed like the waiting-room of a courtesan or an exclusive brothel; I had got there first; then in came the Junior Minister. We sat in stony silence for a time; I was expecting to take the object of our desire out to lunch; the Minister was evidently also expecting to take her out to lunch; it became apparent to both of us that she had made a mistake about dates and was now in some confusion – we could hear noises of consultation with her mother next door. After a time the Minister said 'I'll toss you for it.' Then – 'An apt expression!' I realised I liked the Minister. I said 'Which would you rather, win or lose?' He produced a coin and flipped it and caught it and turned it over onto the back of his other hand and covered it. I said 'Heads.' He said without looking at the coin 'You win'. I said 'I insist on seeing!' He took his hand away and it was heads. I said 'And now she will spend the whole of lunch wishing that I was you.' He said 'Always the pursuit: never the consummation.'

I had sometimes wondered – But he did get her in the end, didn't he?

Now, in the foyer of the hotel where it was considered safe for politicians and media people to stay, I saw my friend or rival the Minister again: I had not seen him since he had left me stranded as it were as a victor on the battlefield. He was surrounded by media people who were asking him questions and holding microphones under his chin so aggressively that they might be bowls into which he might be sick; their questions were not about the atrocities in the villages nor the trade in nuclear materials; they were pressing him about his family – about the reactions of his wife to the latest revelations of his mistress, about what he had said to his children who were at a boarding-school. He was saying 'I've told my children that they will have to learn.' Someone said 'Learn what?' He said 'Learn about people who want to cast the first lump of shit.' I thought – But they will pillory him! Then – He might be using this? I wondered if he had seen me across the crowded foyer; I did not know if he would recognise me: he would not know how much I admired him. Then there came a message for me – would I like to go and have a drink in his room?

I found the Minister in shirt-sleeves: he was a large, florid man. Two or three aides were making notes from a map spread out on a table. The Minister gave me a drink. He said 'It didn't seem to me, later, that our friend had spent the whole of lunch wishing that you were me.'

I said 'That was because by then you were having lunch or whatever with her.'

'I suppose I shall never know whether in the end you got her.'

After a time the aides left. They said they were going to have a look round the town. I thought – They will be feeling smug about the Minister, because he will be left behind like Cinderella.

He said 'I've read your pieces about pollution – about people feeling at home if they land themselves in the shit.'

I said 'We all do it.'

'But as you said – What happens when you know this.'

We were drinking whisky. This was the time when I was drinking quite heavily. Half-drunk, you have the impression that you are leaving the world of one thing or the other and are going through the gates of the world of possibilities.

He said as if he were quoting something I had written '– Orderly society sometimes seems possible only under the threat of organised terror; but how is it possible to accept disorderly society when it seems the job of humans to bring order out of chaos –'

I said 'But there is some order if you let things happen, don't you think?'

'There is?'

'There's usually, after all, some sort of consummation.'

There is a magical moment on the edge of drunkenness when chance encounters and connections do seem to be lit with an unearthly radiance – like an early morning festooned with dew. I thought – I suppose the Minister must be something of a drunk too.

He said 'What's so wonderful about this town? You write about it as if it were some outpost of the old Wild West.'

I said 'There's a nightclub called The Garden of Earthly Delights.'

'After Hieronymus Bosch –'

'After Hieronymus Bosch.'

'He seemed to have the idea that people liked getting themselves buggered by fishes.'

'That's one of the fantasies that children have, oddly enough, when they're questioned about satanic abuse.'

'It is?'

'So they say.'

'The things you chaps know!' Then – 'Not a temptation that has exactly come my way.'

I wondered if there was any way by which the Minister and I might get to The Garden of Earthly Delights. Most journalists after a day or two in the town gravitated in the evenings to one of the drinking-dens or nightclubs. They seldom wrote about these, because to do this would deprive readers of what they liked to hear, which was about misery and hardship; also journalists would lose their heroic image if it was thought that they were having too much of a good time.

The Minister said 'So what is it about this particular Garden?'

I said 'Young girls come up from the country, from over the borders, for the pickings, for the windfalls that can be gathered out of the chaos of war.'

'You're suggesting we should go there?'

'I'm suggesting!'

He said as if quoting me again '– There seems something unavoidable about disorganised terror.'

He rang for more whisky. We watched the soda-bubbles rising up and bursting in our glasses; in our imaginations.

I said 'You know the stories about the trade in radioactive material, fissionable material, or whatever, going the rounds in Eastern Europe –'

He said 'Ah, is that what you're after –'

'But what can you ever find out, when it's in everyone's interest just to make up what stories they like?'

'Don't you make up what stories you like?'

'Sometimes. Of course we often make things seem even worse –'

'You know when you're doing that?'

'I sometimes think, if we did it more, then order might come out of chaos.'

'Oh Mephistopheles!'

He went to the window and looked out. There was the half-blacked-out town shot with flashes of light. I thought – He is still wondering if we might go to The Garden of Earthly Delights?

I said 'Well, things may have to get worse before they get better –'

He said 'You mean, say – Go ahead, children, do your worst –'

'And might not that stop it?'

The new bottle of whisky arrived. The waiter was a hatchet-faced man: it seemed he might be a spy – or a bubble in our imaginations.

I said 'There's a big-time warlord, or gangster, known as the Dungbird. When he's in town, he goes most evenings to The Garden of Earthly Delights. And he's at the centre of most of the arms rackets here.'

The Minister said 'What you're saying is, that we should give the mob downstairs a run for their money – make things worse so they might have a chance of getting better.'

'I'm saying that?'

'Say to them – Make what you like of it boys and girls! for how on earth will you ever know what is really happening.'

'What I mean is, there might be a valid reason for us trying to see this man Dungbird –'

The Minister was refilling my glass. It struck me that he was indeed becoming as drunk as I was. He said 'Oh yes, it's a terrible curse, an affliction –'

I thought – The people downstairs? The Dungbirds?

He said 'You mean, we can use this man as an excuse to go and look at these girls?'

I said 'Or we might be using these girls as an excuse to go and see this man –'

The Minister seemed to consider this. He held the whisky bottle as if it were some pointer by which he might exercise control. He said 'Now let's get this straight. What you're saying is, if we go downstairs, and it becomes apparent, after all our apparent efforts, or no efforts, at subterfuge, that we are on our way to The Garden of Earthly Delights, then there could be no conceivable reason for my thus jeopardising my job, my family, what is left of my reputation, except that I am doing this with the aim of having a rendezvous with the man called Bluebeard –'

I said 'Dungbird –'

'– which is what people in the press are always saying I should do anyway – that is, instead of waffling in official conferences, talk to people who in fact have the power to decide whether the war goes on or not.'

'That's logical –'

'Whereas in fact what we would be doing so far as anyone would know, including ourselves, is just going to The Garden of Earthly Delights to pick up women –'

I said 'Or not.'

As we prepared to set out the Minister and I became involved in games of fantasy about what to do about any secret-service men there might be positioned to keep an eye on things in the foyer of the hotel. The Minister said 'Do you know the story of the man who put on a false beard and spectacles in order to get past his wife?' I said 'No.' He said 'His wife mistook him for her lover.'

Going down in the lift the Minister said 'Do you think he'll really be there?'

I said 'Who –'

The Minister said 'Bluebeard. Dungbird.' Then – 'You know, I really want to get out of this job anyway – with a bang.'

One or two media people were in the foyer of the hotel – waiting, perhaps, for their own assignations. A woman called out to us – 'And where are you going at this time of night?' The Minister said 'To pick up women, of course.' He looked at her blankly.

The woman began to ask – 'Have you spoken to your wife yet?' Then tailed off and turned away.

The Minister and I went and stood on the pavement. There was a man on the door who might be a secret-service person. The air was cold; there were bits of moonlight like pieces of metal coming down. I had been using a particular taxi-driver who hung about outside the hotel: he had been trying to find out details of what I was doing. The Minister was saying to the doorman 'No I don't want an official car. If anyone asks, say that we have taken a taxi to

The Garden of Earthly Delights.' I said to my driver, in German, who had come up in his taxi – 'Oh yes, that's right, we want to go to The Garden of Earthly Delights.'

When we were in the taxi the driver asked us, in German, where we wanted to go.

The Minister said 'You see, no one believes politicians.'

I said 'So then you could tell the truth?'

'If you knew it –'

'Yes.'

'Does he understand English?' The Minister was nodding towards the back of the taxi-driver's head.

I said 'I don't know, try him.'

The Minister leaned forwards and said in a loud voice 'I think the best thing for this bloody country would be if the whole fucking thing were blown up.'

The driver turned and beamed at us with a yellow, gap-toothed smile.

I thought – And now he will take us to The Garden of Earthly Delights?

The Garden of Earthly Delights was a large low-ceilinged basement room in which patches of coloured lights swirled round the floor and walls and tables reflected from an old-fashioned globe suspended from the ceiling. By the entrance was a display-board with an announcement in several languages, the English version of which read – Gather Hope All Ye Who Enter Here.

Within the enclosed space there was so much noise from amplified music that it was as if the walls or indeed one's own skull were the membranes of a speaker. At the centre was a writhing mass of dancers, mostly women, mostly young, which solidified towards the edges where young men stood or sat and watched and occasionally and somewhat stiffly joined the dancing. Around the perimeter was a raised platform with tables and chairs set in alcoves like a circle of boxes in a theatre; within these people of what might be superior status sat, paying more attention to each other than to the gyrations of the crowd below, but occasionally peering down as if into a fish-pond from which they might pick their dinner. I thought – This is indeed some representation of hell: in illustrations of hell the outer circle is usually the most agreeable: here on this

153

raised platform the devils seem to have their offices: why are the working-quarters of devils not shown in depictions of hell; because the job indeed might seem too pleasurable?

The Minister and I were led to one of the few unoccupied alcoves; it was as if we had been expected; the doorman at the hotel might have telephoned? At the doorway here there had been a stir: I could not quite remember whether this was what we wanted or did not want. At the table in the next alcove to ours was a group of men, two of whom carried pistols and one had a large black beard. I thought – I did not make up my story about the man called Dungbird: but this is ridiculous. The Minister was trying to say something to me but the noise was too great: he pulled out a notebook and wrote. There were young girls jerking and shaking on the dance-floor. The Minister had written – I can't remember what we are here for, is it to pick up women? I took the pencil and wrote – Either that, or the man with the beard.

The girls on the dance-floor flipped and writhed like eels: or they were those strange emanations from the sea-bed that sway and weave upwards towards the light and then when you touch them they disappear. You are swimming underwater, you have come from a different medium, air; you have come to prod and hook and spear – you are a devil! This is indeed considered to be a pleasure –

The Minister was writing in his notebook – Is it not supposed to be one of the satisfactions of people in heaven to watch people in hell? I took the pencil and wrote – That's why it has been supposed to be more moral in hell.

A strikingly beautiful woman had left the dance-floor and gone to talk with someone by the door; then she came to the table in the next alcove where she leaned with her hands on the back of a chair next to the man with the beard. She attracted his attention and then nodded in the direction of the Minister and myself. The man with the beard looked at us; the woman put her mouth very close to his ear and spoke; the man with the beard beckoned to one of the waiters who hovered around his table. I thought – We are going to be invited over; we are going to be shot; we are going to be hauled to a bare room and chained to a radiator –

– Or you mean, out of chaos things really may turn out all right?

There was a lull in the music. The girls who had been dancing wandered to the edge of the floor; they leaned with their hands on the backs of chairs by the young men. I thought – Sooner or later this pool will be drained and they may die.

The Minister said 'Did you ever work out whether or not, in the pursuit of women, one exactly wants to win?'

I was going to say – One does not exactly know what it is to win – but the music had started again.

The waiter was coming to our table with a bottle and small glasses of the kind from which you drain the liquid in one gulp. He filled two glasses: the man in the next alcove raised his glass to us; we smiled and raised our glasses; then we all downed our liquids in one gulp. I thought I might say to the Minister – You mean, one of us might try to get off with that beautiful woman: one of us might try to talk to the man with the beard?

There was a slight flurry at the door and people were pushing their way through. I thought I recognised one or two from the foyer of the hotel: they were security men? They were followed by a posse of media people. These jostled, then spread out quietly when they saw the Minister and myself. I tried to work out again – This is as we planned it – or isn't it?

The music crashed and whined like shells going overhead: I thought – Even in getting away from it, people simulate war. The woman from the next table was coming over to us: she was one of those golden-skinned women with dark-red hair and bright-red lips that have their habitat in Eastern Europe: she moved like a leopard through long grass. Such images are welcome but somewhat alarming; even in imagination. The Minister stood up and greeted her courteously: he took her hand and bent over it and was introducing her to me as if they were old acquaintances. I thought – This is his technique? He spoke into the woman's ear; then he left us and went over to the table in the next alcove where he was greeted by the man with the beard. I thought – A good technique! I had stood, formally, to greet the red-haired woman: she sat down. I thought – Somewhere or other this can be what we make of it. The woman poured out two more drinks from the bottle that the waiter had left at our table. We raised our glasses to each other. I thought – And perhaps after all I should not be at that other table; I should be here.

Because talk was impossible through the noise, it was easy for the woman and I, or myself at least, to embark on a shadow-play with our eyes, our minds: I wondered – What would it be like to go to bed with a woman like this? I had no such experience: she would be a leopard and myself a deer? So straightforward, so matter-of-fact: the disrobing, the stalking, in my hotel room; and then the first bite on the neck, the guts spilling out on the floor. And the deer submitting so meekly! Is not this what a deer is for: to be gutted, skinned; it likes it even?

The music suddenly stopped. The silence was, yes, like the draining of a pool – all those shapes, convolutions, collapsing in blobs and strands. The cause of this ceasing – I had taken in the dumb-show out of the corner of my eye – was that after the Minister had been sitting with the man at the next table for some time, and had been trying without avail to make himself heard, the man had gestured to one of his henchmen who had got up and gone over to the glass-protected booth where the man who controlled the recorded music sat like a dangerous criminal on trial, and there had banged on the glass and when the man had not seemed to hear had gone to where a bunch of wires emerged from the booth and had jerked at them so that the music ceased abruptly. And then, after a moment in which it seemed that one could see quite clearly the dying shapes in the pool, the lights went out.

There were candles in jars already alight on the tables. One's eyes grew accustomed as if to a new medium – still that of an underwater world, perhaps, but one in which one could take one's mask off and breathe.

The woman said, 'That's better.'

I said 'You speak English.'

'My husband is English.'

'That's not him at the next table?'

'No.'

The dancers were leaving the dance-floor. They were surrounding and engulfing the security men and the media people. I thought – We really might be able to get up to something, the woman and I, without being too much observed –

– But of course I know that this is not quite the point.

The woman said 'Your friend said you would like to dance with me.'

I said 'And now there's no music –'

'Who cares about music –'

'Quite.'

The Minister was talking earnestly to the man with the beard: there was a man sitting between them like an interpreter. I should be listening. Or might the woman and I really go to a hotel? How could I tell –

The woman said 'My children are in England.'

I said 'You'd like to join them? You'd like to have them here?'

'You see, I knew you would understand –'

'Is your friend at the next table the man they call Bluebeard?'

'Oh he is much more important than Bluebeard!'

'I mean Dungbird –'

She said 'Can you help me?'

Some of the girls who had been on the dance-floor were being chatted up by the media people. In the next alcove the Minister and the man with a beard were like waxworks of historical figures conspiring by candlelight. I thought – But here, now, what is it that is happening?

I said 'Do you or your friend know anything about the smuggling of arms, of weapons, of radioactive material –'

She said 'Oh that, yes –'

'You do?'

'Yes. And there is worse.'

I thought – Of course, she is likely to be making this up. But have I not said that, for what is required, one might as well make it up?

The flash of a camera suddenly went off. I instinctively lowered my head. Then I thought – But is not just this, for some reason or other, what we have wanted – some ambivalence; confusion –

I said 'Where? I mean, where is this material –'

The woman said 'What are you, a negotiator?'

'A journalist.'

'What would you do with this story?'

'Let it be known.'

'Why?'

'Because then people would be frightened.'

'Don't you think people are frightened?'

'Not enough.'

'They quite like it?'

'Yes.'

She watched me with grey-green eyes. I thought – But it doesn't matter if I don't know exactly what she might be up to.

She said 'You think if people were frightened enough, the war might stop –'

'Yes. And you could see your children.'

At the next table the Minister and the man with the beard had stopped talking and were watching us. A waiter was bringing some more candles to our table. I thought – Perhaps they are jealous: perhaps they know an historical event might even be happening here.

The woman said 'There's a place called Brodcic in the mountains. A good new road goes off from there. You'll know the road because it isn't on any map.'

I said 'Brodcic –'

'Yes.' She spelt it.

'Thank you.'

'It is important, I agree, that power should not remain in anyone's hands.' Then – 'I can give you the address of my children.'

The woman and I were gazing at each other across the table as if passionately. I thought – We really are acting out one of those scenes, the poignancy of which depends on the probability that two lovers will not see each other again. Or again – She really might come to the hotel?

I said 'Write it down.'

She said 'Not here.' Then – 'Would you mind if, in a moment, I throw a glass of drink at your face.'

I said 'No?'

'It is important that we do not seem to be colluding.'

'Yes.'

'Where can I find you?'

'At the hotel.'

The man with the beard had been speaking to one of his

henchmen who had got up and was coming over to our table. I thought – So this timing might be right: do you think? The woman picked up one of the small glasses and threw its contents, which were not much, vaguely in my direction. I thought – But you mean, I may be shot, if you come to the hotel? I was making a show of dabbing with my handkerchief at my clothes. I thought – And now, anyone, make what you like of that.

The woman had left me and was going back to the other table. The Minister was leaving the other table and was coming back to me. I thought – Everything is happening in due order. The Minister said 'You're not losing your touch?'

I said 'What did you find out?'

'They seem to think it depends on the Russians –'

'What –'

'God knows.'

'I see.'

He had sat down at our table again. A waiter was refilling our glasses. The man at the next table was once more raising his glass to us and smiling. The red-haired woman was in the chair next to him and was putting her arm through his. We raised our glasses to them. Some flashbulbs went off.

I said 'She seems to think there's rotting nuclear material, or whatever, or worse, somewhere in the mountains.'

'You'd never find it.'

'She might have made it up –'

'Does it matter? If they think it's there: if they think they know –'

The lights suddenly came on again. I thought – And now the music will start up: and that will be the end of anything sensible that anyone might know.

I began to say 'Well we've been seen to be getting information, and goodness knows not sucking up, and that's what we set out –' But then the music did begin again, and all we could do was shake our heads, and smile.

When we got up to leave it was as if we still might have forgotten something we had come for: two of the girls who had been with the media people had come to our table; a security man had come after them; the girls seemed to be posing: some flashbulbs went off.

The Minister and I paused, as if we were conferring. None of this seemed to matter. The security man took the Minister by the arm: the Minister paid no attention: he was nodding at me, frowning. As we went towards the door the man with the beard for what seemed the hundredth time raised his glass to us; the woman with red hair smiled at me. More flashbulbs went off. Patches of coloured lights swirled around walls and chairs and the floor once more like water. When we were out in the street it was as if we had come up for air; the media people followed us; there was our taxi. The security men were leading the Minister towards an official-looking car: I thought – Yes, we should go home separately. I held my hand out to the Minister; he took it; the media people seemed uncertain whether or not to take photographs. The Minister said 'Well, till our next assignation.' I said 'I'm afraid you may not be able to go out with a bang.' He said 'I should have stayed with the woman?' I thought I might say – Oh but I don't know if she'll come to the hotel!

Ten

There was a walk that I sometimes did when I left work early at The Bunker: I caught a bus in the direction of my home and got off near to where there were steps down to the towpath of the canal that ran through this part of London. Here there had once been warehouses and small factories and the marshalling yards of railways; after the war these had been in disrepair and now much of the land had been redeveloped. But here and there were open spaces in which tall gaunt buildings stood with their windows blown out as if they were slaves who had been blinded so as not to witness the self-destructiveness of their masters.

There was one enclave, however, where the towpath came to a lock with gates; on the other side was a lock-keeper's cottage and a sort of Japanese garden that had been constructed out of the wasteland: there were neat gravelled paths and standing stones and ornamental grasses and reeds by ponds. This enterprise had been undertaken by a group of teenage boys and girls under the nominal supervision of a young man from a charitable trust backed by the Council; the lock-keeper's cottage had been refurbished as a recreation centre for visitors; further along the canal there was a space on the bank where canoes were kept. At the other end of the garden there was a gaunt and gutted brick building which the boys and girls had set about repairing, when finished it would add to the amenities of the garden.

I had come across this place in my walk and felt it to be somewhat magical: I had wanted to write a piece about it – about the all-too-rare efforts of the young to create a garden of their own after what they might feel was their abandonment by the grown-up world; about the difficulties of finding a way to do this. I had crossed over the lock-gates and had talked to some of the boys and girls when they were working on the ruined building, they had been somewhat wary; I had wondered – Is it inevitable, this feeling of betrayal between the old and the young? But it had seemed reasonable that they might fear publicity that might render them exposed. Then when I had spoken of my idea of a story to people in The Bunker they had said – Oh but you know what that place is, don't you? It's used as a sort of trading-post for dust. I had said – Dust? They had said – You know: shit, dope, drugs, dust. I had not quite believed this; but one does not want to appear gullible about, nor to become involved in simply condemning, the matter of youth culture and drugs. So I did not pursue my story, and took to passing by on the other side of the canal.

But I continued to be somewhat haunted by this place – it was so secret, so inaccessible: approachable at the far side of the canal only by a footpath across wasteland, and the way over the lock-gates from the towpath soon being barred with a tangle of barbed wire. The gaunt brick building eventually had its roof on but its windows remained carefully boarded up: what might it be used for? those wild parties fuelled by whatever was the latest hallucinogenic drug? The whole place became in my mind something like Kundry's magic garden – the garden of the castle in which the wicked magician Klingsor lived, inhabited by beautiful sirens and through which (for some reason I could not remember) Parsifal had to pass in order to reach the Holy Grail. I began to think – But even if the stories of drugs and orgiastic parties are true, should I not be crossing over the canal to have a look? have I not said myself often enough that without some risk, some exposure, one does not reach a Holy Grail? But then had I not become wise enough to know that this was unlikely to be the sort of crack-up that was required –

though was not the point of Parsifal that he was innocent and not wise at all? These ruminations became part of what generally troubled me at that time – the impossibility of knowing what might be, as it were, a good crack-up. After a time I found I was anyway ceasing to go on my walks along the canal; I found it easier to linger over my whiskies in The Sailing Junk instead. But still, watching the bubbles rising up in my glass, my mind, I could think – might it not have been better if I had crossed over the canal?

In the mid-morning of this day when in the early hours I had arrived back from my journey to Cumbria, I thought I would go on this walk along the towpath again on my way from The Bunker to Billy's Parents' Day at the school. I had not been on this walk for some time: I thought – But God knows, after this weekend, I might be better equipped to deal with the sirens of Kundry's magic garden. I walked beside the canal thinking – Parsifal, Parsifal, what did you mean that your innocence protects you: you have found the right magic herb in the hills? Then when I got to the place on the towpath where I could see the lock and the cottage it seemed there was no one there: stones in the garden had been knocked over; one of the windows of the cottage was broken; it was as if the place had been vandalised, though the gaunt brick building remained boarded up and seemingly impregnable. I sat on the beam of the lock-gate opposite the cottage; the barbed wire on the lock-gates had been pulled aside so that there might be a way through. I saw also that there was a figure of a young man sitting or reclining on the steps up to the door of the cottage; but he was so still that he might have been a dummy; he seemed to be covered in a fine white dust. I thought for a moment that the boys and girls might have been making pieces of sculpture.

The feel of expectation or excitement that had come upon me as I was approaching the garden along the towpath had turned into a more virulent obsession that occasionally came up on me at this time (one does not like to remember these things: there are good and bad reasons why one does not like to remember them). These feelings, invasions, were of a sexual kind: impulses of such a bizarre and unexpected power (where do they come from? what has sparked them off?) that they were indeed like some assault by devils (do not most men, most people, at times feel something like this?

but the compulsion to forget is even stronger). These experiences were like those of St Anthony's temptations in the desert – or rather of a St Anthony who had given up the struggle and was already on his way into town. They were often to do with aspects of sexuality that played no part in my ordinary life, dark corners to do with degradation or self-degradation – powerful presumably just because for the most part they did not come to the light. I had no idea why, or at which times, such experiences arose or would arise: sometimes perhaps when I was tired, sometimes perhaps when there was too much going on and circuits seemed to become overheated in the brain. Or perhaps it was just to do with cycles of systems of the body – or the moon. Anyway, when these invasions came, there they were, yes, like the claws of crabs, the mouths and tails of eels, crawling through the guts between genitals and brain. And what was there to do except in some sense to give in – or so it seemed. On my walk from The Bunker I had increasingly been aware of such an onset – of my turning from Dr Jekyll into Mr Hyde. Perhaps it was because I had been in some sensual heaven with Ellen and Gaby that I now seemed to be attacked by demons from a sexual hell.

I was sitting at the far side of the canal from where the young man was reclining on the steps of the cottage. This place had been present in my heart, guts, mind, as an image of Kundry's garden; but why, as a siren, should there be this young man?

He was leaning back on his elbows with his legs stretched out and apart at an ungainly angle. It was as if this might be an invitation – but not of a kind that had hitherto appealed to me. Or perhaps his was the sort of invitation that is offered by those who are helpless or sick – I was reminded of the semi-autistic boy whom I had watched on video being handled or mishandled by those supposed to be caring for him, and what else could they do, he had seemed to be inviting mishandling. It was not even that this young man by the lock-keeper's cottage looked particularly like a girl: he was just a figure, hot and dusty, such as one might come across outside a doorway in an eastern country. He wore jeans and a T-shirt and his hair was brushed forwards on his forehead like feathers; he had high cheekbones and a narrow face that might, all right, have been that of a faun. I could not remember any previous dark invasion with

164

regard to a man: usually the handlings or mishandlings I dreamed of were narcissistic or to do with women. But now it was as if this dusty young man was a figure outside a shanty-town brothel and the compulsion was to use, to be used, to be abused by him – this was not just appalling, exciting, it was ridiculous? I had time to work out – Yes perhaps I have become too fantastical, too head-in-the-clouds, during these three days; perhaps I need to be brought down to earth with a crash: you really mean that? But I was already moving – of my own free will; but it did not feel like free will! – towards the lock-gates and the damaged barrier that I could step around. My heart was thumping: I could still explain to myself – Would it not after all only be right that I should enquire about what has happened to this magic garden? There was scum and refuse trapped against one side of the lock-gates; on the other water splashed to the lower level lethargically. I had a constriction in my throat: I thought – My mind is blocked like the water piled up against the lock-gates: there scum is trapped; what I need as it were is to spurt down lethargically. When I got to the far side I said in the direction of the young man 'What's happened? has this place been vandalised?' The young man watched me as if he were waiting for me to say something more. After a time he said 'Yes.'

I could not think what might be the next step. I was hanging onto the blockage in my mind: I wanted there to be some eruption, explosion, so that water might rush down to the sea.

I said 'Who by?' Then – 'I used to drop in here sometimes on my way home. There was someone in charge I spoke to, was it you?'

He said 'You've been here before?'

'Once or twice.'

'You wanted to come here now?'

'Yes.'

He stood up slowly. I thought – What I have imagined about the place has only been imagination! But why should he have been sitting outside the door like a prostitute in an eastern country –

He said 'Come inside.' I felt somewhat faint. I thought – but he will make all the running; all I have to do is to follow. We went up the steps into the cottage. Because I was so nervous, I said 'What sort of thing do you do here?'

He said as if amused – 'Whatever you like.'

'I don't know what I like.'

'A common predicament.'

Within the cottage the walls or partitions had been taken down so that there was just one long room; there were blankets and bedrolls and sleeping-bags neatly folded at one end, some cooking utensils and a stove in a corner. I thought – But I have been here before! in that barn, in Cumbria –

– But in that case –

I said 'I mean, what usually goes on –'

He said 'People use it as a sort of refuge.'

'A refuge from what?'

He laughed and put his hand on my arm. He said 'From people like you.'

I was hardly listening to what he said. He had white teeth and pale down on his upper lip. I wanted to back away. I wanted to be told that I could not back away. I wanted something overwhelming to happen to me, so that the pressure and pain would be taken from my mind, heart, groin –

I thought – I am like that man with the dead grey face in Cumbria: the one whose car went up in flames?

Then he said 'I thought you'd come about Billy.' He let go of my arm and moved away.

I said 'Billy?'

He said 'Then what did you come here for?'

I said 'You know Billy?'

He had gone to the window and was standing with his back to me. He raised himself on his toes. I thought – But then this is the disaster, the floodgates have opened and it is the whole of me that is rushing down towards the sea.

He said 'Though it's true that it's the other stuff that people are now trying to come here for.'

I had sat down on a packing-case with my back against a wall. I thought – For God's sake, Parsifal, what is innocence –

I said 'How do you know Billy?'

He said 'I used to teach at Billy's school. You know that –'

'No.'

'Billy said he'd told you –'

'No.'

'Well, boys and girls come here. It's a home.'

I thought – It doesn't matter that Billy didn't tell me. Then – But what is the other stuff that people come here for?

He said 'Billy helps.'

'What sort of boys and girls?'

'There are enough, God knows.'

'And Billy helps?'

'Though they're extraordinarily good at looking after themselves.'

'What is the other stuff that people come here for?'

He had turned and was smiling at me. I thought – He is trying to tell me that he knows: he knows why I came here: and it doesn't matter. My mind went blank.

He said 'Never mind. It hasn't happened yet.' Then – 'And we're packing up, as you see.'

After a time I said 'What did you teach at Billy's school?'

He said 'Environment, Nature Studies –'

'What Billy called Scouts?'

'Did he? I don't know. I took them canoeing.'

'When was Billy last here?'

'You know when Billy was last here.'

'No.'

He said 'Oh dear.' Then – 'Billy needn't know.'

I kept losing track of what was happening, just when I thought I had found it. I thought – What is it that Billy needn't know: about my being here?

After a time he said 'Billy was here last night.'

I said 'But he was with me last night.'

'So he got back all right?'

'Yes.' Then – 'Was that when the place was vandalised?'

He laughed and came and put a hand on my arm again. He said 'Things get muddled, don't you think?' Then – 'That was some of our own people who were angry that we were having to go.' Then – 'I didn't really think you might be one of the others.'

I said 'Who are the others?'

He moved away. I thought – But he is on my side: he is trying to tell me that things are all right.

I said 'But Billy didn't come to any harm –'

He said 'No.'

I said 'You mean boys and girls come here, have come here and you look after them –'

'Yes. It's been a good place. It's near the station.' Then – 'Billy says you're quite good at that sort of thing.'

'What sort of thing?'

'Helping people. Children. Wasn't there something I read in the papers?'

'Oh that, yes.'

He came and stood in front of me again. He put his hands on his hips. I thought – He is teasing me: he is keeping options open –

I said 'And you say Billy was here last night –'

'Yes.'

'And Jenny?'

'Yes. You know what they call us? The kiddos –'

'I know. But what are the other people who were here last night –'

'They want to take this place over. But you needn't worry about them unless you want to.'

'Why not? I mean, why do they want to take this place over?'

'Because it's been a good place, a special place, a place on its own. These are the sort of places that get taken over, don't you think?'

'So Billy and Jenny won't be coming back –'

'They're back with you, aren't they?'

'I mean –'

'I know what you mean. They may come back to pick up their things.' He had gone back to the window and was looking out. He said 'It's up to you, now, isn't it?'

I felt as if the crabs and eels that a short time ago had been crawling up my spine had been let out and the whole lot of us were now back in the sea. I thought – So we have been liberated? Then – Who was it who said that?

I said 'I was just on my way to Billy's Parents' Day at school.'

He said 'Look, I'm sorry if I haven't been helpful, but it's sometimes difficult to know how much to say. Billy sometimes came here in the evenings after school. Yes, he once or twice stayed here the night, when things weren't too good at home. You don't mind my saying things weren't too good at home? What's so wrong about that. What's wrong is people who say there's never anything wrong at home.

I said 'I'm not a good father.'

'Take that as read.'

'But he wasn't into drugs?'

'No, we were into stopping drugs.'

'But the people who broke the place up?'

'There are always some yobbos. But it's the others who frighten me.'

I thought I might say again – What others? But he said quickly – 'Billy's learning: you'll see.'

I could not think of anything else to say. I might ask once more – But you're sure Billy's all right? But it seemed best just to get to Parents' Day – where, I wondered, I might see?

I said 'Thank you for looking after Billy.'

He said 'I don't look after them. They look after me.'

He went out of the lock-keeper's cottage and down one of the paths that led to the gaunt brick building. He was a short, strutting figure: I thought – Perhaps he is Parsifal, now the guardian of the garden. The brick building was like a small-scale model of the reprocessing-plant – a windowless fortress within which fantasies might be bottled or be let out. I had left the cottage and was crossing the lock-gates to the side of the canal where there was the towpath. I thought – So what is it that these children, Billy, might have learned: that you have to look after yourselves –

– And after a time people are, or are not, on your side?

I was walking along the towpath. The canal ran in a straight line ahead and there was nowhere else to go: a wall was on one side and the water on the other. Across the canal were brick buildings like the one behind me in the garden – structures with no entrances to them for people by the canal. I was trying to imagine what it might be like to be the children: they had knowledge of, were cautious towards, other people's paths; but what could anyone know of these – that if you followed your own, you might have contact with the whole? In imagining this I was following my own path: how appalling that I knew so little of Billy's life! But how miraculous if I might be coming into contact with it – like walking on hot coals. And what is the experience of people who walk on hot coals? Oh of course terror; but then the vision that everything may be all right –

– A brazier in the darkness; of hot coals!

I was having to leave the canal and go up steps into the network of streets. This was where children grew up, learned to fight, learned that they had to fight; learned that their life-line from grown-ups was also the noose around their throat. Of course grown-ups feel impelled both to nurture and to smother children, as indeed they want to be nurtured and smothered themselves: out in the cold there is fear – from others; from oneself. Billy had been a night – or was it two – away from home: what was I supposed to say? Surely not – Damn you, for causing me such fear – but – Well done: for that which has not been lost cannot be found. And so on. I had a vision of those mothers and children being shovelled alive into pits. And then on the other side of the hill –

– It's all right, Billy: it's all right –

– There are millstones around our necks –

– Grind corn with them: use them as lifebuoys –

– They are what were rolled away from that tomb?

I had jumped on a bus: jumped off again. I was coming towards the gates of Billy's school. The road had been cleared: there were no more signs of the bomb. I thought – That did work quite well for us, didn't it?

Within the gates of the school there seemed to be the same crowd of parents that had been there in the morning: they had never gone out; they had come back; what was the difference. There is a Buñuel film in which a crowd of people at a banquet are prevented from leaving by an unknown fear; a lion is glimpsed prowling in the corridors; but it is in the mind that there is fear. The parents within the school playground were there out of kindliness or convention: in what way did they seem trapped? Here were stalls on which were laid out the objects that the children had made or that the parents had collected and brought that morning: these were on sale to provide money for new equipment or some outing for the school – or to provide this opportunity for parents and children to be seen together. The children were bright-eyed and amused behind their stalls; they were like people looking down from a circle of boxes in a Roman amphitheatre; the parents were like the gladiators, the victims, the born-again Christians or whatever – how helpless they looked in their arena! But the children looked down on them quite kindly: here was no real cause of fear – only occasionally a temptation to be overcome by giggles. I had been struck before by the idea of how strange it was that such lively children should have sprung from and would later presumably turn into such somehow ungainly adults: what catastrophe is it that happens to humans between the ages of, say, fourteen and forty, so that some potentiality seems to be extinguished, and humans seem to be going the way of dinosaurs. I thought now – But why might there not be some rejuvenation to and fro: it makes sense that they should see grown-ups as kiddos?

I was looking for Melissa. I had been looking for Melissa that morning. I needed Melissa in order to say – You do see, don't you, that we have something to learn –

I saw Billy behind a stall on which were laid out boxes and ornaments that he and other children had encrusted with shells. I thought – I knew that Billy was collecting shells! I could have brought him some from Cumbria –

– Even ones that have two spirals, or whorls, as if in an effort to make something different.

I went up to Billy and said 'Oh Lord, I forgot to bring you any shells!'

He said 'Oh that's all right!'

'There were one or two where I was which had such strange formations: with spirals, or heads, as if one were trying to grow out of another.'

'Yes, I've heard about them.'

'You have?'

'Yes.'

I watched Billy. He was looking down at his shells. It seemed that in some other world there might be a version of myself shouting at Billy – Where were you yesterday! or the night before! Tell me! – and then disappearing into the void.

I said 'Is Mum here?'

'Yes, she was looking for you.'

'Oh was she, good.'

'You've said you won't be angry —'

'No.'

'You're sure?'

'Billy, I ran into that teacher, or scoutmaster, or whatever, this afternoon on my way back from work. The one who used to take you canoeing on the canal.'

'Oh yes, he was the one who told us about the shells.'

'He was?'

'Yes.'

'He said you had some trouble there last night.'

'Not really, no —'

'But Billy, you were supposed to be staying with the Armstrongs.'

'No, that was the night before.'

'Was it?'

'There were just some people trying to turn us out.' Then — 'Jenny can't go on staying with her parents.'

'Why not?'

'I don't know. You must ask her.'

'You could have come home.'

'I did.' Then — 'What should I say?'

I thought — About your parents? About Jenny's?

When Billy looked up at me there was some hurt behind his eyes as there had been with the people in Cumbria. I wanted to say to him — It's all right, Billy! I said 'Don't say anything then. And I won't.'

I was feeling in my pocket for some change with which I might buy one of Billy's boxes of shells. I came across something that felt like the two-headed shell that one of the fair-haired boys had given me on the beach. But had I not given this back to him? Or had I just not paid for it — I could not remember. But now there it was, with its two whorls independent and yet growing one from the other and then a small bump in between. I said 'Look, after all, I have got one of those shells!'

Billy said 'Look, there's Mum!'

'Where —'

'Let me see.'

He took the shell that I had handed to him. I looked at where

Billy had been looking and there was Melissa at the far end of the playground talking to Mr and Mrs Armstrong. She had seen me. She had her teeth bared as if she were in a high wind. I knew this look of Melissa's, it was as if she were on some journey past rocks and sirens strapped to a mast –

Billy said 'It's beautiful. Can I keep it?'

'Yes do.'

'Thanks, Dad.' Then – 'Yes, don't say anything to Jenny's parents. Or say what you like.' He laughed.

I walked across the playground. Should not Billy have said – I'm sorry? Should not I have said – I'm sorry? So many chances: so many possibilities. Or should one be sorry only for everything – or nothing? Melissa was watching me as I approached – me on my hot coals; she in her high wind. I thought – What a furnace! But we are on the sea?

– And what strange songs the sirens sing!

I said 'Hullo.'

She said 'Hullo.'

'I've been looking for you.'

'I've been looking for you too.' Then – 'You know Ted and Jill Armstrong?'

Mrs Armstrong said 'Yes we met this morning.'

Melissa said 'You met this morning?'

Mr Armstrong said 'Yes. And I thought we'd got things straightened out.'

I said 'And haven't you?'

Melissa was frowning. I thought – But this is all right: I've come to join you at your mast: and bring you a nice warm brazier of coals –

Melissa was saying 'Jill was saying that Billy and Jenny weren't with them last night.'

I said 'No, they were with me.'

'And where were you?'

'You know where I was.'

'I don't.'

'I was at home.'

'Oh I see.'

Melissa seemed to be crumpling slightly in her high wind. I

thought – She is laughing, she is crying; does one do both, to the songs that sirens sing?

Mrs Armstrong said 'But it's not last night, it's the night before that –'

Melissa said 'Weren't they with you the night before that?'

Mr Armstrong said 'Yes.'

Mrs Armstrong said 'No.'

Mr Armstrong said 'Which night are we talking about?'

Melissa said 'Where were they then –'

I said 'And where were you –'

Melissa said 'That doesn't matter –'

I said 'All right it doesn't.'

Melissa was hanging on. It was as if she had come to a fork in the road. I thought – How can you come to a fork if you are strapped to a mast? There is a gibbet, you mean, that creaks like a sail in a high wind?

Melissa said 'You know where I was –'

'No I don't.'

'I left a number –'

'With Billy –'

'Yes. When did you get back?'

'Last night.'

'Did you have a good time?'

'Yes.' Then – 'Did you?'

Mr and Mrs Armstrong were watching us. I thought – We are putting on this show and not only for their benefit. We are two old escape artists managing to wriggle round to face each other on the mast: if we wriggle sensuously enough the ropes may fall away: might not people have a tremendous orgasm strapped to a mast –

Melissa said 'No I didn't.'

I said 'I'm sorry.'

'Are you?'

'No.'

Mr and Mrs Armstrong seemed to be half-embarrassed, half-enthralled. I thought – Sea-monsters might indeed be upstaged by such a show?

Mr Armstrong said 'So the night before that, at least, they were with you –'

I said 'Rather than with you –'

Mrs Armstrong said 'Why do you say that –'

Mr Armstrong said quickly 'No harm seems to have been done then –'

I said 'That's right.'

Mrs Armstrong said to Melissa 'It's a pity you weren't here this morning –'

Melissa said 'I got held up by the bomb.'

Mr Armstrong said 'Let's leave it at that.'

I wanted to put my arms round Melissa. In some other world we might be singing, singing, on a moonlit stage.

Mrs Armstrong said 'Look! There's Jenny –'

I said 'She's coming to stay?'

Jenny was standing by the stall where Billy was selling his boxes encrusted with shells: Billy was showing her something that he held in his hand – presumably the shell that I had given him. Jenny looked at it: then at us, across the width of the playground. I thought – There are all these messages: and we can't even tell what they are.

I said to Melissa 'Is that all right?'

She said 'Is what all right –'

'Jenny coming to stay.'

'How many more people are coming to stay?'

'What?'

Mr Armstrong said 'She can always stay with my sister.'

Mrs Armstrong said 'Now don't start that again.'

I thought it imperative that we get away from Mr and Mrs Armstrong. They must be wanting to get away from us. They were watching Billy and Jenny. I took Melissa by the arm. I said 'Melissa and I are about to have a slight family contretemps.'

Melissa said 'I don't think what we are about to have is a slight family contretemps.'

Mr or Mrs Armstrong said 'Oh, no problem!' They laughed.

I thought – We can now take our curtain calls: find a quiet corner off-stage.

I was leading Melissa away. Melissa was resisting. It was as if she were saying – I won't be taken in by any of your tricks –

And I could say – But I don't want you to be taken in by any of my old tricks!

She said 'Who's Gaby –'

I said 'I told you who's Gaby –'

'No.'

'Well, I told Billy. She's the girl in Cumbria.'

'You've asked her to stay?'

We had reached a corner of the playground. There was a wire fence on each side. I thought – But perhaps there is always some sort of audience watching.

I said 'She's twelve, thirteen. She wants to go to school.'

She said 'You're mad. I didn't know when you were coming back. I didn't know if you were ever coming back –'

'I told you –'

'You didn't –'

'And so on and so on –'

'I thought Billy was with the Armstrongs –'

'Well he wasn't.'

'Where was he then?'

'Look, I'll tell you. But it doesn't matter now.'

'Of course it matters –'

'You couldn't know –'

'I feel so guilty.' Then – 'I suppose Billy told you I wasn't at home –'

'No.'

'Well he did. I mean I wasn't.'

I thought – All right, all right. You've said you feel guilty? You feel guilty about Billy?

I said 'Well, I've asked you. Where were you?'

'I was with Malcolm.'

'With Malcolm? I thought you were with Jack.'

'I know you did.'

'What were you doing with Malcolm?'

'Not what you think.' Then – 'What do you think I was doing?'

'I didn't even know you knew Malcolm!'

'Of course you did!'

'You mean, I didn't want to know you knew Malcolm –'

'What?'

176

'Oh never mind.'

I thought – You mean, we might appear to be a married couple having a normal row? We might be Christians being torn apart by lions? We might be workers on a rubbish dump sifting through the litter –

She said 'Malcolm rang me up about Janice.'

'But you knew about Janice –'

'About him and Janice. He was suicidal. At least he said he was –'

'I see. And he wasn't?'

'I don't know.'

I thought – But something must have happened; or why didn't you tell me? but so what: for goodness' sake –

– Oh well, something happened between me and Ellen in Cumbria.

I said 'Well that makes sense.'

She said 'Jack had to come and rescue me.'

'You rang up Jack?'

'Yes, Jack didn't tell you?'

'Is that how Jack got his black eye?'

'Has Jack got a black eye?'

'Of course Jack didn't tell me!'

'I thought he was your friend.'

'He is.'

'It isn't funny.'

'Isn't it? Then from what did Jack have to rescue you –'

'Do you remember what happened between us – what – only three days ago?'

'Yes.'

'What –'

'I gave you a black eye.'

'Well you did –'

'And that wasn't funny –'

'No.'

'I'm sorry.'

'Well it wasn't, I suppose, much of a black eye.'

I said 'So how about going to one of those small hotels in the streets in front of the station?'

She stared at me. I thought – All right, the music stops: and then we can, if we like, leave the theatre.

She said 'I told Jack to tell you that we're finished.'

I said 'Sex is sometimes very good between people on the point of breaking up.'

'You think we are breaking up?'

'No.'

'You were so awful. So awful!'

She took hold of my hand and began kneading it.

I said 'Yes.'

I thought I might say – But you must have managed to have quite a good time, really –

She said 'Look, if you really would like to go to a hotel –'

I said 'But I know, I know – what about Billy: what about Jenny –'

We were walking hand in hand across the playground. Billy and Jenny were watching us. I thought – It's all right, children: the kiddos will be having their supper soon, and then will be going up to bed.

Melissa said 'Why did Jenny and Billy want to leave the Armstrongs?'

I said 'I suppose for the same sort of reason that they didn't want to stay with us.'

'But they did –'

'Oh yes.'

'Perhaps Ted Armstrong got up to no good with Jenny.'

'Except that everybody thinks that.'

'Did you get up to no good with Gaby?'

'No! I think up to a point, I got up to good.'

Billy and Jenny had disappeared from behind their stall. I was thinking – Now perhaps they need not worry if they think we are all right –

– But what a predicament for grown-ups to be in: all right!

Melissa said 'Who is this Gaby?'

I said 'She's the girl who organised the group of children who set themselves up in the hills. Except that they weren't really on their own, they were looked after by an old woman called Mrs

Ferguson. Mrs Ferguson says she'll pay for Gaby if she goes to school in London.'

'She wants to go to school?'

'Yes.'

'But why should we look after her?'

'I don't know. It's just what's happened –'

'You know she and Billy have been in touch?'

'Have they? Yes, I know. I mean I didn't really.'

We were hanging round by the stall on which there had been boxes encrusted with shells. All the boxes seemed to have been sold. I thought – And they have gone out like seeds into the universe –

Melissa said 'Billy told me.' Then – 'But what will we tell Billy –'

I said 'About what?'

'I told him we're splitting up.'

'Well he wouldn't have believed that, would he?'

The parents were drifting from the playground into the school building: and then there would be speeches and cups of tea. I thought – But if we can't really quite go to a hotel –

– What on earth do couples do who are all right?

Melissa said 'Look, I think there are just one or two more things I'd better do.'

I said 'What?' Then – 'No, I mean just yes.'

'I said I'd see Malcolm this evening. I told you, he's suicidal.' Then – 'Can this Gaby look after herself?'

'Oh yes, and others –'

'What others?'

'When you go off with Malcolm or Jack –'

'I'm not going off with Malcolm or Jack!'

'Oh no, no, I was joking –'

'Though perhaps I wouldn't mind Jack.'

I felt, as I had felt before, that there was too much coming in. Melissa and I seemed to have been standing too long on hot coals. Perhaps if the stage burned down, we might be able to leave the theatre –

I said 'Look, anyway, I've got to go and rescue my car.'

She said 'I'd better go to the tea-cakes and speeches.'

'Then you'll see the children home?'

'Yes I always see the children home!'

'Yes I know you do.'

'I don't think I did too badly with Malcolm.'

'Good.'

'And thank you for looking after the children.'

'Oh thank you for looking after the children!'

'I would like some time to go to one of those hotels by the station.'

Eleven

Another place that I sometimes stopped off at on my walks home from The Bunker was the church, or lodgings, of the priest, Father Watkin, whose advice I had asked when I was doing my first story on the children in Yugoslavia. Father Watkin had become a friend: he had also become involved in organising pilgrimages to go out to the shrine in Yugoslavia. I liked dropping in and talking to Father Watkin. He did not try to proselytise; he talked about his attitudes and his ideas in a detached way as if it were not up to him if no one paid attention to them.

This afternoon when I left Melissa and the children at the school it was true that I had to get my car: but also I felt that for Melissa and me to become accustomed to whatever was happening we needed time for things to settle down. Also I needed to talk to Father Watkin about my plans for going out to Yugoslavia, and about the aftermath of my last trip there.

My car was where I had left it on the pavement; there was a notice on the windscreen threatening various prosecutions. I drove to Father Watkin's church which was no longer in parish use; it was in disrepair with its windows boarded up, though Father Watkin still said Mass in it. He used to say – Perhaps one day at an appropriate moment the roof will fall down: not a bad way to go.

There was a house next door where Father Watkin had lodgings; I rang his bell and waited. It had begun to rain. I realised that I was hungry; I thought – I am getting used to fasting, but what about prayer? Is it prayer that Father Watkin is doing when he seems to be listening to something else when he is talking? There was no answer from the lodgings. I noticed that there was a light on in the darkened church; this could be seen through a gap where one of the boards over the windows had been pulled away; it seemed that the church might have been broken into. I pushed on the door, which was usually locked; and it opened. I thought that Father Watkin must be inside – or some intruder.

I went quietly into the church: there was a light on in the nave; one or two saints were still in their niches on the walls. I thought – One day I will find out about praying: are you aware of what you are being attentive to? or is just it a way of not feeling trapped?

There was a light coming from underneath the door of the vestry – at least I presumed this was the vestry: it was a room at the back of the choir-stalls and the organ. I went to this door and put my ear against it; I pushed; it was locked. There was a scraping and gasping noise coming from within. I thought I might murmur – Father Watkin? It's me! But this would hardly help if there really was an intruder and Father Watkin was being strangled. I looked for another way into the vestry: there was definitely a groaning sound. There was an organ loft above the choir-stalls where Father Watkin sometimes played the organ; this was an ancient instrument that itself made a wheezing sound; perhaps the organ had mysteriously come alive? Its working parts backed onto the upper part of the vestry; there was unlikely to be a solid partition, more likely a baize hanging or a screen. I climbed up the steps to the organ loft: the organ was still and silent. I thought – Perhaps Father Watkin is wrestling with prayer in the vestry like Jacob with his angel: I should not intrude? But what on earth was that story – the angel had caught Jacob with a blow below the belt; then Jacob had got hold of the angel by whatever they were called in those days and would not let go until God or the angel had blessed him. What on earth were these stories? what did they mean –

– You battered away –

– You took your chances?

In the organ loft there were pipes on either side of the console like a waterfall that has frozen; behind this were the delicate working parts of the organ – pieces of wood finely cut and redolent like boxes that contain spices in an eastern country. And beyond these there was, yes, a green baize hanging that separated, presumably, the organ from the upper part of the vestry. I was squeezing between the framework and the working parts of the organ when, alarmingly, the whole structure did seem to come shudderingly to life: there was a deep heaving noise, slow at first but then rising; this might be heralding the arousal of indeed a massive all-in-wrestler type of god – or it might just mean that I had inadvertently pushed against, trodden on, some operative part of the organ. Whichever, there seemed an urgency to do something; I lurched and tripped forwards; my fist went through the somewhat decaying green cloth that separated these parts of the organ from what was beyond, and like this I toppled slowly – one foot trapped – head first through the cloth into the upper part of the vestry. In this position the top part of my body projected and became wedged like the figurehead of a ship – or indeed like some airborne angel. I was some distance above the ground; I could not get much of a handhold on the structure at my waist; I thought – Since I am stuck, should I not give a blessing?

The vestry contained the usual assortment of church furnishings – in particular a life-size crucifix, presumably the one which, so Father Watkin had told me, he had been accustomed as a young man to carry through streets when taking part in missionary pageants. This crucifix had tilted and toppled forwards from where it had been propped; it was being prevented from falling to the floor by one of its arms having caught hold of a Mothers' Union banner – I mean it seemed that the figure on the cross had clutched at this banner which was suspended from the ceiling in order to prevent itself from falling further. And it seemed that the figure on the cross might indeed be alive; it was twitching; it had a bald head. I thought – I cannot remember another Christ with a bald head.

Then I realised that the figure on the cross was Father Watkin. I thought – Oh well, yes, this is, isn't it, one particular wrestle with an angel or devil. I said 'Just a minute, I'm coming.' Father Watkin appeared to be in considerable difficulty on his cross; he had a rope round his throat; his feet and one hand were tied; the other was clinging to the Mothers' Union banner. I thought – Well, this may indeed be a way to see angels. I was struggling to get down from my peculiar projection from the back of the organ: I could get little leverage with my hands; my foot was still stuck; I might perhaps topple further and hang upside down, but then I would be like St Peter and in no better position than Father Watkin. But anyway, people in Father Watkin's situation often do not wish to be rescued, do they? the point is, to feel oneself ravished – whether or not by angels. But Father Watkin did seem in some extremity; the top of his head was going pink; this was unlikely to be an emergent halo. I managed to jerk and twist my foot and then slither like a snake down the vestry wall; turn a somersault, and then gaze up at Father Watkin. He was in his underpants; his body was white and rather bulbous; I thought – He is like a potato that has been left too long in a cellar. I stood and got my hands under an arm of the cross and pushed; it pivoted and became wedged back in its corner. I got my shoulder under one of Father Watkin's shoulders and pulled at the knot of the rope round his neck: this was in an easy-to-release bow: I thought – Well sometimes you are sensible even if you want to see angels. With one hand free he took over the job of releasing the other; I knelt at his feet in order to untie the cord there, but then I thought – I am overdoing this: or I am putting off the moment when I have to face him? I stood up and brushed at my clothes which were covered in a fine white dust. I remembered – There was a fine white dust on the body of the young man by the canal. Father Watkin untied his feet and stepped down from the cross. He said 'Thanks.' Then – 'Phew, that was a close one!'

I said 'I was just passing and I saw a light on.'

He said 'The synchronicitous Samaritan!'

I realised that the noise from the organ had stopped. I thought – That old God was trying to be helpful?

I sat on a chair. Father Watkin sat down opposite me. He was wiping his face with a cloth. I wondered if it was a cloth with which he wiped things on the altar.

It was as if Father Watkin and I were in some confessional, but with the walls fallen down so that we found ourselves face to face. He seemed to be waiting for me to speak, which might seem reasonable, except that it was he who had been carrying a burden. I thought – But I do not want him to feel guilty.

I said 'Do you find it helps, to do something like that?'

He said 'In the short run, yes. In the long run, I don't suppose so.'

'When things get too much, you mean? With too much pressure coming in?'

'Yes.'

'But if you stuck things out –'

'That would probably be better.'

'But you might do something worse?'

'Or something worse might happen?'

'But that might be made use of –'

'Certainly, yes.'

'But not this?'

'I don't know.'

He did not seem to be embarrassed. He was sitting with his hands on his knees, his eyes half-closed, taking deep breaths.

I thought – Did he have time for that flower, that *chakra* or whatever to grow out of the top of his head?

I said 'I only ask because I sometimes have compulsions, not quite like that, but to some sort of destruction or self-destruction. And then I wonder if it's better to fight them or just to get them over quickly, in private –'

He stood up and went to a cupboard. His strange bulbous body was like something that in various places had been trying, and failing, to give birth. He said 'You're being very kind.'

I thought – He knows of course that I won't talk.

I said 'It seems just human nature.'

He said 'I sometimes think it might be better if it were out in the open.' Then – 'I know you're telling me, thank you, that you won't talk.'

'That human nature were out in the open? That this sort of thing were out in the open? But surely it is —'

'One may know it about other people. One hardly admits it to others about oneself —'

'You think if one did, it might change?'

'It's a chance. Perhaps.'

He had taken a black cassock out of the cupboard and was pulling it over his head. He was like a candle being snuffed out. I thought — You mean, if you moved about naked in front of the altar, for instance, people might understand more about the need and nature of redemption?

I said 'But people know about the Crucifixion —'

He said 'People don't know just how much or why they might like it.'

'That was a problem for Jesus?'

'Oh that, well, yes. There are lessons to go on being learned.'

He had come and sat on the chair opposite me again. I thought — Somewhere, here and now, there is some wrestling with angels.

I said 'But still it's better to do it yourself than to get someone to do it for you —'

'Why do it at all?'

'You've said — If it's out in the open, it might effect change.'

'Well it did, didn't it —'

'Oh I see.'

'But you can't exactly commend it.'

We seemed to have come to some end in our confession. I thought — And then you go out into the outside world?

I said 'I'm thinking of going out again to Yugoslavia.'

He said 'Oh yes, I was going to ask you about that.'

'I want to write about how if people like doing mayhem to themselves, then why not let them: just say — Yes, if that's what you like —'

'And that might change them? But they like doing it to others: can you say yes to that?' Then — 'Have you seen the parents of that child?'

'No, I was going to ask you about that.'

'There are always the innocent. Though God can make use of what he likes.'

186

'That child seemed to know what he liked.'

'Well yes, perhaps God especially can make use of that.'

There had been an incident at the end of my last visit to Yugoslavia which was one of the things I had wished to discuss with Father Watkin: this was what he was referring to when he spoke of 'the parents of that child'. This was also the story I had been reminded of when I had been talking to the man by the canal.

I said 'And when things are being worked out, the present can affect the future and the future affect the past –'

'Oh I suppose so.'

'I mean, it was in order to talk to you about that child that I turned up just now. And before this you weren't obliged to help me with that child –'

'Oh yes I was.'

'Well yes I see.'

He had stood again and was tidying his ropes and putting them neatly into a cupboard. He straightened the cross and the Mothers' Union banner. I thought – At such moments one can talk about this sort of thing, before it goes –

– When it seems to be happening?

He said 'The great stumbling-block about God for many people is the suffering of children. But this is a feeling of grown-ups. Ask the children.'

'And what would they say –'

'Some of them might say – But for most it doesn't seem to be a problem.'

'Why not?'

'They think it's their responsibility.'

'They think they're like God –'

'Yes.'

'And this is true.'

'Yes.'

'And then we stop them.'

We had both stood up. He said – 'Well no one likes a grown-up responsibility.' I thought – But we're trying?

I said 'Oh well, if I do get to Yugoslavia, I might have a chance of seeing that lady in blue.'

He said 'Sister Bernardine –'

'Yes, Sister Bernardine.'

'But I've told you, she doesn't wear blue she wears grey.' Then – 'You haven't yet written your proper account of that story?'

This story that I became involved with after my trip with my friend the Minister to The Garden of Earthly Delights was not the one (as it might have been) to do with the rumours of rotting nuclear dumps in the hills: I saw no chance of making anything of this yet: the village of Brodcic was unapproachable at this stage of the war, and I had no incentive at this time to take what might be undue risks for this story. I stayed on in the town where I had been with the Minister and went in pursuit of a story (and indeed what incentive might I have had for this?) about the large numbers of children, babies, that had been abandoned in orphanages and hospitals in this part of Europe as a result of turmoil and now war – children far too young for there to be any question of their surviving on their own; and such babies being of little interest to the local grown-up world at war except that from time to time they might be used to publicise the other side's atrocities. And for people in the West they might provide pictures of suffering when required – when there had not been more dramatic horror stories for some time. Most people could get their *frissons* and then put the pictures out of mind. But sometimes there were couples whose circumstances of life and heart were such that they were moved to do something practical about these children; and since the money that one might give to charitable organisations apparently seldom reached its proper destination, these couples found themselves landed with the idea, compulsion, that they should adopt one or two of these children. But then authorities did suddenly find a role to play – which was to put a string of obstacles in the way of couples wanting to adopt children. At home this was to some extent unavoidable because of well-established rules; but in Eastern Europe there had evolved a game by which authorities and lawyers used children as bargaining counters in the business of exercising power and making money.

The first time I visited one of these orphanages I found the experience unnerving. This was with regard not only to the condition of the children, though this was bad enough, nor even to the attitudes of the people who ran the place and of some of those who had come with me to visit it – I had come with a group of reporters and photographers after we have been told there was a selection of children being put on show. These were children that might be seen as destitute enough to evoke charitable aid from the West (which might then be misappropriated), but not so far gone that those in charge might be blamed. The photographers had gravitated to another part of the huge bare dormitory where some of the worst cases had been set apart with screens placed round them: arguments were going on about what pictures could be taken and what could not: such arguments were diverting concern from what might have been felt more properly about the children. I had followed the photographers: I was thinking – But indeed what virtue is there in simply being appalled? and yet, for the most part, what else is there to be suffered or done. Babies lay and stared sightlessly; there was no crying; it was terrible that there was no crying. There was one child with malformed limbs like the one that I had seen swimming in the lake: I thought – But that one did get as far as the lake! I wandered through to another and smaller dormitory where there were slightly older children, between two and three, who also seemed to have been set out of bounds: a few of these children did not seem to have given up hope: they were watchful, belligerent; one was even standing and holding onto the bars of his cot or cage. What alarmed me about this situation – I mean alarmed me apart from the condition of the children or the attitudes of the grown-ups – was to do with the fact that it was indeed conceivable that one or two of these children might be 'saved': but then, if one was a would-be adopting parent (oh yes, I had such fantasies!) how on earth would one choose? How conceivably could one say – You or you will live: you or you will probably die. And yet this was what, as it were, a God would be or was doing all the time – with regard to children, at least those not old enough to be making any choices. Perhaps that was why it seemed there could be no God – why adults could not believe there was a God – how could a God or indeed themselves bear to take such responsibility? I was thinking this while I was watching the one particular child standing and holding onto the bars of his cage. I was wondering – Perhaps God indeed began to feel too tired, too guilty; and so, like humans, has wanted to die. But this is not relevant to children?

The child who was standing up and holding onto the bars of his cage was doing this in such a way that he seemed to know he was imprisoned; and thus that there might be some state of getting out. There was not much he could do about this himself; he would depend on someone or something from outside. It was this, strangely, that he seemed to know. He had been watching me as I approached. It was this that I found unnerving – not only that I might be someone who might have to make a choice, but that this child was observing me as if to see whether or not I would choose: not only what would my choice be, but would I have the courage! I thought suddenly – But it is as if this child is making a choice: he has chosen to ask – What are you grown-ups: are you human? you think you should not be like gods? The child had thin dark hair and large dark eyes: I had seen representations of creatures like this on the columns of mediaeval cloisters – figures with huge wide eyes as if wondering at the strange world on which they had landed. His attentiveness seemed to set him out from the others. He stared up at me patiently. I found I was talking to myself as if I were talking to him; as if by this he might understand. I was saying – Oh my dear, but what can I do? you are one out of thousands or millions; all over the world there are children spilled onto the ground like seeds, like sperm: you survive or not by chance: I cannot choose. Then – You think I can? But I have a wife and a child at home: so even if I were a god what could I do? Can everyone be saved? I put my finger through the bar of the cage: the child clung onto it.

I thought – Oh you lady in blue, walking on the hillside! pray for us now and at the hour of our birth.

I did not know how to get the child to let go of my finger. I said to myself – or to him or to whoever – I'll do what I can.

In the hotel in the town in which I was staying was a couple of whom I shall call Mr and Mrs Smith. I had heard that they had come to this part of the world with the intention, or on the chance, of adopting a child. (There are often coincidences as well as fantasies about such heartfelt things?) I had heard that Mr and Mrs Smith had become disheartened because of legal and financial difficulties – it seemed that no one in this country or at home was being of much help to them. They had come out to this town with some hope of bribing officials; some bribes had been given, but there were always more officials, lawyers, more real or pretended relatives of a child to be satisfied and paid off; and so Mr and Mrs Smith had reached a state of despair. I had not yet myself at this time become accustomed to the idea of things turning up – though I had been made to wonder about odd coincidences when I had been involved with the Minister and the red-haired woman and the man called Dungbird in The Garden of Earthly Delights.

I met Mr Smith in the bar of the hotel. He said that he and his wife were indeed thinking of going home. They had been to the orphanage that I had been to – this was the one currently open to visitors – and they had seen a child that they would have liked to have chosen; but this child had a grandmother who, it was said, as next of kin would have to give permission; and this grandmother could not at the moment be found, and a search would take time and money, and the grandmother would require compensation, and lawyers would have to be employed to get a permit for the child to leave the country – and so on and so on. Mr and Mrs Smith had already paid out considerable sums and there were no signs of the demands growing less, nor of an eventually successful outcome; and there were still the formalities to be gone through at home. Also, Mr Smith said, they had become uneasy about the difficulty of choosing one child rather than another; perhaps after all it might be better not to meddle in ways in which humans seemed set to go to perdition. Mr Smith and I were getting somewhat drunk. I knew I should ask – Which was this child you had in mind? But it was as if an answer might occasion a familiar white light to come down – and not because I had managed to anaesthetise myself with drink, but because I had not.

Mrs Smith joined us at the bar of the hotel and she described the child that she had wanted to choose; and then it seemed evident, yes, that this was the child that I would have chosen; or rather – and this seemed to be the point – that had chosen me. I told them that I had been out to the orphanage that afternoon and had noticed this child – I was sure it was the one they had described – and it seemed in some sense to be expectant. They did not say – as they might have done – How strange! – or – What a coincidence! They stared at me. Mrs Smith began to cry. I said 'I might be able to help.'

Mr Smith said 'How?'

'I have some contacts here, and at home. And one of the good things about a state of chaos or war is that you can sometimes out of it produce some sort of order of your own.'

Mrs Smith said 'I do believe in coincidences.'

I said 'But will you take the risk?'

I had seen the possibility that if one could get the child away from the orphanage, then in order to get it out the country I might be able to make use of the bands of pilgrims that went to and from the shrine where the children talked to the Virgin Mary: these pilgrimages were continuing even in time of war, though in a somewhat haphazard way. I could make contact with Father Watkin in London: I might at last be able to have some contact with the lady in blue. And in London my editor, Jack, might be interested in the story; and this could put pressure on the authorities if there was any difficulty about getting the child accepted at home.

I explained this to Mr and Mrs Smith. I said 'But of course, it will still depend on chances.'

Mrs Smith said 'I knew something like this would happen when I was doing my charts.'

Mr Smith said 'She really believes all that stars rubbish.'

Mrs Smith said 'I believe what happens.'

I thought I might say – It is easier when you're drinking.

I managed to get through on the telephone to Father Watkin in London. It seemed to me that my plans, and requests, were hardly making sense: Father Watkin said 'Oh I expect that should work out all right.'

I said 'But who should I ask for at the shrine?'

He said 'Sister Bernardine. I'll give her warning.'

I said 'Does Sister Bernardine wear a blue uniform? I might have seen her on that hillside –'

He said 'No, she doesn't wear blue, she wears grey.'

Mr and Mrs Smith and I made a plan that we would go to the orphanage the next day and they would tell the superintendent that although they had collected a large sum of money for the lawyers and the child's grandmother, and so on, they had got fed up with the delay and had decided to give up the project – unless, of course, the superintendent could see a way by which they could take away their chosen child here and now. In this case, of course, the money would be available, and no questions asked. I said 'I don't know if this will work, but I can't think of anything better.'

We went out to the orphanage in the taxi of the driver who had taken the Minister and me to The Garden of Earthly Delights. I had made friends with this man, and he had attached himself to me for the time that I remained in his country. Mr and Mrs Smith and I went over our plans in the car. I told the driver that if we got the child away from the orphanage, I would ask him to drive us all the way to the village where there was the shrine. He turned to me with his yellow-toothed smile and said 'The Holy Mother no?' I said 'The Holy Mother yes.' He made the sign of the cross and the car nearly went off the road. Mrs Smith leaned forward and said 'You believe in the Holy Mother?' The driver made a gesture of drawing his finger across his throat. He said 'She say we all going to be blown up, no?'

The superintendent of the orphanage was a hard-faced woman whom I had not liked: she had not liked me the day before when I had wandered off on my own. I left Mr and Mrs Smith to talk with her and an interpreter in her office. I wandered off again now through the huge dormitory to the smaller room at the end. There was the child sitting up in its cot: but this time it was not looking at me, as if this might not be polite. I thought – Or perhaps it knows that all this does not really depend on me.

So – Come on, Mary, you can do your stuff about birth as well as about death.

After a time Mr and Mrs Smith and the superintendent and the interpreter appeared at the far end of the huge dormitory: they were arguing volubly. The superintendent was waving her arms; they had been joined by a short fat woman who seemed to be being briefed hurriedly by the interpreter and who then went to a cot and picked up one of the sickly-looking babies and held it out to Mrs Smith. Mrs Smith seemed to be undecided whether or not to take it: the short fat woman put the baby back in its cot and took up another baby and held it out to Mrs Smith. I had gone to the doorway between the two dormitories; I called out to Mr Smith 'What are they saying?' Mr Smith said 'They say we can have one of these babies, this is the grandmother, she seems to be the grandmother of all of them, we can have one if we pay the money now.' I said 'But why can't you have the one that you want?' The interpreter said 'The babies in that room are not possible.' I said 'Why not?' Mr Smith said 'Apparently those in that room are not ethnically correct.' I thought – Ethnically correct? You mean that child, although healthy, has been earmarked to die? Then – Oh yes, there was that massacre of the innocents, was there not! Mrs Smith was not taking in her arms the baby that was being held out to her. I said 'Just a minute.' I turned back to the smaller dormitory and saw that the wide-eyed child was now standing up and was holding onto the bars of its cot and was putting a foot up as if trying to get out. I thought – So we are going to play God after all, are we, you and I. I picked up the child and carried it through into the larger dormitory; it was turning its head to see where it was being taken in my arms. I said to Mrs Smith 'This is the child that you wanted, isn't it?' Mrs Smith said 'Yes.' The superintendent and the interpreter and the fat woman started talking all at once; the superintendent tried to take the child from me; I hung onto it: I thought – Oh come on, can we not defeat King Herod's soldiers? I noticed that my taxi-driver had come up the stairs to the doorway of the dormitory; he was carrying a shotgun over his shoulder; I had not seen him before with a gun. Mr Smith was holding out a wad of notes to the superintendent: he said 'Don't you just want the money?' The driver said 'Give me the money.' Mr Smith said 'Shall I?' I thought – How do I know? Then – I do owe him money. The taxi-driver took the money out of Mr Smith's hand; he peeled off a few notes and gave them to the superintendent; then he gave one each to the interpreter and the short fat woman. They all started talking and shouting and waving their arms: then the driver began talking at them and they all shut up. After a moment the superintendent stood aside as if to show us that we could go: the driver gave the short fat woman some more money and spoke to her and she put the sickly child she had been holding back in its cot. The driver put the rest of his money in his pocket. Then he signalled to Mr and Mrs Smith and me to follow him out of the door. I gave the child that I had been carrying to Mrs Smith, and it turned to her and put an arm round her neck. As we were going down the stairs the driver patted his pocket and said to me 'This will pay for the journey.' I said 'Yes.' He said 'But you do not come too: I will telephone a friend of mine to take you back to town.' I said 'Why do not I come too?' The driver said 'Because I have told them you will be going back to talk to your very important friend in town.' I thought – Who is my friend: you mean the man called Dungbird? Then – But now I will miss meeting that lady by the shrine! Oh well, there is always a cost. Mrs Smith said 'This is a miracle.' The driver said 'No miracle. I just told them that they do what you want double quick or their whole fucking place would be blown up.'

Twelve

Walking back through rain from Father Watkin's church to my home I was recollecting the story of the orphanage and the child. I had been reunited with my taxi-driver and he had told me how Mr and Mrs Smith had arrived at the village of the shrine; they had been looked after by a lady, Sister Bernardine or whoever, who wore either blue or grey. They had been seen onto a plane: they had survived. Jack had run the story quite prominently in the paper at home; this had helped to clear the way for the Smiths' adoption of the child. I had written the story in a style intended to encourage this outcome: I had made it a cloak-and-dagger affair in which ingenuity and determination had combined to rescue a life. I had left out much of what seemed to me to be the real story – of the complex interactions between attentiveness and chance. Jack had said – You can write your own story when you like. I had said – I don't know how to write about what is or is not chance.

I spoke on the telephone to Mr and Mrs Smith. I said I would come to the country to see the child. I never did. I thought – Perhaps things can't be dwelt on, even with gratitude, too much – if a story is to come out right.

Walking back through the rain I tried to remember what Father

Watkin and I had talked about or rather not quite talked – a world of possibilities spread through space and outside time: a world in which connections were made which in ordinary life appeared as chance, but on which attentiveness to the present might have an effect. This was a world believed in by visionaries and mystics and schizophrenics: how could one tell which were which? Perhaps one never did: this was what was implied by faith: certainly there seemed no virtue in talking about it too much.

But mad people did not feel wonder? or the desire to give gratitude for what otherwise might seem mad?

I was approaching the terrace above the canal where there was my home. Here three days ago I had seen Melissa as a gorgon above rooftops. She had spat at me; I had hit her; so I had gone to Cumbria and she had gone – wherever. But these had not been, after all, quite separate ways because – those who have been truly together are never entirely apart? This could be vertified? and so one was talking about the nature of the universe – or love?

Melissa was in the downstairs sitting-room of our house; she was smoking a cigarette, which she did not usually do: she was backing away as if the smoke were coming after her. I thought – She is trying to put up smokescreens: but I left her happy only such a short time ago! Never mind, we have seen this is a journey. I know almost nothing of what she has been doing these last three days; she knows almost nothing of what I have been doing. Things may not be able to be talked about but they have to be suffered, learned.

I said 'Where are Billy and Jenny, are they all right?'

She said 'They've gone to get Jenny's things.'

'Why, where are Jenny's things?'

'I thought you knew.'

I sat on the sofa. This was a room in which I never quite felt at home – where the family were supposed to come together in the evenings. I thought – But of course families never do quite stay together, except at those magical moments when there seems to be a breakthrough to or from that life behind the stage.

I said 'They told you?'

She said 'Look, you know how pleased I was to see you, but you know nothing of my life –'

'Then tell me –'

'But you never listen.'

'I'm listening now.'

I found myself adopting the attitude of someone quite painstakingly listening – an attitude by which, I knew, families can set about sending each other mad. I thought – But how does one stop?

Melissa said 'I know I said that Malcolm was suicidal. And so he was. But he'd also been trying to help me.'

After a time I said 'Do you need help?'

'I'd been going to this group, did you know?'

'No.'

'You see, you know nothing –'

'I've said I don't know!'

'Don't shout!'

'I'm not!'

I thought – All right, all right, we need help.

When I had been with Gaby in Cumbria she had told me of a story, a fairy story, she had been told by Peter, in which it was supposed that there were watchers from outer space who were trying to prevent humans from destroying themselves; they could not interfere directly because this would abrogate humans' freedom of choice which was somehow necessary for the correct functioning of the universe; but watchers could give them nudges –

Melissa was saying 'This group was run by a psychoanalyst who was experimenting with drugs. He asked for people who were interested as volunteers, and Malcolm took me along. Of course it was also true that Malcolm was after me.'

I had said I thought Peter's story a good story: also – You mean it might be useful to act as though it were true? Gaby had said – Oh true, how do we know what is true? I had thought – Well at least these watchers might be parts of ourselves.

Melissa said 'Don't you want me to tell you?'

I said 'Of course I do!'

'Anyway, I thought Billy was staying with the Armstrongs.'

It was true I was finding it difficult to listen to Melissa. Perhaps it would be easier if I just jumped up and started smashing the furniture. But then it did not seem to be the job of whatever might be watching to suggest that things should be easy –

Melissa said 'Oh I knew you'd be angry.'

I said 'I'm not angry!' Then – 'Or what does it matter if I am.'

'It doesn't?'

'No.'

I thought – No jealousy nor games we play with jealousy matter.
Then – But what does one do: recite some holy mantra?

Melissa said 'Well that evening, two nights ago, everything went
wrong. There was just me, Malcolm, this analyst, and a young man
who I thought must be the analyst's boyfriend. But I didn't know.'

I thought – Well come on, watchers, whoever you are, give us a
nudge –

– Mary Mother of God, start praying for us double quick, or it
seems we might be blown up?

Melissa said 'I was supposed to be the one looking after them. I
mean, not taking the drug. I mean, they were taking the drug. At
least they said they were. They were crawling around on all fours
making noises like animals. I found that I wanted them all dead –'

I said 'Well that was sensible –'

'You're not listening!'

'I am!'

There was a fax-machine in the corner of our sitting-room
which was used for messages sometimes for me and sometimes for
Melissa; also lately there had been messages in a strange code from
friends of Billy's. This machine was now giving its indications of
coming to life. I thought – Hi, watchers, here we are!

Melissa said 'Then sometime later the young man had disappeared. I was afraid he might have jumped out of the window.'

I said 'And had he?'

'I don't know.'

'Melissa, none of this matters.'

The fax-machine had embarked on its grinding noise as if in the
stages of a birth. I thought – And now out may come a message to
preserve the universe.

Melissa said 'What do you mean, none of this matters?'

I said 'It may do to you, but you're not really telling me what
happened. You're playing games – to defend yourself; to make me
feel jealous.' Then – 'And anyway, it's only a few feet from the
window to the terrace.'

'I didn't say it was in this house!'

'Oh didn't you? Then what —'

The fax-machine had come to the end of its birth; had died of exhaustion: it made its crunching noise as if a baby's head were being chopped off.

Melissa shouted 'All right it was!'

I thought — Now surely this is the chance for me to jump up and start striding around the room: then I can have a look at what has come through on the fax-machine.

I stood and walked up and down. I thought — But now I am playing games! But if I know this —

— I must not do it too frenetically, or Melissa may jump out of the window.

Melissa said 'Then Malcolm said that they hadn't really taken the drug after all, this was part of the experiment.'

I said 'What experiment —'

'To see what I would do.'

'Well what did you do —'

'Nothing.'

I thought I should say — Well now that's all, Melissa.

When I got close to the machine and glanced down I saw that there was more than one message on the holder; a previous message had come in earlier. The top message was in handwriting and seemed to be signed Janice, though this did not seem to be in Janice's writing —

Melissa said 'Then Malcolm said it was I who might have been given the drug —'

I said 'Melissa, for God's sake!'

'What —'

'Stop!'

It seemed that I could now take up the top piece of paper on the fax-machine and look at the piece of paper on the tray underneath; this had just one line of typing on it which said — Gaby will be arriving at 6.45 this evening — and then underneath this a line in Billy's writing — Dad I'll do this.

I said 'When did this come in?'

Melissa said 'Did you hear what I said?'

'Yes. Were you given a drug?'

'I don't think so.'

'Are you on drugs now?'

'No.'

'Then what does it matter.'

I was holding the two pieces of paper in my hands. I thought –
These are nudges, yes; they can turn us from what is happening –

– Can they tell us what we should be doing?

Melissa said 'I wanted to kill Malcolm.'

'I'm not surprised.'

'God I hate you.'

'Stop playing with drugs. Stop playing games. Stop going with
people like Malcolm.'

'You're never here –'

'I'm sorry. I'll try. But none of this boring stuff matters.'

'And anyway, what about Gaby.'

'I don't know about Gaby. I don't know if she's been abused, if
she makes things up, if she's radioactive, if she's seen the Virgin
Mary, if she's bumped off one of the Social Services people even.
None of this stuff matters.'

'Then what does?'

'That she's arriving at 6.45 at the station –'

'And Billy's gone to meet her.'

'Yes.'

I thought – So that is that then: all right, Melissa?

The first piece of paper which I held in my hand, and was in
writing that was strange to me, said – I am writing this in clear so
that no one will understand it. Janice and Charlie have come to
London and would like to meet you in The Sailing Junk after
seven. They have something important to say to you. The next part
of this message is in code. Love from Janice.

I thought – But this is not from Janice: it is from Ellen?

I said to Melissa 'How much do you know about this place
where Billy and Jenny have been staying?'

Melissa said 'It's run by one of the masters. They've stayed there
before. He takes them sailing.'

'Have you been there?'

'No.' Then – 'Oh I know I shouldn't have let them go on their
own to the station! But I wanted to be here when you got back.'

She had put her head in her hands. I thought – She is acting? she is not acting if she knows she is acting –

– Perhaps we can talk about things sensibly again now.

I said 'And have you seen Malcolm? Where is he now?'

'He had to go to the hospital. I did say I'd see him.'

'You're sure this drug didn't hurt you?'

'Malcolm said you were quite right about the scare in Cumbria. It had nothing to do with what they were saying it was.'

'What was it then –'

'He said those children were being used as guinea-pigs.'

'Malcolm knew?'

'I suppose he wanted to show off.'

I was thinking – But if Billy had gone to the station, or has gone to pick up Jenny's things, then they still might not want to come back here if they think Melissa and I are quarrelling; or indeed on some nonsense with drugs –

Melissa said 'Do you think I shouldn't mind when you go away? When I know you are with Janice?'

I said 'No, I think you should.'

'But you think that doesn't matter –'

'Oh yes that matters. We should just stop.'

'Have you stopped with Janice?'

'Yes.' Then – 'What else did Malcolm say –'

I thought – Perhaps children are some sort of watchers; or attentiveness to children; or just the children in ourselves that can still look down on our demented grown-up world as if through the banisters of a landing –

Melissa said 'He says that anyway the authorities are now doing something –'

'About what –'

'The children.'

'What children?'

'Aren't they going to some special school or something?'

'The triplets? Malcolm knew about the triplets?'

'He admitted you might have had something to do with it –'

'Me?'

'By butting in. I thought it might be something to do with that woman in Yugoslavia.'

'What woman –'

'The one you met in a nightclub. Didn't she have children?'

I put a hand over my heart. I thought – Melissa! Melissa! Then –
All right, all you watchers who have been bursting to come on
stage: you have done enough; now you just stop!

– Or you mean: it really might have had something to do with
that red-haired woman?

Melissa said 'Or perhaps I have got it wrong, I usually do.' Then
– 'All right, I don't care what you got up to with anyone, or that
woman!'

I thought – But I didn't get up to anything with that woman!
You mean, because she didn't come to the hotel? Then – Oh for
goodness' sake, let's get back on stage –

I said 'This fax is from Janice. At least it says it's from Janice.
They want me to meet them at The Sailing Junk.'

'Yes I know.'

'How do you know?'

'Someone called Charlie rang.'

I thought – We may never again wholly be able to get back on-
stage.

I said 'Charlie's the man Janice went to see in Cumbria when I
thought she might have wanted to be going with me.'

Melissa said 'This young man I was telling you about, he was
someone who told me to stop playing games, you know, even
before you.'

I thought – What young man? Oh that young man –

Then – But I don't want to regret, do I, not doing anything with
that woman in Yugoslavia.

I said 'Do you have to go to the hospital? I think I'd better go to
The Sailing Junk.'

'No, I've been to the hospital. But I think I should go and see if
Billy and Jenny are all right at the station.'

'Yes you do that.'

'Couldn't you come too? No, you needn't. Perhaps it would be
better if I meet this Gaby on my own?'

We seemed to be quite steady with one foot on and one foot off
stage: to be on a knife-edge; a correct position. Melissa was looking

very beautiful. I thought – If we were wholly on stage, perhaps at this moment we would go upstairs to make love.

I said 'I want to make love.'

She said 'I do want another baby.'

'Then why not –'

'The timing should be right.'

Melissa came and put a hand up to my face. A hot wind seemed to go through me. I thought – By the timing, you mean what Mrs Smith called her charts?

She said 'Jack says that you want to go out again to Yugoslavia.'

I said 'You might come with me.'

She said 'Oh no, by that time we should have got the timing right.'

On my way to The Sailing Junk I was thinking – But how can I possibly live like this: wandering across plains and over mountains taking direction from the stars; carrying with me on a handcart my own portable stage, props, backcloth, box of tricks; picking occasional travelling companions: but part of myself watching as if from where – the stars? the branches of a tree? – together with my wife Melissa, saying – That was not much of a performance last night, do you think? But what a wonder, that on our journey we can watch from that tree!

In The Sailing Junk there was the later evening crowd – the one getting down to serious drinking. The noise of chatter that was like machinery had risen to such a pitch that it seemed reasonable to look round to see what might be produced – something moulded, spun, by the end of the day – was it conceivable that there should be nothing? As a watcher should I not ask – How is it that the fate of the universe might depend on such a mob: in the face of the rush to perdition, what are the chances for humans to become like gods? In The Sailing Junk it was as if the uproar were producing pollution – the rain on that dark lake, the smoke that Melissa backed away from as if devils were coming after her, the clamour that was knocking a hole in the roof of our minds through which we might drift away – but not to heaven. Janice and Charlie were at a table on the covered terrace. Here the noise was less intense: it might even give cover for watchers, for agents, to pass on messages. I said

'Hullo Janice, hullo Charlie.' Janice said 'Charlie has something important to tell you.' I said 'I know.' She said 'What do you know?' I said 'That Charlie has something important to tell me.'

I sat at their table. I thought – I am setting up my portable stage beneath this tree: what is the performance tonight, children?

Janice said 'There really was a scare. We were quite right to take precautions. But in fact it wasn't coming from where we thought it was.'

Charlie said 'I never thought it was.'

I said 'Yes I know.'

Janice said 'Why do you keep saying that you know?'

I said 'Malcolm told Melissa.'

Janice was sitting with her fingers round the stem of a glass; it was as if she might be prepared to throw it in someone's face. I thought – Oh but this is a comedy! I have seen something like it before. People do it to cover up what is going on off-stage.

Charlie said 'They know what direction it's coming from, but they don't know exactly where. But then there's Mr Kempinski –'

I said 'Mr Kempinski from Yugoslavia –'

Charlie said 'Yes.'

Janice said 'I didn't know there'd be a scare.'

I said 'When did you two first meet?'

Charlie smiled as if he was pleased with what I had said. Janice stared down at the bubbles in her glass.

Charlie said 'When I got back from Bosnia.'

I said 'You were in Bosnia?'

'Yes.'

Janice said 'You must have read about it. He was quite a *cause célèbre*.'

I thought – One searches for one's lines: what is a prompter, except a nudger just off-stage?

Charlie said 'Have you rung up Ellen?'

I said 'Not yet.'

'She sent you a fax –'

'I got two. They were both from her?'

'She wanted to talk to you.'

Janice said 'Is that what you two want to talk about?'

I thought – But Janice has always seemed to be a slightly different play. She was looking away to the main part of the bar.

I said to Charlie 'Is that man Fred Ellen's father?'

Charlie said 'No.'

'Who is then?'

'I think Mrs Ferguson's husband.'

'And what happened to him?'

'He shot Mrs Ferguson.'

'Is that why she's in a wheelchair?'

'Yes.'

I noticed that Malcolm had come into the bar. He had some sort of plastic support round his neck. I thought – It was he who jumped out of the window?

I said 'Why didn't Mrs Ferguson shoot him instead of him shooting her, if he's Ellen's father?'

Charlie said 'I think he was trying to shoot himself.'

'I see.'

Janice said 'Look, there's Malcolm!'

I thought – We are not getting this quite right: though it is interesting, isn't it, like the stuff one sees on television.

I said to Charlie 'You didn't want to stay with Ellen?'

He said 'No, I think she only ever wanted to make him jealous.'

'Who?'

'You don't know?'

I thought – Peter?

Then – These are all nudges. But I am still not sure just what I have to do.

Malcolm, at the bar, seemed to be deliberately avoiding looking at us: Janice was now avoiding looking at Malcolm. I thought – You mean, what have I come here for? I should have gone with Melissa and the children?

I said 'You mean Peter.'

Charlie said 'Yes.'

'That's what she wanted to talk to me about?'

Janice said 'I should have thought you would have been more interested in talking about Melissa.'

I set off round the back of the covered terraced on a route by which I thought I would avoid Malcolm. I was going to the telephone. The telephone was on a ledge by the Gents' lavatory. I dialled my home, but there was no answer. I dialled the number of the hotel in Cumbria. I stared at the woodwork. I thought – You nudge and are nudged: there is a knock-on effect like that from an albatross's wingbeat. I thought – I have nothing really to do here: except to find out what I should be doing. Then – But is this what for the last three days we have been doing for one another? I said 'Ellen?' She said 'Yes.' I thought – But I did adore her!

Ellen said 'I've been trying to get hold of you but I've only been able to get hold of your wife.'

'What was she like?'

'She was pleasant.'

'Ellen –'

'Yes.'

'Are you really Mr Ferguson's daughter?'

'And Mrs Ferguson's step-daughter –'

'So Peter's your half-brother –'

'Yes.'

'But that doesn't matter –'

'No. He used to think it did.'

'But he doesn't now –'

'No.'

'What changed it –'

'I wanted to tell you –'

'What –'

'Why I made use of you –'

'Why –'

'I adored you.'

I rested my head against the woodwork. I thought – The images go down like the patterns on Mrs Ferguson's screen; to ever greater and more beautiful levels of complexity.

I said 'Where's Peter now?'

Ellen said 'He's here, do you want to talk to him?'

'No. What about –'

'He took those tapes.'

'Oh I see.'

I banged my head slightly against the woodwork. I thought – I do think I see? Then – I might be able to have a look at them in the evenings.

Ellen said 'He was confused. Can you blame him –'

I said 'No.'

'I don't know who my mother was. I think that's grander than not knowing who one's father is, don't you think?'

I thought – I have been sitting too long in this tree.

I said 'But Peter and you are all right now –'

'Yes. After you've come up here sorting us all out like some great bird –'

I shouted 'Ellen!'

'Yes?'

'It's you who've sorted out me.'

There was silence for a time. Then she said 'Then that's the best, isn't it, in the best of all possible worlds.' She rang off.

I thought – Well here we are then. Where? I'd better go back to the table.

Malcolm had joined Charlie and Janice. Malcolm did not look at me. It seemed he might have difficulty in turning his neck.

Charlie was saying 'It's a situation in which indeed anything can happen. How can anyone begin to know what in fact is going on? There are certain reports from certain people, certain readings on certain instruments, but that's because those particular people and instruments were at a certain place at a certain time. People can make of these what they like. No one has any means of knowing the connections –'

Janice said to me 'We're talking of Bosnia.'

Malcolm said as if to no one in particular – 'What did you think we were talking about?'

Janice said 'Malcolm is upset because I let him think I was going away with you.'

Charlie said 'Apparently he wouldn't have minded if it was me.'

Malcolm said 'It wasn't that, it was Melissa.'

I said 'Oh I see.'

Malcolm was dabbing at his clothes. It seemed that Janice might have thrown her glass of wine at him. I was trying to remember why I had not gone with Melissa to the station. I thought I might say to Charlie – Could Peter have been evil?

I said 'How well did you know Peter?'

Charlie said 'Not well.'

I said 'He took a film –'

Charlie said 'Oh I thought that was the Social Services people.'

Janice said 'There's a film of Charlie in Bosnia.'

Malcolm said to me 'Is Melissa all right?'

Charlie said 'I never had much to do with the children.'

I said 'They had that hold over the Social Services people?'

I thought – It is not evil, the use that you can make of evil –

Then – I must know if Billy and Jenny have got back from the station.

Malcolm was saying to Janice 'I'd like to see that film.'

Janice was saying 'The point is, no one's seeing it.'

Charlie said 'What film are we talking about?'

I said 'Just a minute.'

I set off round the back of the terrace again to the telephone. I dialled the number of my home. There was still no answer. I listened to the tone on the answering-machine. I thought – But I have no message: I am learning.

I dialled Mrs Ferguson's number in Cumbria. Mrs Ferguson answered. I said 'I was trying to ring my home, but there's no answer. So I thought I'd ring you.'

She said 'Hasn't Gaby arrived yet?'

'My son and wife have gone to meet her at the station.'

'She may not want to come to you.'

'Why not?'

'Though I think she trusts you –'

'And she trusted Peter –'

'I didn't know about her and Peter.'

'But that was all right –'

'I didn't want him to see Ellen.'

'But now you don't mind?'

'No.'

'So that's how it's worked out.'

Somewhere floating beyond the woodwork in front of my eyes was the vision of Gaby and myself in the cornfield: from there I had had a vision of myself with the lady in blue by a stream. I thought –

One learns that these are connections; one waits for what these are to turn up.

I said 'Look, I'd better see if they've got back from the station.'

'Yes, you do that.' Then – 'What was that place that Gaby talked about in London?'

'I didn't know Gaby talked about anywhere in London.'

'Yes, she spoke to your son.'

'She did?'

'Yes.'

'Where?' I thought – You mean, they might have talked about that place by the canal?

I said 'Thank you.'

'What for –'

'For being so good to us.'

She rang off.

I was staring at the woodwork. There was nothing to see in the woodwork. I thought – It's not possible that there really might be watchers from outer space?

I went back round the terrace to our table. Malcolm had gone. I thought – But he was not wholly in someone else's story. Janice seemed to be waiting for me. She said 'I think you ought to write Charlie's story about Bosnia.'

Charlie said 'I don't want anyone to write my story about Bosnia.'

I had been intending to say – Look, I must be going.

Janice said 'It is important that people should know.'

Charlie said 'The point is that people should not know.'

I sat down at the table. I thought – All right, all right: nudges might go down to even further levels of connection.

I said 'When were you in Bosnia?'

Janice said: 'He was asked to be present at the killing of some hostages.'

Charlie said 'I chose to be present at the killing of some hostages.'

I thought I might say – Do you know a place called Brodcic? It's somewhere in the hills –

Janice said 'They had arranged a photo opportunity for the shooting of these hostages –'

Charlie said 'For the delight and doubtless profit of people both on the spot and at home.'

I thought – You mean, to show contempt for people? This is a story about the observer and the thing observed?

Janice said 'The hostages were to be shot one by one in front of cameras. So what were the people behind the cameras going to do –'

I thought – You mean, what was Charlie, or what are we, going to do?

Janice said: 'It might have escalated the war, or it might have brought it home to people –'

I said 'What –'

Charlie said 'Was I right?'

Janice said 'Charlie said: For every hostage that is shot, I will shoot one of your men.'

I said 'And so you did?'

Janice said 'But Charlie won't say what happened then.'

Charlie said 'Charlie says it might not have happened if he says what happened then.'

I said 'Look, I've got to go to the station –'

Charlie said 'Yes, you do that.'

'Do you know a place called Brodcic?'

'I don't think so, no.'

'Look, what you did must have been right –'

Charlie said 'How –'

Janice said 'Jack says you want to go out again to Bosnia –'

Charlie said 'I'll give you some addresses.'

I said 'You survived.'

Thirteen

Before I left The Sailing Junk I tried to telephone again to my home. There was still no answer. The tone on the machine was like a summons to a journey.

I had not talked to Melissa about what to do if the children were not at the station and had not come home. It seemed reasonable (though what had things in this area to do with reason) that I should go home by way of the lock-keeper's cottage – where Jenny might have gone to collect her things; where the children might have chosen to go anyway; which was the place (this was the nudge) that Mrs Ferguson was surely referring to on the telephone?

But impressions might still come in and out of one's head at random. The summons was – Are you listening?

It was by now getting dark. These three days had been amongst the longest of the year. Perhaps in darkness there would be the chance for things to settle down and happen in due order: one would no longer be dazzled by the bright lights on a stage.

I could run through streets to the steps down to the towpath; jump on a bus, jump off again. Underneath my feet the world would turn: I might look down from my tree on events as if they could be captured like the captions to a film –

— Adam, having caught that old Dad walking naked in the garden, takes his clothes so that he can move unobserved into the outside world —

How steady the streets were! everything holding to its expected groove. We cannot see to the backs of walls and houses; what an opportunity to make what we cannot see! There is nothing beyond the speed of light? What of darkness —

— The traveller, finding himself at the edge of the known world, sees that the light pervading everywhere is darkness —

I was coming to a bridge beyond which there were steps down to the towpath. At night the gates to the steps would be locked. I had climbed over these gates at night once before: I had felt myself somewhat daring — encroaching on a forbidden zone of muggers and robbers and fantasies. I had not gone far: just enough for me to think now — This is indeed a mythological world: there are the shapes of possibilities in darkness.

The gate was set back from the road beyond a patch of grass. There was a street-lamp overhead which was not working. A body was slumped or impaled across the metalwork at the top of the gates; at least I assumed it was a body — of some intrepid but star-struck traveller who had tried to go faster than the speed of light? Or perhaps it was a shield, or cushion, by which I could climb over: did not bodies pile up at the edge of a stage? So that the angel's flaming sword might become fused, confused —

I could climb upon these images: it was to myself I was talking?

When I got closer I saw that the body was that of a woman. She was half-way over the gate; she was caught, collapsed; a leg waved back from a white exposed thigh like a flag or a token of surrender: was not this a chance for which men dreamed —

I said — 'Melissa?'

— The watcher, having travelled in the realm of darkness, finds that he is back at the gate of the garden and he can see that his wife has got there first —

When I got close enough to see more of the situation it was the fact, yes, that the woman was Melissa: and should I be surprised? I knew those thighs, that darkness! and had I not wondered, half known, that she might be coming this way? For having gone to the station — having not even got as far as the station — would she not have had her own intimations that the children might come this way? I need not say — What on earth are you doing here? What on earth was anyone doing anywhere: why is it that some things are, and others not. I went up to Melissa and put an arm around her; I tried to lift her off, or over, the metalwork at the top of the fence. She did not say — What are you doing here? She would have known what I was doing there —

> — *The exiled couple, having learned to get the timing right, find that they can help each other into the forbidden zone —*

I heaved at Melissa and she slithered down at the far side of the gate; she stood at the top of the steps to the towpath and brushed at her clothes. I stood back and put a hand on top of the wire and then went sailing over like a bird. Melissa watched me. I thought — It is not necessary, quite, to believe this: what you have to do is watch. When I was beside Melissa I put an arm round her and she laid her head on my shoulder. We did not talk. Words were like bodies piled up against the wire. Somewhat awkwardly, we moved down the steps towards the canal.

There were patches of yellow sky from the lights of the city. The water of the canal was black and silver. Behind us was the area which had been made desolate by abandonment and disuse; things crumbled around and within a forbidden zone. A few roads went over bridges to the north: the canal ran underneath them as if it were a vein. Melissa and I reached the towpath and we looked down at the water. *Together the betrayed couple reach what might be their inheritance.*

We walked hand in hand along the towpath. I was taking Melissa to where I had been before: perhaps she was taking me to where she had been before — at least, in the imagination? All my life I had been haunted by an image, a story, which was that of a serene couple walking hand in hand on a beach while just beyond them, to one side of them, was a temple in which hags were dismembering a child; and it was in the light, the shadow, of this temple that the couple were so together and so serene. Occasionally and increasingly in my life I had thought – But what is it to be so serene? the couple can split up, come together, can't they? can take a closer look at the temple with the hags and the child. Then might they not see that all these have been parts of themselves – the hags and the serenity and the temple and the child. When I had been on the towpath before at night there had been one or two loving couples; they were wrapped round one another; trying to climb into one another; were they not like hags in a temple? And so what might their beautiful children be doing – going fishing from a beach?

Melissa and I were coming to a long stretch of the canal where there was a turning: it was here where you walked and things did not seem to get any closer or further away. But you learn – something is (or is not) being built in quite a different dimension. For how many years had Melissa and I been walking: sometimes we were closer and sometimes further away: but step by step – what might there be – a tower up to heaven? You place a stone here, some earth there – it is hardly yourself that keeps one stone on top of another: the thing is held together by – gravity? Gravity is not light; it has no speed. It is the darkness in which light travels?

We were coming to the end of the long straight path by the canal. Somewhere round the corner, on the other side of the water, there would be the large brick building which the children had been rebuilding inside their garden: but what had they been building it for – not just to demonstrate the miracle of one brick remaining on top of another. But this was the place that others wanted to take over – grown-ups – and so the children had let them? The building was squat, ungainly: it was like some prison: I thought – And so the children might entrap them?

We could hear the sound of drumming even before we got to the bend in the canal: it was the sound of a heartbeat by which an unborn baby is enclosed: before it is freed by the angel with the flaming sword. As Melissa and I came to the bend in the canal we could see the bare brick building ahead of us across the water; it was like a frog that might once have been a prince or princess: a mutant that had been pissed on instead of kissed. It was from this building that there was coming the sound of drumming. The building itself might be the membrane of a throat: as if the frog might be preparing to spit out poison – to effect some further metamorphosis? There were chinks of light coming through cracks in the boarded-up windows: or it was as if the building might be on fire, with the walls too hard, like those of a crystal, for any new life to break out. Melissa and I had stopped on the towpath. It seemed, yes, that we might be approaching some mythical apocalypse; or hell.

In the painting of *The Garden of Earthly Delights* the people in heaven had seemed more attentive than serene: and those in hell whom they might be watching – those being consumed or violated – had appeared simply bored.

The large brick building pulsated like a cell: it seemed of a hostile order to that which was around it. There are cancer cells like this: they proliferate, explode: there is no mechanism to tell them when to stop; they produce chaos and ruin around them by insisting on just their own form of order. I thought – This is a mutation that has flourished outside the garden: back in the garden one might assimilate, make use of it; might even tell it to stop?

Melissa was taking her hand away from my own. It was as if she were drawing a weapon from a sheath: not a sword? might one not yet see what better job could be done? You wish to cut out that which can kill you: but if you cut out that which has grown so naturally, then indeed the whole body may still die: what right to life or death has one part more than another? Such cells, configurations, are inside us, part of us; they proliferate, yes: but if you watch them, with care, then might their life be not simply their own and so their loneliness die? To the hags and the child could one not say – Go on, good luck, do your worst – if one said this to oneself? And then walk on along the beach to the sea; and see what died. Melissa and I walked on. We were coming to where the canal opened out by the lock-gates. The noise that was coming from the bare and boarded-up brick building at the other side of the canal was evidently that of some party in progress – one of those parties that occurred from time to time in this part of London – in buildings on bare and desolate ground so that there might be no restraint on the drumming – or the violence. And the drugs? It was these that were like a cancer? and could one say so what – with bodies writhing in that happy profusion that could indeed be seen as hell. But then – why not? If there was a pattern. Occasionally there was a cry – of indignity or triumph. Melissa said something under her breath: or perhaps she was just letting her breath in and out more carefully. I thought – But you have to make a choice which way you yourself will be going.

For the first time since we had been on the towpath I looked at Melissa; until now it had seemed so necessary to watch and listen where we were going. Melissa had the sad, attentive look on her face of – what – a mother and child in a painting? And someone who would know about perdition. It seemed that I should go on my own across the lock-gates to the lock-keeper's cottage: I could say to Melissa – Look, you have done enough; you must stay now and rest. There was the half-dismantled barrier I had scrambled round that morning. Melissa sat on the beam or arm that controlled the lock-gates: I thought – But do not use your power to open the gates and let life-blood drain away! there can be learning. I stepped onto the narrow walkway at the top of the gates. There was the piled-up refuse on one side and the drop on the other; more refuse swirled at the lower level onto which water splashed lethargically. I thought – All right, this is in the outside world and in the mind: I will be crossing.

The lock-keeper's cottage was in darkness. A hedge made it difficult to see through to the ornamental garden. The noise that was coming from the gaunt brick building was just of drumming; there was no music. It seemed – music might divert non-attention? The door of the cottage was ajar; but why was this in darkness; there were plastic bags and a suitcase lined up outside the door. I had seen these this morning; I had seen them – where – in the barn in Cumbria: but then I should not feel fear? I was clambering round the obstacle half-way across the lock-gates; my fear could perhaps be of falling: but I then might hide within the refuse onto which the water splashed. In the strangeness of meeting Melissa I had not dwelt upon what we had exactly come here to do: to find the children? but those plastic bags outside the cottage door – they could be belongings of victims? I stepped onto the ground in front of the lock-keeper's cottage: how on earth was it I had tried to explain the dismemberment in the temple: there was no need for fear? I turned along the path towards the ornamental garden. Here were the paths bordered by stones and wooden platforms beside ponds; the land rose gently from the bank of the canal so that water could run down through a garden of rather barren rocks. The garden had in fact always seemed somewhat unfinished: order had been made out of chaos but to what end – did not life require some observation; consciousness? Now, in the yellowing light of a far-away city that might be burning, from what seemed to be flickering fires within the boarded-up building, it appeared that there had, yes, been added some dimension to the garden; some form to give it life: there were figures dotted about here and there like statues or indeed as if they might be members of an audience. They were observing the gaunt and pulsating brick building: they sat attentively with their arms round their knees: I realised that they were children. They were like those watchers and listeners on the side of a hill – I mean that hill where stones had been made smooth by pilgrims with bare feet or on their knees – or they might be that young couple watching from a hillside the children themselves in the farm buildings – or like that lady who watched and walked away when bodies were being disinterred from graves. I was, of course, looking for Billy and Jenny: and Gaby? Why should I not be looking for Gaby: when there had been so much to get us here. Billy, was, yes, amongst the children; he was sitting on his own, on a rock, or on what might be a haversack or suitcase: his feet were on one of the pathways that went down towards the building. Had he seen me: he might not have seen me: he was making it easier for me to see what I would do? But it was as if we all knew what we would do – I went and stood by Billy and with him watched the gaunt brick building. It was as if we, myself and Billy and the other children, formed some precise pattern, representation, in the half-darkness; some notation like that of music, the unheard music, that might give resonance, shape, to the trapped drumming that came from the prison-like building. Two of the children had gone right up to the wall of the building and were looking through what seemed to be a crack in one of the boarded-up windows; another two children stood in an open space behind them as if awaiting their turn to see inside. But what was it that there might be inside – the unholy of holies where hags had their dream of dismembering a child? Or had there indeed been some mutation, assimilation – not so much within the cancerous cell as from what might be made of it from that which observed. Melissa had come to the edge of the ornamental garden; she would have followed me across the lock-gates; I wondered if she would see us; of course she did. I thought I would put a finger to my lips: but she would recognise the unheard music. I noticed that none of us cast shadows in this strange darkness and light: it was as if what caused shadows were all trapped within the building. The two children who had been standing at the crack in the window were moving away; they were coming towards me and Billy: I saw that they were Gaby and Jenny. Melissa had come up beside me and when Gaby and Jenny saw us they stopped and smiled. I thought – Hullo, Gaby. Billy was watching the building. Gaby and Jenny waited for a while and then made gestures which seemed to invite Melissa and me to take what had been their place at the crack in the boarded-up window. The two children who had been in line behind them were also standing aside: I thought – It is as if they knew Melissa and I might be here? I looked at Billy; but I thought – He will know we have to be doing this on our own. I felt for Melissa's hand: I found it: the two children who had been waiting in front of us had sat down. Melissa and I went down the path towards the building. I thought – Now laugh, we must laugh: Melissa and I will ourselves be absurd as we lean to look throught the crack in the window.

Within the enclosed space of the barn-like building was a scene which might indeed have been a contemporary theme-park representation of hell – not one such as that of the painting of *The Garden of Earthly Delights* because that was a somnolent, dream-like version of hell; nor even that of one of the currently fashionable dungeon-museums in which ancient horrors are set out in fetching dinginess and shadow. This was an energetic, practical, working vision of hell where the inmates were going about their business with application and gusto. It was perhaps more like the nightclub of The Garden of Earthly Delights but here with everything spot-lit and exposed that might be the pleasures of war. There were both men and women, mostly naked, some in what might have seemed to be fancy-dress – masks and chains and bits of leather like loosely fitting skin – in pairs and groups conscientiously ministering to one another's needs: like teachers, like nurses; like workers functioning efficiently on a factory-floor: whose *raison-d'être* and indeed whose product were special requirements of human nature – in full recognition of the moral injunction that one should only do to others what one might like to have done to oneself. Nearest to us was a man being nailed to a block of wood; he was watching attentively while a nail was driven through his scrotum; it was as if he might be saying – Just a little higher, or more to the left, do you think? and then I will know just where I am, I will be tethered, I will not be blown here and there by every passing wind. The person ministering to him was a woman, also naked, except for a belt from which hung carpenters' tools; these were like dugs from which the needy might feed. At some distance was the body of a woman (or man? I couldn't tell) tied face-down to a sloping trestle with hands and feet spread; he or she had a large and slightly dented behind; beside this was a figure dressed as a chef; he was heating up an implement on a small electric grill. The man (or woman) on the trestle was looking over a shoulder expectantly like someone at a table taking care that a steak of his choice should be properly done; the steak, presumably, was his or her behind. There was a stove in the centre of the room giving off red and purplish smoke: the atmosphere was such that it must have been difficult to breathe – but the point would be, wouldn't it, to make it difficult to breathe – was it not then that you saw devils; or angels? The drumming was coming from two huge speakers that were, yes, like a devil's elongated ears: a devil does not listen; he simply gives out noise? There were further scenes, tableaux, on which, as if with a surfeit of too rich and exotic sweets, the mind or stomach might not want too much to dwell – a figure on its back with its legs in the air having something pushed up its behind (not a fish? a doll? there really are these images?); someone lifting a skirt as if above a lavatory in order to straddle a face – oh yes, we know all this: but do we? do we not rather keep it in some dungeon theme-park of the mind, where it rots and festers? And then it comes out in war; in the burying alive of women and children? There were not many whips; I thought – It is too conventional to have whips! From the surfeit of what I was seeing I began to dream – This is something at the heart of humans, all right: but is not this also what has enabled humans to survive – this terrible ability of fragile creatures to suffer hardship, pain; the necessary satisfaction in such endurance. Or how would they have survived? And for this has it also been necessary to afflict others – can this be admitted? If we are to stay alive, I mean, is it conceivable that this sort of thing should be denied? But if you observe it, know it and remember it, was it not this that a god taught us by coming down? Had not this god felt guilty: said – Sorry if I've landed you in this; but what else could I do? and you do it to me: and so now you can be like gods coming down. I mean, if you see this, know it, you can watch it as it goes on in the mind; and gods and you can be kind to each other, and let it go? I had also been wondering – But what on earth do Billy and Jenny and Gaby and the rest make of all this? Then – But it is just this that Billy and Gaby and the rest are making of it – they have seen what human nature is, and are learning how to live with it and get over it. And they are the generation of children of this world who are wiser than the children of light.

I could feel Melissa growing restless beside me. There was a man in a cooking pot with just a hole in the lid for his head: a woman had hooks through her nipples from which weights hung as on a pair of scales. I thought I might say to Melissa – Oh but let's just wait to see that person being branded on the behind! the instrument is nearly ready; the waiters are gathering round the table: we may not see such a presentation again. The branding, when it came, made a slight sizzling sight; no sound could be heard above the drumming. The figure being waited upon threw its head back wide-mouthed as if indeed it might have seen angels.

I stepped back from the window: Melissa had already stepped back. She did not look at me or try to take me by the hand. I thought – Well, this is quite practical, this operation on the human heart. Melissa and I walked up the path to where Billy and now Jenny and Gaby were sitting. The two children who had made way for us were now taking our places at the window. I thought – And from this cell, children might go out into the world? Billy was standing up. He took hold of the suitcase on which he had been sitting. I thought I recognised it as the one that had been in the back of my car in Cumbria. I thought – Oh Gaby, Gaby, in what other world, in what seed-pod, did I know you?

Gaby and Jenny set off along the path towards the lock-keeper's cottage. Billy waited till Melissa and I had joined him; it seemed that he wanted us to know he would look after us. We set off after Gaby and Jenny; Billy followed; we came to the exit of the garden by the cottage, and Jenny went and picked up one of the plastic bags. There was a path across wasteland to a road at this side of the canal. I thought that this was the way by which the children would have come and might be going now; the road came from the station. But Jenny and Gaby started down a path that I had not been along before, which ran parallel to the water and away from the garden but on the same side of the canal. Then suddenly a flare like a firework went up from the direction of the road across the wasteland: I turned to watch this: it was an alarm? a warning? Then almost immediately there were children running past us from the direction of the garden; we stepped aside to let them pass. They were keeping clear of the wasteland; they did not seem to be crossing the lock-gates; it was as if they knew where there might be danger for them. Gaby and Jenny waited till the children had gone past, then we followed them along the path at this side of the canal. This path led through undergrowth; there was an occasional glimpse of water, then it curled down towards the canal. I remembered this place; I had noticed it on my walks on the far side of the canal; it was where the children kept their canoes, drawn up on the bank by a small quayside. The children who had got there ahead of us were launching canoes; they were pausing to listen; there was the sound of a police-car siren from the direction of the road. I realised that the sound of drumming had ceased. The children in their canoes were sliding away on the canal. Melissa and Billy and Jenny and Gaby and I were in our group at the quayside.

Billy and Jenny went to a half-hidden boathouse and were manipulating the door with a piece of wood; they disappeared inside, leaving Melissa and Gaby and I on the bank. Melissa and Gaby were in some communication with one another, it was as if they did not have to say – Hullo, hullo, I don't think we've met? but of course we know each other, don't we. Billy and Jenny appeared from the far end of the boathouse in a small rowing-boat which they manoeuvred to the quayside; Billy climbed out and held it for Melissa and Gaby and me to get in. But it did not seem possible for us all to get in, it was like one of those coracles or cockleshells in which saints and missionaries used to travel across uncharted seas. I thought – But they didn't sink; or did they? Gaby was handing to Jenny in the boat the plastic bag and suitcase: Billy was holding his hand out to Melissa. Melissa climbed in and Jenny moved over to the far side of the boat to balance it; Billy guided Melissa to the prow and Jenny sat on the back seat. Gaby was holding the side of the boat and was stretching her hand out to me: I thought – We have got where we want, Gaby. I stepped in and settled on the seat in the middle: it was, yes, as if there might just be room for one in the front and two in the middle and two on the seat at the back: but the balance would have to be kept very precisely; the water was already nearly up to the boat's rim. I thought – But it is always touch and go, isn't it: with life (can I not say this?) or what is called death. There were sounds of banging and shouting from where we had come; an impression of pursuers and their quarry. I thought – But that too is what they have chosen! Gaby and Billy were pushing off. There was a moment when they were each on one knee at the sides of the boat like the wings of some great bird; then they folded themselves carefully into the boat – Billy to sit by me in the middle, Gaby to join Jenny at the back. We had floated into the middle of the canal; we were heading away from the lock-gates. Jenny and Billy were lifting oars from the bottom of the boat, one of which Jenny handed to me. I took it and fitted it into the rowlock. Billy and I rowed gently. We were heading in the direction in which I used to walk home along the towpath in the evening. I had never before seen any rowing-boats on the canal; how was it that the canal was so seldom used; it seemed to be waiting?

It was indeed as if our boat was like a shell or a cell precariously making its way along a canal in order to form – what – some new brain, liver, heartbeat? Naturally on such a journey it would be vulnerable and somewhat absurd; with the likelihood at any moment of capsizing. The towpath was on one side and the wasteland on the other: on either of these there might be dangers: how had we come here – by means of what butterfly's wingbeat far out in the ocean or jungle? Or where were we going: but this do we ever know? What we do is just balance the boat so carefully; so we survive wherever we are going. Billy and I were rowing so carefully, hardly making any disturbance on the surface of the water. We seemed to be going along with the water, we were so gently rowing. I could not see Melissa behind me in the prow; she might have that look on her face as if spray were beating into her – but attentive, gratified, like that mother with her children. Jenny and Gaby were facing Billy and me so close that our knees were almost touching; I thought – You mean, Gaby and Billy might in fact have come across each other before in that garden? but I did know you, oh my daughter! Behind us the gaunt brick building was now out of sound and out of sight: there were just a few sparks or stars from another flare that had gone up. We were going under a bridge; this was like the wings of an enormous bird to cover us.

It had seemed we might have set out to row the whole way to our home, but there was a tunnel in this direction some way along the canal through which there was no towpath and at the entrance to which there was a notice saying that it was forbidden for any boats except powered boats to go through. It was here that on my walks I had had to leave the canal; but the children in their canoes must be already on their way through, and they would be going where pursuers could not follow them. I thought – If this is the edge of the known world, of course we will get through! And there will be a landing-place beyond from which we can reach our home.

So watch out for your head, Melissa, as we go through the tunnel –

– Let us look after you, Gaby and Jenny, if you see yourselves as our parents –

– And you and I, Billy, will have something to hand on.

Fourteen

The front-line (so-called) town in which I found myself when I
went back to cover the war in what had once been Yugoslavia had
become symbolic of what was characteristic of the fighting: it had
been a place where Serbs and Croats and Muslims had for some
years lived amicably side by side; they had intermarried so that it
seemed they were losing the distinctions of nationality: then
suddenly Serbs were butchering Croats, and Croats and Muslims
were butchering Serbs, and then Serbs and Croats were joining
forces to butcher Muslims – and so on and so on – until it seemed
that these groupings and regroupings were being used as a
justification for whatever butchery might be available. Politicians
and journalists of course could not allow things to be seen like this:
for the sake of their jobs, their sanity, they had to explain – these are
struggles for national identity: when these people lived peaceably
together they were under the heel of a repressive empire – that of
the Turks, of Austria-Hungary, then that of Russian Communism
– they returned to tribal allegiances when such tyrannies were
removed, and one does not wish for a return to tyranny, does one?
An explanation about a return to international allegiances was also
trotted out – the Croats had traditionally been aligned with

Germany, the Serbs with Russia, and the Muslims – well the Muslims could be seen as part of resurgent Islam. These lines of reasoning provided politicians and journalists with endless means of talking and travelling hither and thither and staying in four-star hotels; and people who had a taste for butchery could feel themselves the centre of attention.

When it became evident that whatever territory was won or held, whatever publicity was given for whatever atrocities, whatever lines were drawn on maps in agreement that such or such a group would remain here and others there – when it became evident that in spite of any of this the fighting and atrocities continued just the same (peace is likely to be boring: how much more exciting for young men is life with a gun!) then, after a while, it was the politicians and journalists who got bored with so much repetition, and there were after all fresher and just as ghastly areas available for analysis and description elsewhere. And it was then for a time that the fighting did seem to get less: had ordinary people learned something? or was it just that fighting was less publicised. I sometimes wondered – Could not people who like cruelty and pain, when the fit takes them, simply retire to a work-out such as there was in that gaunt brick building by the canal: or is what is generally required a more public form of suffering?

I had written as much as I could of the story of Charlie and the hostages – of the invitation for cameras to be present at a public execution. I had set the scene – the hostages, women and old men, lined up in front of an open grave; a man like Dungbird and his troupe with their automatic weapons ready; a henchman designated to go down the line with a pistol shooting the hostages one by one in the back of the head. And the film crews behind their cameras – this was a scoop? were they expected to interfere? surely this would be up to Charlie and his men: everyone had their own jobs to do. But it was Charlie's job not to interfere – those were his orders – he was there just to watch: but even if this entailed the observation of atrocities? This was a question about which traditionally not much had been said: what was unspoken was – Was it or was it not up to the individual? Charlie and his detachment had stood in the dusty square. Charlie would have wondered – But by what criteria would an individual know what was up to him? He had said to the man who was like Dungbird (so I had written) – All right, if one of your men shoots one of the hostages, then one of your men will be shot. And the man like Dungbird had said – Then the man who shoots one of my men will be shot – and so on and so on. And both Charlie and the man like Dungbird knew that this might provoke a larger war; that in the mêlée they themselves would probably be shot; and where is the glamour anyway in a much larger war. But how could they climb down without firing one shot? That would be no glamorous form of war! I had written – Of course no one is telling the precise outcome; one wants neither to provoke nor condone any war. But Charlie had been sent home under something of a cloud; so he is likely to have shot one or two people – or not! I wrote – With such an open-ended story there is some glamour – but not in war!

The war had not stopped. But from a butterfly's wingbeat – you cannot tell the effects?

One of the most generally hidden things about this war seemed to be what was happening to the children. There were enough stories about young children with their mothers as victims of atrocities or grievous hardships: there were adolescents in the groups who were doing the fighting. But of those in between – the children, say, between the ages of eight and thirteen – I had read, and seen, almost nothing. There were mentions from time to time of such children in the more stable areas living or running wild in the streets: scrounging, stealing, bartering, surviving. There was a rumour of children in war-torn zones hiding in woods and living in caves: but no one seemed to be following up such stories. There had been abandoned children surviving like this at various times of slaughter and starvation in Russia: there were said to be gangs of such children in Eastern Europe now in the wake of the crack-up of totalitarian order. It seemed likely that children might form groups when everyone else was forming groups: that in such gatherings they might be learning to manoeuvre on their own.

I had tried to understand what I had imagined might be special aptitudes of children: what might make them, in spite of their vulnerability, candidates for survival. It had been a conceit of Western imagination that the cruelties and violences of the grown-up world – arising from the drives of sexuality perhaps, as well as

227

those to exercise power – were present even in an untrammelled form in the natures of children: children did not have to wait for sexual adolescence or rat-race contamination by the grown-up world to enjoy the urge to dominate (perhaps even the more subtle power of allowing oneself to be dominated); these were there from the beginning, it was said; they were the same forces, mainly biological, which, as well as being destructive, encouraged the growth of increasingly complex structures. But it seemed to me that this did depend on some yielding by children to the attitudes of the grown-up world. At some stage of their development, however, children were able to see these with amusement; and if this tendency was allowed to develop naturally, then surely children might learn to go their own way. And might they not have a chance of doing this especially in times of war – grown-ups are so obviously childish in times of war – and might not children learn to see this as not so much childish as ridiculous. Might they not become, that is, like those bacteria that learn to survive under stress – that produce mutations necessary for survival in times of stress. Children in times of war, of terror, goodness knows are under stress. But what might be the mutation by which they might survive? Watching the killing and the atrocities they might indeed feel – God knows there has to be something different if we are to survive. What might be both different and possible would be not in terms of fighting the grown-up world (how would this be different) nor indeed ignoring it (how would this be possible) but in learning to use it perhaps – to take advantage of its being under stress; to come into some symbiotic relationship with it, as it were. Oh of course this was fanciful! But it would seem to be following some course of nature. What I had learned from the children in Cumbria – what I had imagined when I had been with the children watching the gaunt and pulsating building by the canal – was how by being shown so obviously the self-destructive ways of the grown-up world they might be learning what they were up against and not only in others but in themselves: and they needed to use the knowledge if they wished to stay alive. They needed to manipulate, to dodge: in this they were what might be called children of darkness: but it had seemed to me with the children in Cumbria at least, that they were also taking on an aura of light.

They were finding out, that is, that if they trusted it then the world would work for them – even figures in the grown-up world. What was required after all was assimilation rather than destruction; and they were finding that there were at least some grown-ups who saw patterns within darkness and light. This Melissa and I had accepted – that we should play our part in whatever patterns turned up. But for these to be followed there had to be discovered such trust on an even more startling level: some knowledge that in the outside world – outside oneself, outside others – there was that which itself made these patterns; even those which occasioned, if recognised, things advantageous to oneself to turn up.

When I arrived in what had once been Yugoslavia for this second time to try to describe something of the war, I recognised in the town in which I based myself the conventional pictures that people had of war: there were the burnt-out houses, the old people picking their way through the rubble, the scurrying across open ground to obtain food and water. There was also, indeed, the underside of war that I had previously glimpsed but which was not much talked about: the jollity, the drinking dens, the easy couplings and uncouplings of lovers without the weight of convention to fear. But I found I did not want to report any more of this: so people liked war, yes: what I wanted to look at was what in these daft circumstances might make war ever stop. Did in the end people just get bored: or was it more true that war never stopped? Or might there ever come a time of as it were transcendent boredom or fear, in which even grown-ups at extremity of stress might stop: and then something of a different nature, if anything, might survive.

The town in which I found myself had become a headquarters for the peace-keeping forces: I had an introduciton from Charlie to the officer in charge of the British contingent. Major Burt was a short, moustached, round-faced man who was managing success-fully to come to terms with his role as a fighting soldier forbidden to do any fighting; he observed the terrible but often untouchable scenes around him unperturbed and sometimes smiling. He had set himself up in the basement of a half-gutted house where he was ministered to by a red-haired woman in her thirties: he would say – Well, what have soldiers traditionally been accustomed to do if they are not to do any fighting. The media people were gathered within the protection of a one-storeyed caravanserai or hostel: most of them accepted this restriction not so much because the soldiers could thus keep an eye on them as they could keep an eye on one another in order not to be upstaged. I found a room in a wooden house with a first-floor verandah; here I would sit and survey the scene in the evenings – the corner where an old woman had been shot carrying her basket of laundry; the battlements of a house which could give cover for a sniper. I thought – I have to take some risks in order to find out what I am doing here? Major Burt came to visit me in the evenings. He said 'So you know old Charlie. What's happening to old Charlie?'

I said 'He had a job as a security officer at a nuclear plant in Cumbria. But he's giving this up.'

'Why?'

'He's got a girl in London.'

'He was a great success with the women, was old Charlie.'

I liked Major Burt. We sat and drank whisky. I thought – We are like two old colonialists looking out with grim satisfaction on the ruins of empire.

I said 'How many people did Charlie have to kill? I mean, that business with the hostages.'

He said 'I think I have categorically to deny that I know anything about that.'

'I should guess no more than one or two. After that, it would have gone either one way or the other.'

'He's not supposed to tell that story, old Charlie.'

'He hasn't. I'm trying to trick it out of you.'

We drank our whisky. There is a special pleasure in getting drunk in times of danger, you are not so stuck with fear; you are in a world of possibilities.

I said 'Do you think it made any difference?'

'What –'

'To the war.'

'The war hasn't stopped.'

'I mean, if there was more like it. On a grander scale.'

'Have you written the story?'

'No, I couldn't really.'

230

'Why not?'

'It's the unknown, the fear of the unknown, that might make this sort of thing stop.'

At the corner where the old woman with her laundry-basket had been shot there were still a few bits of clothing in the gutter; and now a bunch of flowers. I thought – Perhaps Major Burt and I get on so well together, as I did indeed with the Minister, because there is the chance that we might be shot.

Major Burt said 'We're waiting for a convoy to come up from the coast. Do you want to go with it? You could write about that.'

I said 'About how we're keeping the war going by providing with supplies the gangs who take their cut?'

'Or by providing them with hostages –'

'I've written about that.'

I'd come to Bosnia to try to find out about the nuclear arms dump or installation that was supposed to be in a dangerous condition in the mountains. There were rumours that an area was already contaminated; that the contamination might spread; that the authorities knew about this but were keeping quiet so that there should not be panic. I had thought – But what would be wrong with panic? Surely what is required is a recognition of the need for panic –

I said to Major Burt 'Do you know anything about a nuclear dump in the hills?

He said 'Oh Good Lord, I really am supposed not to say anything about that.'

'Why should not news of it get out? Even if it's a rumour. That might be an occasion for the war to stop.'

'That's what Charlie thought.'

'Charlie might have started the rumour?'

'I hadn't thought of that.'

I had not been able to find the village called Brodcic on a map. There was a town called Krodvic up in the hills. I said to Major Burt 'Where is the convoy going tomorrow; does it go near the place called Krodvic?'

He said 'If it gets through.'

I said 'Could Krodvic be the same as Brodcic? I mean, in some different language or script.'

He said 'I don't know?' Then – 'It's true there are no-go areas in the mountains.'

'I could try to do that story.'

'Not if you're dead.'

We sat and watched the sun go down. I thought – Perhaps that's the point: you find out what stories survive, are effective, by either being or not being dead.

Major Burt said 'Are you married?'

'Yes.'

'Children?'

'One or two.'

I thought – I mean, one on the way.

He said 'I sometimes wonder why we bring them into the world.'

'They may be the chance to alter it.'

'Chancy buggers.'

'Do you know any stories about gangs of children in the hills?'

He said 'Oh for God's sake, yes, but we can't think too much about them.'

We watched the bubbles rising in our glasses, in our minds. I thought – They dissolve and float away over forests and cornfields: some sort of rain, some sort of hope, my children.

There was a walk I had done on a previous evening after my whisky: this went round the outskirts of the town to a ruined church on the top of a hill. From this I had watched a blood-red sunset: life spilled out onto the ground. I had thought – One cannot choose Armageddon: one can say it might be there. Now, when Major Burt had left me, I thought I would do this walk again. The path started off through narrow alleyways: here an assassin might jump out – with a knife, with a gun – so you wonder, as usual, what you are doing here. In the church there had been stains of what looked like real blood on the altar: I had thought – Well sometimes indeed reality breaks through. Now on my second walk I could see from the high ground at the edge of the town the lights of the expected convoy grinding up the road through the dusk: the lights were like the torches of pilgrims in procession. I thought – But what is the use, either of pilgrimage or charitable relief, if all that is achieved is to provide comfort and sustenance for killers rather than their victims. This is the best that humans can do? Then hurry on, whatever might be more than human.

I became aware that there was a figure following me up the narrow alleyway from the town. I was coming out onto the open ground in front of the church. The figure had a shawl over its head; it might be that of a woman: she was carrying a basket: she might be on her way to the church; the basket might contain a bomb or a gun. I was clambering hurriedly across the open ground. I thought I would get into the shelter of the church: but when had it ever helped to seek shelter in a church? This church itself had been bombed. I thought – Or perhaps a true church is always one that has been bombed: one finds better shelter in rubble. I was treading over broken stones and I moved behind the altar: the woman was following me into the church. It appeared that what she was carrying in her basket was flowers. She began to lay these out on the altar. I came out from behind the shelter of a pillar. The woman seemed to be laughing. I thought – She is laughing because I have been hiding? It was suddenly as if I were stepping into almost unbearable light. I thought – This is happening too quickly. Then – But of course, I know her! She is – but I could not quite say it even to myself. She said 'I know you will be thinking that this is some sort of miracle, but it isn't: I knew you were here.'

I said 'How did you know I was here?'

She said 'From one of the Sisters. I think Father Watkin told her. I mean I knew you were in the town.'

'How did you know who I was?'

'I think I've seen you, haven't I?'

She continued to lay out the flowers on the altar. She arranged them in a cross, with other flowers in a circle round them. I did not know whether or not to say – You saw me on the side of that hill?

She said 'I knew the family who were killed here. There was a mother and a father and two children who were very young. They were killed as they sheltered behind the altar.'

I said 'Yes.'

'Some of the older children got away.'

When she had finished setting out her flowers she knelt down and prayed. I stood and watched her.

I thought – But I am going to be able to bear this.

When she stood up she said 'Would you like to come with me into the hills tomorrow?'

I said 'Yes.'

She said 'We'll have to start early. We'll leave with the convoy. Then we turn off. I need someone to share the driving.'

'Yes.'

'As a matter of fact I suppose this is rather odd.'

'Where will you be, in the square?'

I walked with her back down the hill. It was as if the hot coals we might have been walking on we were carrying in our hands. I thought – But things will not now always be like this?

She said 'I think it helps if one sees things as rather funny. You looked so alarmed when I saw you in the church! As if I might shoot you, or you were seeing a vision.'

I said 'I saw you on that hillside years ago.'

'Yes I know.'

'You remembered me?'

'Yes.'

'What do you say when you pray?'

She seemed to think about this for a time. Then she said – 'I sometimes say – Jesus laughs.'

In the morning there were the usual delays before the convoy could proceed on its way – arguments with the local militiamen who had roadblocks on the outskirts of the town, with representatives of different militias further up the road. These arguments were about nothing in particular, they lasted as long as those instigating them got satisfaction from them. The woman with whom I was going to drive waited by her truck: she wore grey overalls and a grey cap; in stronger sunlight I suppose I might have mistaken the colour of her clothes for blue. Her truck was a small four-wheel-drive and was loaded with cartons of what looked like medical supplies: it seemed she was working for her own charitable organisation rather than any more official agency. I still was not asking questions: I assumed she would be looking for children: I had become imbued with the idea that unnecessary questions might divert the course of understanding or even of what would happen. The woman seemed to accept this: after we had greeted

234

one another in the morning we stayed quiet and slightly apart. I thought – This is a form of praying?

I said 'You'd like me to start driving?'

She said 'Yes, would you?'

When the convoy eventually set off we joined in at the end. We sat side by side. I thought – So long as I have something to do such as driving, this is bearable.

We passed through roadblocks and ground up into the hills. There was the impression, as so often, of something slightly different happening elsewhere. We entered a forest where there were tall trees like antennae: perhaps if you looked through them, into them, then like one of those magic pictures you might glimpse what was going on elsewhere.

I said 'When I saw you on the hillside I thought you were the Virgin Mary.'

She said 'I don't think that's after all so flattering'

'Why not?'

'She seems nowadays such a grumbling mother! Always blaming the children; not taking responsibility herself.'

'But not at the beginning –'

'Oh not at the beginning! But things become what we make of them, no?'

We trailed along at the back of the convoy. Figures came to watch us, silently, from the often ruined farmhouses that stood back from the road.

I said 'We can make things one thing or another?'

She said 'Your friends told me about you when they brought us that child.'

'And then you heard from Father Watkin? That's an explanation for how we're here now?'

'Oh if you want explanations!'

After a time she pointed and we left the convoy and turned up a track through the trees. I thought I might say – You know where we're going?

– But then we might lose our way in the trees?

The tack emerged eventually from the forest onto a huge flat plateau of broken stones. I did not know how long I had been driving: time seemed sometimes to go faster and sometimes almost to stop. I had been wishing that I might go on driving for ever: then I wished to rest and lay my head on her shoulder.

I said 'You look after children –'

'When we can find them.'

'You bring food and medicine –'

'Yes.'

'Do they manage?'

'They survive.'

It was as if there were something keeping her faintly amused. I thought – Perhaps it is because we are not after all angels but a man and woman in the front of this truck. Then – Jesus laughs?

She said 'Would you like me to drive?'

'If you like.'

I stopped and we changed places. I bounced for a while in the passenger-seat: then I found I was half-dreaming with my head against her shoulder.

Images came into my mind – the Virgin Mary holding the child, holding the crucified Christ, sheltering beneath her skirts all the children of the world: there was a picture of this –

I dozed, woke. When I looked around, the truck had stopped and was some way off the track; she had pulled up by a stream. She was out of the truck and squatting by a rock, peeing. I thought – The Virgin Mary? So all right, children, you would have had to get out from under her skirts –

She said 'Would you like some food? a cup of tea?'

'Yes I'd like that.'

'I don't think it's much further.'

She had camping-gas equipment in the back of the truck. We made tea, and ate bread and cheese and biscuits. I thought – This is the place by the stream that I have seen before; I mean, in that vision.

She said 'Thank you for coming with me –'

I said 'Oh I thank you!'

'There might be some sickness. I should have warned you.'

'I wanted to come here. I knew what I might expect.'

This time it was she who seemed to be falling asleep. I thought – Perhaps we are sickening: perhaps we are being given grace.

I said 'Lay your head against me.'

236

She said 'Just for a moment.'

She did this awkwardly, as if she had never done such a thing before: I thought – But we are laughing? With her head on my lap I bent over her and it was as if like this I might enfold her: as if we might be two of those cells that grow into one. She had a slightly worn but still beautiful face; with wrinkles of such finenees that her skin might be transparent.

Then it was as if I were in the small boat again with Melissa and Billy and Gaby and Jenny: we were entering the tunnel; the tunnel was long and dark but it was as if it were filled with the light that was not visible unless there was something for it to bump up against: but were not we ourselves of the nature of light? and thus free to go down the tunnel. At the end of it there might be – what – that man in a white robe whom you see on the threshold of death? And he would say – All right, boys and girls, we've done the dying: and now let's get on with life. We had carried the boat up to the house – Melissa, Billy, Gaby, Jenny and I. And that night Melissa and I had made love. And I had thought – We have got the timing right?

I was looking down at the woman's face in my lap. I thought – Who is the parent; who is the child.

When she woke she said 'Didn't you know back at home some children who came from this part of the world?'

I said 'Yes I did.'

'I heard some story.'

We drove on again. It appeared from the position of the sun to be late afternoon: the place by the stream where we had been sitting seemed to be quite close to the stream's source: the huge boulder-strewn plateau rose up to a distant ridge. The sun was setting behind our backs: the ridge in front seemed to be burning with an even more intense than usual glow. There was the time when we did not seem to be getting any closer or further away: then we were almost up to the ridge, ourselves bathed everywhere in light.

I was driving. The woman was peering across me out of my side of the truck. I slowed and stopped. Just short of the ridge, at some distance from the track, were some flat smooth shapes that in the odd light seemed at first to be formations of lava; then it seemed they might be the roofs of low stone buildings of some settlement, designed perhaps even to appear like rock. There were some goats nibbling. This was the first sign of life we had seen for a long time. I said 'This is where we're coming to?'

The woman said 'Do you see anyone?'

I said 'No.'

I drove to the top of the ridge. It was suddenly as if a curtain had been raised in front of us: the rough track over which we had been travelling for so many miles became abruptly a metalled road just over the ridge: it stretched away from us into blue hills in the distance. Not far ahead on the road military vehicles were drawn up in a line: they were pointing away from us down the road. Beside them was a watchtower by a gateway with a high wire fence going off on either side: behind this was an area of some huts and a few large and grassy mounds that might indeed be those of a military camp with underground storage facilities. I thought – Or a burial ground? There were soldiers in and around the trucks; they were carrying crates from the camp through the gateway and loading them onto trucks; some of the objects carried were on stretchers with coverings; many of the soldiers had makeshift masks over their faces. I thought – But it does not look as if those stretchers contain dead bodies – yet?'

I had stopped on the brow of the ridge. A group of soldiers nearest to us had turned to us and were standing with their hands shading their eyes; it must have been difficult for them to see us with the bright sun directly behind. One beckoned to us as if ordering us to approach; he bent down as if to try to get his eyes into the shade; he was holding a gun. Another man, an officer, was hurrying down the line of trucks gesticulating as if to get the soldiers to finish what they were doing quickly; he wore a more elaborate mask over his face. I thought – Perhaps he will not be able to see us in the setting sun. The soldier who had been pointing his gun at us got into the back of the truck at the end of the line; he was still beckoning; it seemed that if we did not obey him, he might shoot. The woman beside me said 'Turn in through the gate.' I thought – You mean, that is somewhere where they will not want to go back to – to come after us? The soldiers seemed to have carried the last of their loads to the trucks; tailboards were being raised; the front of the convoy was moving off even as people were still jumping in. I thought – Dear God, yes, this must be urgent: we are lucky? unlucky? I drove down over the brow of the hill as if in obedience to the soldier who had the gun: I followed the last truck as it moved off – not too close and not too far away – and then when we were parallel with the gateway I swung the wheel and turned in. I thought – The soldier might not shoot because then he might still have to come back for us. I drove fast round the inside perimeter of the fence until it seemed that I was as far from the road as I could go; then I stopped, behind the shelter of one of the large mounds. There was a door into the mound which had been pulled off its hinges; there were crates inside of what seemed to be a different kind to the ones the soldiers had been carrying. I thought – But I don't know what the soldiers were carrying. We may never know; what does it matter.

One of the larger mounds in the centre seemed to be open at the top and to have suffered from some small explosion. I thought – Or it might have been just refuse they were burning.

The woman said again 'Do you see anyone?'

I said 'No.'

I thought – What does she expect to see: children?

I was sitting at the side of the truck which was next to the perimeter fence. The mesh of the fence at this point was sagging: it was as if people might have used this point to break in. It reminded me of the fence at Billy's school. At the far side of this, as if in an illustration of a time-warp, were two children facing the curve of the net looking in. They were a boy and a girl, perhaps ten and twelve. I thought – Oh well, for God's sake, here we are. Then – Sooner or later, I can go home?

I said 'Yes, I see two children.'

She leaned across me to speak to them: I opened the door. The three of them spoke in a language that I did not understand. The children stepped across the sagging piece of fence as if they were walking on water; they went to the woman's side of the truck and went on talking there. I was thinking – This is as far as I will go with my story: if it is to have effect, I mean, I cannot tell any more.

The woman said 'This is where they get their provisions.'

I said 'Oh yes.'

'They're in the old living-quarters.'

'I see.'

'I don't think they're sick, as a matter of fact, but I'll stay with them.'

I thought – Then I'll stay too.

She said 'You can take the truck back. You know where to go.'

She held the door open for the two children; they hoisted themselves and clung to the side of the truck. I thought – They are like Billy and Gaby on the edge of that boat like wings. I drove back round the inside of the perimeter fence to the gate: I thought – It seems, yes, that we all know where to go.

I drove back to just short of the top of the ridge: here the metalled road swung round towards the settlement of low stone buildings and there stopped. I followed the road. As we came up to the settlement children were appearing as if out of the ground to greet us: I thought – All right, all right, not from dragon's teeth like angels; there would be underground shelters here and what better place to hide – pursuers being loath to come because of stories of dangers and death on stony ground.

I stopped just short of the low stone buildings. The children gathered round the truck. They were bright-eyed, attentive: some were in clothes too big for them: some had fitted themselves out in coverings of their own design. The woman had got out of the truck and she and the children were unloading stores from the back. There were food and medical provisions: there were tools and books and even a blackboard. I was thinking – I don't want to go; I want to go: it is because all this makes sense, rather than that it does not, that it is almost unbearable. The woman said 'You will find the way?' I said 'But you can't stay!' She said 'Of course I must stay.' I said 'Then I don't want to go.' She said 'Of course you must go: the truck will be needed, it would be noticed here. And you must get back to your family.'

I stood and watched her. I did not know what to do. She and the children would be – for how long – in this wilderness. They had provisions. The sun had gone down beneath the level of hills. There would soon be darkness.

I said 'You'll be in danger –'

She said 'I don't think as a matter of fact much has happened.'

'But you can't know –'

'And so you can write your story.'

The last time I saw her she was standing with a group of children and the light from the gathering dusk was making her clothes strangely blue. She and the children were waving to me: it was as if they were her family. She said 'And tell Sister Bernardine where I am, will you?'

I said 'I thought you were Sister Bernardine!'

She laughed: she said 'Oh no I'm the Virgin Mary!'